THE
HONEYCRISP
ORCHARD
INN

Also by Valerie Bowman

The Austen Hunks Trilogy
Hiring Mr. Darcy
Kissing Mr. Knightley
Marrying Mr. Wentworth

THE HONEYCRISP ORCHARD INN

A Honeycrisp Orchard Romance

VALERIE BOWMAN

An Imprint of HarperCollinsPublishers

FIRST EDITION

Interior text design by Diahann Sturge-Campbell

Library of Congress Cataloging-in-Publication Data

Names: Bowman, Valerie author
Title: The Honeycrisp Orchard Inn : a novel / Valerie Bowman.
Description: First edition. | New York, NY : Avon, an imprint of HarperCollinsPublishers, 2025. | Series: Honeycrisp Orchard romance ; book 1
Identifiers: LCCN 2025021076 | ISBN 9780063454033 trade paperback | ISBN 9780063454040 ebook
Subjects: LCGFT: Romance fiction | Fiction | Novels
Classification: LCC PS3602.O8996 H66 2025 | DDC 813/.6—dc23/eng/20250516
LC record available at https://lccn.loc.gov/2025021076

ISBN 978-0-06-345403-3

Printed in the United States of America

25 26 27 28 29 LBC 5 4 3 2 1

To my hometown, the village of Rantoul, Illinois, my own little Harvest Hollow

Chapter 1

Y ou're fired, Eleanor."
It takes a moment for the words to filter through my eardrum and present themselves to my brain in a way that makes any sense. I'm 99 percent sure the look on my face remains pleasant, but inside panic is throwing a rager, and I wasn't invited.

Did I just hear Steve Gibbons, my boss *for the last seven years*, say that I'm fired? That can't be, and yet . . .

One glance through the glass doors at the shiny brown oval conference room table provides more evidence. All three of the clients, execs from the Bolt Hotel Group, are sitting there, blinking at me in sympathy. They just heard my presentation. The one I've been working on all summer. Right before Steve asked me to step into the hallway for a private conversation.

Steve's eyes are slightly narrowed in that way he does when he's trying to seem as if he cares. Like the time I told him my uncle died, and I needed one day off work. And Geoff, my coworker and ex-boyfriend for all of *twelve hours*, has his head cocked to the side, his fingers steepled in front of his chest, and is nodding in a clearly fake-sympathetic manner. I recognize his look. It's the same look he gave the ladies at the animal shelter when we volunteered there last spring and they told him how many dogs need homes. Fake. As. Hell. Geoff doesn't even like dogs. He's allergic to them. He only volunteered because Steve asked us to, and he took so much allergy medicine, he had to lie down. Plus, I never should have dated a man who steeples his fingers. Finger steepling is ridiculous.

"I don't . . . understand." Those are the three uninspired words that decide to slide on out of my mouth as I continue to stare into the conference room. How eloquent. How professional. Five stars.

"This is really embarrassing," Steve says, shaking his head. "I never would have allowed you to present to the Bolt Group if I knew you were planning to copy Geoff's presentation."

Wait. What? "Geoff had a presentation?" I ask. I thought he was only sitting in while I gave mine. My presentation began promptly at nine a.m. as scheduled. What the hell is Steve talking about?

"Yes, it started at eight. I thought you knew," Steve replies, giving me a look that can only be described as patronizing.

"It started at eight? You thought I knew?" Apparently, all I can do is echo what I just heard like some sort of a well-dressed parrot. And I *am* well dressed. At least I have that going for me. I put on a suit for this. All long, sleek, black trousers with a wide leg, sky-blue satin shell blouse with a keyhole neckline, and one-button black blazer. I'm wearing heels. Expensive heels. This is serious.

And I deserve this account. I've been working on the event plan for the Bolt Hotel Group's new brand launch party for the last three months. Our firm, GMJ Events, had been chosen by the biggest hotel group in the country, and Steve had given *me* the account. After years of weddings, bar and bat mitzvahs, and small corporate shindigs, I was finally getting a chance at the big league. Bolt Hotel Group owns over eight thousand hotels and has twenty brands. It's huge.

I'd planned the hell out of their event, the unveiling of the first of their newest brand: Barn and Branch. A set of unique country inns the Bolt Hotel Group will purchase around the country and make over in their exquisite style. Their gorgeous boutique-like rooms start at a thousand dollars a night. The launch event must go off without a hitch, and it will. Because I've planned it that way.

There will be farmhouse flowers in milk jugs, and pumpkin-and-cinnamon-scented votives in tiny glass holders on every table. Thick off-white tablecloths and gold flatware. Pumpkins and gourds spilling from every surface, making the entire dining room feel like a cornu-copia from an autumn harvest. I planned *every single* detail down to the pesto-encrusted broiled salmon entrées and the apple-crisp bread pudding topped with semi-melted white chocolate chips. Delicious perfection, damn it.

This meeting today was supposed to be a formality. A check in the box. Steve had assured me we already had the account. Hell, everything was already planned, and now I was fired? What happened between me leaving work last night and this morning when I walked into this conference room? Other than Geoff dumping me, that is?

"I didn't know," I assure Steve. "What's going on?"

Steve's eyes crinkle again. This time he adds a wince. "Listen, Eleanor, I didn't want to make a scene in front of the clients, but Geoff told us what happened."

"What *happened?*" I frown. Did Geoff tell them he broke up with me last night? After living together for two years, being together for four, he unceremoniously dumped me the night before my big pre-sentation. It sucks beyond belief, and I still haven't processed it yet, but after watching a depressing documentary about the meteoric rise of dementia in the US and getting about two hours of sleep on the uncomfortable Ikea couch in our apartment, I woke up this morning determined to forget about it long enough to make the *biggest presen-tation of my career.* But what the hell does Geoff dumping me have to do with it?

"Look, Steve. I'm fine. Really. What happened last night won't affect my performance in the least. I—"

"I don't think you understand, Eleanor." Steve puts a comforting hand on my shoulder and squeezes ever so slightly. "Geoff gave us the heads-up. He *thought* your presentation might closely mirror his."

What the—? "I didn't—"

"I didn't totally believe him," Steve continues, "but then you came in with yours and it was nearly word-for-word the same thing. It makes us look bad, Eleanor."

I *know* my face must register my shock. I was born without a poker face. "I'm sorry, he *what*?"

"Look," Steve continues. "We work in a competitive business, Eleanor. I know it can be tough, but GMJ is not an organization that tolerates this type of behavior. Passing off a colleague's presentation as your own"—he shakes his head sadly—"is grounds for termination."

What the hell? Geoff didn't have any ideas. And I certainly hadn't stolen any of them. In fact, if anyone needed to steal ideas, it was Geoff. And apparently, that's precisely what that snake had done. He'd heard my presentation fifty times. He knew all the details, had been there when I'd worked day after day to make them all come together. I'd practiced my presentation for him to get feedback multiple times a night every night for the last month.

My vision blurs slightly. Is going rage-blind a thing? It sounds like a thing. "That's it? I'm fired. You're not even going to hear me out? What if I told you that Geoff stole the presentation from *me*?" I don't want to appear unprofessional, but I'm not about to go down without a fight or at least an attempt at telling the truth either.

Steve's face crumples in faux sympathy. Very faux. Plus, another freakin' wince. "I'd believe you if Geoff hadn't been bouncing these ideas off me the last month or so. We'd already talked about his plan at length, he and I."

I squeeze my eyes shut and pinch the bridge of my nose. "Geoff's been giving you details of the plan for the last month?" Was this really happening? It wasn't some sort of test, was it? See how the event planner responds to having her ideas stolen by her recent ex? Am I on a reality show and don't know it?

"Yes. And it's a brilliant plan. I see why you would choose it over your own."

I press my lips together. It *is* a brilliant plan. Because it is *my own*. I'd perfected every detail. The white pumpkins and hot toddies with cinnamon sticks swirling inside. The hayrides in honest-to-goodness wagons with honest-to-goodness horses. Horses with jaunty orange bows tied to their manes. And I'd told every single one of those details to Geoff MF-ing Herringdon, only to have him steal them from me.

And now it hits me. Like a fist to my middle. The memories flood back. Every time Steve and Geoff exchanged a look or laughed about their dumb golf handicaps or made their little inside jokes about their shared college fraternity. I'd always known this company is a boys' club. But GMJ is the premier event-planning company in the city. Every planner out there wants a job here. I thought I had proven myself, but Geoff set me up perfectly. He took all my ideas and fed them to Steve over the last month to ruin my credibility and make it look like they were all *his*. Meanwhile, I'd been keeping my plans close to my vest so I could wow both Steve and the clients at the same time. Today. It was supposed to be today!

I drag air into my lungs as a red cloud covers my vision. "I spent the last seven years working sixty-hour weeks for this place, and this is the thanks I get?"

Okay, fine. I may medal in the cliché Olympics for that statement, but it feels good to say something, *anything* to get a little of my own back.

I'd given up weekends to attend the firm's most important events. I'd missed family milestones to seem like a team player. I'd skipped the last several Thanksgivings at home to bring the apple pie to the annual dinner Steve holds for the top brass at the firm, thankful to have been invited.

"You've been a valued employee for years. I understand that," Steve says. "Please, let's keep this professional. I'll call HR. You can stop there on the way out. They'll tell you all the details of your termination."

Termination details? Like I give a flying eff about termination details right now. "Can I at least get the stuff from my desk?" I ask, pointing toward the door at the end of the hallway that leads to our offices. I want my hot-pink water tumbler and the gray sweater I keep hanging on the back of my chair for when the AC makes it really cold in there.

"I don't think that's a great idea," Steve says, shaking his head. "I can send them home for you with Geoff if you like."

"Don't bother," I huff. "Geoff broke up with me last night. I'm moving out." My voice rises, and I turn red—I can feel my face heat. There. Let Steve think about *that* for a few minutes. If the event plan was Geoff's idea, why did he dump me last night? Only Steve probably assumes Geoff dumped me because I was trying to steal *his* brilliant idea. Gah.

Steve clears his throat. "Don't make a scene, Eleanor. You don't want to burn any bridges, do you?"

Don't make a scene?

Did he really just say that?

Something breaks inside of me. I don't give a crap about any bridges, I want to burn down the whole building. But I will happily start with Steve's stupid Patagonia vest. I've wanted to tell him about those vests for years. It's *go time*. I turn on my heel and stalk toward the elevator yelling, "You're not a finance bro, Steve! Lose the vests."

"Best of luck to you, Eleanor," comes Steve's calm and still-fake voice from behind me. "I hope you land on your feet."

To my credit, I resist the urge to reply by lifting a middle finger in the air toward him. Instead, I wait until the elevator opens and swallows me before I allow the tears to sting my eyes. Why do tears have to be my visceral reaction to anger? I don't want to sob. I *want* to punch both those jerks in the stomach. But here are tears, nonetheless. Right on cue.

Determined to keep it together, I tug on the hem of my blazer, clear my throat, and lift my chin. I blow out a breath and stare at my reflection in the glossy silver elevator door. It's a little blurry, but I don't *look* like I just got fired. My straight, brown, shoulder-length hair is on point. My dark-rose lipstick isn't smeared, and my hazel eyes might be swimming with tears, but none have fallen. Yet.

I'm hoping to get all the way to the lobby without a stop. I don't want anyone climbing on the elevator to witness my watery eyes. At least I have my bag and my keys with me. I'm not stopping in HR. I'm not stopping anywhere. I'm going to . . .

Going to . . .

Damn it. I can't go home. It's not even my home any longer. I'd moved into Geoff's place, and the lease was in his name. We'd already established last night that I'd be the one moving out. ASAP.

Where *am* I going now?

The elevator dings at the lobby, and I step out into the wide marbled expanse just as my phone buzzes. *Mom* comes up on the screen. I inwardly cringe. The last thing I want to do is explain to my mother what just happened. Mom always wanted me to stay home out in Harvest Hollow on Long Island. To work for the inn she and Dad own. When I was a kid, it'd been fun to think of working with Mom and Dad, but by the time I graduated high school, I was looking forward to a new adventure in the city. Harvest Hollow is a small town, and the city just seemed so full of possibilities. And I'd loved it here . . . until today.

Now that I think about it, Mom had also always warned me about Manhattan being "dog-eat-dog." I'd dismissed her concerns the same way I did when she told me I needed to have bottles of pepper spray in every drawer in my apartment. I mean, that's a lot of pepper spray.

But I take a deep breath and answer the phone, because what else do I have to do? "Hi, Mom."

"Hi, Ellie, how are you?"

She insists on calling me Ellie. Everyone at home does. I'd dropped the nickname and started going by Eleanor when I began working at the firm. I thought it sounded more professional. The name of a future partner. "I'm . . . okay. How're you?"

"I know you're busy, but . . ."

Mom begins every conversation we have this way. "I know you're busy, but Mrs. Timkins is having a garage sale this weekend, and I wondered if you wanted to come. I know you're busy, but the Harvest Hollow Community Theater is doing *The Music Man*, and I thought you might enjoy it." I always say no. I'm always too busy.

This time, she says, "I know you're busy, but we need your help with an event."

Wait. What's this? "An *event*?" I echo. By this time, I've walked across the lobby and am staring out the three-story glass windows at Madison Avenue and the morning traffic streaming up it. I may have just been dumped and fired, but at least it's a bright sunny day in late September. Wait. Are those storm clouds in the distance?

Of course they are.

"Yes, your dad and I and the Parkers have entered the inn and orchard into the Autumn Harvest Parade, and this year we thought we'd do an Autumn Harvest Festival out here that same weekend. I told Lyn I'd ask you to help."

Lyn Parker is the owner of the apple orchard and the rest of the property where my parents' inn sits. The Parkers and my parents have been in business together since before I was born, and our families have always been close. I'd been raised alongside their two kids, Aiden and Charlotte. Aiden is a year older than me, and Charlotte is several years younger. I think she was in eighth grade the year I graduated high school. As kids, Aiden and I had been tight in that way all kids who are thrown together because of their parents' friendship are. But once we'd hit high school, the differences in our personalities had become obvious. I'd been more of a student-council, straight-A, homecoming-court type, and Aiden had been more of a Future Farmers of America sort. I think he was also the president of the Wood Shop Club or something like that. He never went to school dances or participated in anything fun. I'd gone off to college in the city, and Aiden had . . . I'm not really sure. But the last I'd heard, he'd come back to live in our hometown and works on the orchard farming the trees. And Charlotte works there too. Somewhere. I hadn't really kept tabs since moving away.

"I told Lyn not to get her hopes up," Mom continues.

I frown. "What does that mean?"

"You know. You're busy, dear. I understand."

I *am* busy. Or at least I had been, the dozens of other times Mom had called and asked me to participate in the hometown hominess of Harvest Hollow, New York. But at the moment, I am decidedly free . . . and without a place to live. Which means I can go out and stay at the inn under the guise of helping Mom and Dad without having to admit I've been fired and dumped just yet. I'll work my way up to that confession.

"You're in luck, Mom!" I say. "I just finished a big project, and I'm free for a little while." Best to be vague.

"You are?" Mom's voice sounds delighted and shocked. Which makes guilt slither through me.

"Yep."

"Oh, wonderful. You can stay in the attic apartment, of course," Mom says.

The attic apartment is a two-bedroom place at the top of the inn all tucked up under the eaves. It's cute and cozy, and smells of sweet cinnamon and cloves, just like the rest of the inn does. And I always stay there when I come home. Which, admittedly, isn't often. But I'm pretty sure Mom and Dad built it for me to live in after college. So, I think of it as mine.

"When can you be here?" Mom asks next.

"How about tonight?" Might as well get going. It's not like I have the money to stay at a hotel. I'll have to use my savings to get another apartment and pay for things until I find a new job. The only other option is my best friend, Maria, who has a tiny studio in Chelsea. She would definitely let me crash on the couch, but her hospitality would come with a side of I-told-you-so. She's always hated Geoff, especially the way he spells his name. I have pointed out numerous times that it's his parents' spelling, not his, but she insists it doesn't matter.

"Tonight?" Mom says in a flabbergasted voice, as if I'd just told her she'd won the HGTV dream house, which, by the way, she enters to win every year. "That's wonderful, dear. Your dad and I are going to the Moose Lodge tonight, but the apartment key will be at the front desk for you."

The Moose Lodge is our town's hottest venue for residents of a certain age (and Donny Briggs, the bellhop at the inn). Mom and Dad (and Donny) never miss bingo night at the lodge. Though Donny is the only person under the age of fifty who participates.

"Sounds good, Mom. I'll catch the train out tonight. I should be there by nine."

"Oh, honey. Your father's going to be so excited. Lyn and Kevin too."

I'm pretty sure the Parkers don't care whether I show up. But I don't bother pointing this out to Mom. Instead, I thank my lucky stars that I have a place to go and a reprieve from explaining the dumpster fire my life has just become.

An Autumn Harvest Festival might not be the Bolt Hotel Group's extravaganza, but it's an event. Something small and relaxed and pressureless might be fun for a change. Not to mention I can probably do it with my eyes closed. Not that I will. My eyes will remain firmly open. I subscribe to the if-something's-worth-doing-it's-worth-doing-well theory of life and work.

"See you in the morning, then, Mom," I say, before clicking off my phone.

I take a deep breath before I walk over and hop into the revolving glass door to leave the building for the last time. It's insane to think about that. I hit the street filled with the crowded, noisy traffic that is Manhattan on a Wednesday morning. I glance at my smartwatch. Nearly ten a.m. First, I'll go back to the apartment and pack. But I will only stay there long enough to get my clothes. And maybe rearrange the pantry so the canned goods are mixed in with the boxed goods. Geoff will hate that. That level of petty feels right. Otherwise, there will be no lingering. Then, I will text Maria to tell her I'll be out of town for a bit. I'll confess the rest to her later, hopefully over cocktails at our favorite bar in the Village.

When I woke up this morning, I never would have thought that by nightfall I'd be on my way back to Harvest Hollow. But here I go.

Chapter 2

Twelve hours later, I pull my rain-soaked self, including hat, coat, scarf, and enormous suitcase, through the ton of mud that currently makes up the front of the Honeycrisp Orchard Inn. Has this mud always been here, or did it just materialize tonight because the dumping, the firing, the long, smelly, delayed train ride, *and the rain* haven't been enough for a bad day? Mud is a nice touch, though. Truly. Chef's kiss to the Universe.

All I need now is—

And there it is. First, I hear a telltale bleat, and then Miss Guinevere gallops directly into my hip. I fly into the mud pile, landing on my left side with a loud "oof."

"Good to see you, Miss Guin," I say to the goat, who is staring down at me, chewing something, and bleating.

The orchard is also a working farm, and schoolchildren come out here on field trips most of the year, so, in addition to the other animals, the Parkers decided to buy some goats. Kids love goats, so I hear. Goats and weary travelers, however, are a different story. I've also learned from Mom's stories that goat owners are subject to all manner of indignities, including spitting, theft, and oh yes, the best one, being rammed into and toppled over. It's fun. Sort of like living with a mischievous linebacker who pops out of nowhere every so often with no warning.

Miss Guin is the most egregious of the lot when it comes to headbutting. Mom and Dad had to increase their insurance because of her.

Yep. Goat insurance. It's a thing.

I struggle up to my knees and use my suitcase to pull myself out of the muck. I look down at myself. Oh. Good. If I didn't have enough mud on me before, now I do. It's all over my wool coat, my adorable suede shoes I clearly should not have worn here, and my retro seventies-style jeans that I just bought at a little boutique in the city south of Houston.

Miss Guinevere, who clearly doesn't care about fashion, trots off. She is no doubt plotting her next tackle.

I lift my head and stare up at the inn. Despite the mud, the place looks like an autumn postcard. It's a huge white farmhouse with autumn wreaths filled with orange leaves and pine cones, glowing candles in the windows, pumpkins and gourds scattered along the balustrade, white wooden rocking chairs, and large planters filled to the brim with bright yellow and orange mums. It couldn't be more bucolic. It may be a tiny part of a tiny town, but I have to admit it's a beautiful place. No doubt about it.

And it is my home.

Most people would probably think it odd to live in an inn, but I didn't know any different. Dad built us a two-bedroom apartment behind the front desk. I had my own room and grew up helping at the inn. Everything from maid service to room service is second nature to me. The part I liked the best, though, was the event planning. Whenever anyone wanted a wedding or a baby shower here, I begged Mom to let me help. That was back when I actually thought I'd stay here and plan events solely for the inn. Before I realized there was a whole big, wide world out there.

The lights are on inside the inn, and the soft, warm glow filters out into the soggy night. A little pang of regret unfurls in my chest. It's been a long time since I've been here. Too long. The regret turns into a dull ache as I stare at the inn, an outsider looking in. Everything is so homey and cozy. It's flannels and hot tea and warm socks. And I've missed it. I've *missed* this place.

The last several Thanksgivings, I'd gone to Steve and Barbara's apartment in the city, then stayed in town to work. The last four Christmases, I'd gone to Geoff's family's house in Connecticut. He insisted that his mother would *die* without him on Christmas. Plus, he never really showed much interest in spending time with Mom and Dad. He met them when they came to the city and a couple of times after that, but he never visited here.

I made excuses for why Geoff never showed up. I was too embarrassed to tell my parents the truth, that he wasn't interested. Visiting without Geoff, each time needing to explain his absence, had taken a toll on my desire to visit . . . until I just stopped altogether. It really has been a long time since I've been back here.

I've seen my parents since then . . . well, once. They came into the city to see *The Phantom of the Opera* before it ended. Dad was a big fan of "The Music of the Night." We had dinner before the show, and I took them to my favorite brunch place the next morning. Mimosas were enjoyed by all. And that had been, what? Uh. More than a year ago? Two? I scrunch up my nose and wince. Not great.

Okay, no matter. I am here now, and it's right on the cusp of the very best season for it. The leaves have already begun to turn crisp with orange on the edges, and there's a decided chill in the air. I thump, bump, thump my suitcase up the wide front stairs. Once I'm standing on the huge wraparound porch, out of the rain, I decide to take off my coat. No need to slop mud all over. I kick off my boots too, right there next to the front door, and drop my hat beside them. There is no help for my muddy jeans. They've got to come in with me.

I push open the big wooden front door with the apple-shape brass door knocker and step inside. It's like stepping back in time. The first thing I notice is the scent. Cinnamon sticks are simmering on the stove. They are always simmering on the stove this time of year. I breathe them in. It makes me the slightest bit melancholy and a lot happy. A smile curves my lips.

The next thing I notice is Pumpkin snorting. Pumpkin is a pug Mom rescued from the Harvest Hollow Humane Society when he was a puppy. He is a little chonk, and like the rest of his breed, he has trouble breathing, which causes a constant wheezing sound wherever he goes. Poor dog can't sneak up on anyone. He is also eternally dressed in an orange jumpsuit. It is a set of dog pajamas that Mom put on him one year for fun. However, Mom could not have anticipated Pumpkin's attachment to loungewear. The first time she tried to take it off, Pumpkin emitted a ferocious growl and in general wasn't having it. Mom was forced to buy a second set of orange PJs, which are quickly put on Pumpkin the moment the first set is occasionally removed to be washed. But even with the new set on, Pumpkin sits in front of the washer and dryer staring until the original set is ready. How he knows those are the OG PJs is anyone's guess. It's really quite unsettling.

Pumpkin waddles over to me and stares up at me, his tongue hanging out, his perpetual pug smile on his little round face. "Good to see you, P-dog," I say.

Pumpkin barks twice, and I squat down to rub his fat little neck because I know he loves that. And because he'll keep barking if I don't. His curly pig tail gets me every time. It sits on his back like he can't be bothered to hold it up. It's just cute. No two ways about it.

"Ellie! Is that you?" comes a bright voice from behind the front desk.

I look up to see Charlotte Parker standing there.

"Hi, Charlotte," I call back, waving. "You look great."

And she does. Her long dark hair is pulled back in a ponytail, and her dark eyes framed by long black lashes are blinking at me brightly. She's always got a smile on her face, and tonight is no exception. I usually say I never trust anyone who's *always* happy, but right now, after the day I've had, Charlotte's sunny demeanor makes me feel good.

Leaving Pumpkin and his PJs to waddle behind me, I straighten and make my way over to the front desk.

"What are you doing here?" I ask.

"Your mom didn't tell you I work here in the inn now, Ellie?" Charlotte asks, her smile somehow widening.

"Oh, she must have." I flutter a hand in the air. It's no use trying to tell anyone in Harvest Hollow that my name is Eleanor now. They won't say it. They're quirky like that. Childhood nicknames are not changeable in these parts. Or so Mrs. Lawrence at the drive-in movie theater told me once when I attempted to correct her years ago.

"Yep." Charlotte splays her hands over the front desk. "I'm here most days. And Wednesday nights when your parents go to bingo."

"How's business?" I ask mostly to be polite.

A strange look passes briefly over her face. "It's . . . good . . ."

"Oh yeah?" I bob my head back and forth. "Lots of bookings? Got twelve tonight?" The inn has twenty rooms. Sixty percent occupancy is a good night.

"Something like that." Charlotte snaps her fingers. "Oh yeah, here's the key to the apartment upstairs. Your mom asked me to make sure you get it."

She slides a physical metal key toward me. It has a big piece of leather attached to it by an orange ribbon. The words *The Penthouse* are printed in white on the leather. I shake my head. Mom insists on keeping actual keys around here. I explained to her a dozen times why key cards make more sense, but she and Dad both refuse. "People don't come here for the technology, Ellie," Mom says. "They come here to step back in time. To keep things simple. Keys are simple."

I wish I could really step back in time. Back to when Geoff asked me out over our lunch hour one day. "It's just drinks, Eleanor," he said. Then he'd gone on to be charming. He asked me to dinner, and even though I had a strict policy about not mixing business with pleasure, I somehow ended up dating him and eventually moving in with him. And he ended up stealing my brilliant ideas and dumping me.

Yes, a time machine would be welcome right about now. Where's the TARDIS when you need it?

I shake my head. I have more important things than my crappy past to think about right now. Like taking a long, hot bath in the claw-foot tub upstairs in the attic apartment. And then tomorrow, I will think about how to explain to Mom why I have time on my hands. And then I'll think about stealthily conducting a job search from here and getting back to the city and exacting my revenge on both Geoff and Steve. Okay, maybe not that last part. How long does it take after a bad breakup to stop fantasizing about revenge, though?

But there will be time to think about all that tomorrow. When I'm not freezing cold, bone tired, and caked in mud.

"Thanks," I say to Charlotte as I grab the giant key. "I'll just . . . go up the back way?" I point toward my parents' apartment behind the front desk. The attic apartment has two entrances. One is accessible via a staircase inside my parents' apartment. The other is from an innocuous-looking door out back. The key works in both locks, but I'm not about to go outside again in the rain, not with Miss Guin lurking around like a land shark.

"Sure!" Charlotte says, pulling open the swinging wood half door that leads behind the front desk.

I pull my suitcase behind me and enter Mom and Dad's place. The smell of cinnamon is stronger in here because the sticks are simmering on Mom's stove. She leaves the pot on low, completely unconcerned about the fire hazard no matter how many times Mr. Peyton the fire chief tells her to stop.

The memories the apartment conjures bring another little smile to my face. Me and Mom baking sugar cookies with apples on them. The cider donuts we used to make. The pumpkin carving and the mums planting. It's pure Norman Rockwell up in here.

I make my way through the living room to the door that leads to the staircase up to the attic on the fourth floor. I thump the suitcase nearly the entire way up. It takes a hot minute. The suitcase is huge, and nearly all my clothes are stuffed inside of it. The good stuff, at least. I couldn't risk Geoff the Traitor burning them or giving them to his new girlfriend, who he probably already has moving in. Jerk.

By the time I get all the way to the top of the stairs, I'm winded and have definitely made a racket the entire inn heard, which I regret. I make a silent promise to be more quiet on the way out. I'll get Donny to help. I'll make sure it's not bingo night when I go.

I balance the suitcase on the stair behind me and wrestle with the big metal key. Once I get a good grip on it, I fumble it around where I *think* the lock should be. It's too dark to see, so I use my fingers to feel around until I figure it out. Only, I don't figure it out, and I clatter around for a length of time that is honestly embarrassing. I double majored in marketing and business at Columbia, yet I somehow can't get an old-timey key in an old-timey lock. Wasn't this the white chocolate chips sprinkled on the top of my crappy day?

"All right! All right!" comes a deep male voice from inside the apartment. "I'm coming."

I have about two seconds to process this surprising turn of events before the wooden door swings open to reveal a half-naked man standing there with a white towel slung low over his hips.

My jaw drops. Because this isn't just any half-naked man. It's a *super-hot half-naked man*. A man who has the body of Adonis. A man with chiseled abs and a six-pack that should seriously be illegal. Or come with a warning, at least. I slowly force myself to lift my gaze from his body to his face. His dark, slightly curly hair has fallen over one brown eye, and he is frowning at me.

"Ellie?" he says. "What are *you* doing here?"

Ellie? He knows me?

I gulp. I've met Adonis before? You'd think I'd remember. Do I have dementia?

I study his face. In that moment, he swipes the wet hair to the side, and oh damn. I know. I know exactly who he is. And I *have* met him before. Only I haven't seen him in *a while*, and he did not look *anything* like this. I am certain of it. *Certain.*

Mr. Hotness standing in front of me is none other than Aiden Parker. And oh holy Mary mother of God, has he changed.

Chapter 3

Aiden Parker!" I yell his name as if a) he doesn't already know it himself, or b) he's hard of hearing. Both are idiotic.

He shifts to his other bare foot, still holding open the door, still clutching that towel at his hips. I keep my eyes trained on his face because I swear I *cannot* look down at the line of hair on his flat lower abdomen that disappears under the towel. I want to. But now that I know who I'm staring at, it feels . . . wrong. I mean, Aiden and I used to play hide-and-seek together. And now he's . . . I press a hand to my warm cheek.

I shake my head and clear my throat. "What are you doing here, Aiden?"

There. That is a reasonable thing to ask, especially given that he's in the apartment where I'm about to post up for an indeterminate period of time. "Don't you have a house or something?"

I'm still standing on the second step down, one hand balancing my huge suitcase behind me, so I have to crane my neck to look up at him. I try to make it sound casual, like we just ran into each other at the grocery store instead of me desperately trying not to look at his happy trail. Or think about it.

"Would you like to come in?" he asks, as if it's totally normal to invite someone in while wearing a towel.

But yes. Yes, I would like to come in. Because I have every intention of staying here tonight, and possession is nine-tenths of the law or something like that. And even if that's not true, I will quote it as if it's true later, if I must.

I grunt and start to heft my big suitcase behind me, but Aiden stops me by nudging my shoulder slightly and steps down. Still clutching the edge of that towel that is going to haunt my dreams for a *hot minute* with one hand, he grabs my heavy suitcase with his free one and easily swings all of my stuff up onto the top landing. It's over in a matter of seconds, and I expel my breath in a heave as if *I* were the one who just slung a hundred and fifty pounds of clothes up three stairs in one fell swoop.

"Thank you," I say as I step up into the apartment. First, damn. He's tall. Like, really tall. And second, double damn. *His shoulders.* Watching them flex as he lifted that suitcase was . . . *something.*

Aiden closes the door behind me. "Just a sec," he says. "Let me throw on some clothes."

Or not. You could stick with the towel. That would be fine. I wouldn't mind.

I scratch the back of my head, as if I can scrape those types of thoughts from my brain. What was happening? Why was Aiden Parker in Mom and Dad's attic apartment wearing a towel? And when had he become so tall and so hot? And most importantly, with all the inane things Mom mentions on the phone, why had she failed to mention said hotness?

I mean, Aiden and I were kids together. Running around the property and helping our parents with chores. Then we hit high school, and it was like our relationship changed overnight. I was Miss School Spirit, and Aiden was a grumpy loner type. I was busy with schoolwork and extracurriculars, and Aiden was busy with . . . I don't know . . . wood shop and grumbling? He spent more time with his dad learning about farming the apple trees and less time in the food barn and the inn, and we just sort of . . . grew apart. The next thing I knew, I was off to college, and I only saw him in passing here and there over the years. But this is definitely the first time I'd seen him in *at least* four years and *for sure* the first time I'd seen him wearing nothing more than a towel.

I rack my brain, trying to remember everything, *anything* Mom has said about Aiden in the past. He'd gone to college. That seemed right. Where? I don't know. Damn. Why didn't I listen more? He'd moved back to Harvest Hollow. Did Mom tell me he had a house? I may have just made that up. But he couldn't have been living up *here*. Mom wouldn't have offered me the apartment if it wasn't vacant.

Oh God. Does Mom have dementia? She'd sounded okay on the phone earlier, but dementia is tricky. It comes and goes at first. What if she's been steadily going downhill for years, and my failure to listen intently to her phone calls made me oblivious? I am a bad daughter. We need to get her a good doctor. Immediately.

There's a rustling in the bigger of the two bedrooms, which distracts me from my medical intervention plans for my obviously ailing mother. Aiden comes back out wearing nothing but a pair of shorts. Oh, great. So, still a clear view of his fully bare chest. Fantastic. He is scrubbing a towel over his head to dry his hair, and I never knew until this moment that I have a thing for men messily scrubbing their wet hair with towels.

"Hey, there," he says, grinning at me as if I'd just popped by to borrow a cup of sugar. Out here, neighbors do stuff like that. I try to imagine asking to borrow kitchen items from my neighbors in Brooklyn. They'd probably call the cops on me.

"So, yeah. I do have a house," Aiden continues, causing me to stop thinking about borrowing kitchen items, "but there was a pipe burst this week. The plumbers are going to give me an estimate as soon as they finish a job at the Moose Lodge. My place is pretty much flooded at the moment."

"So, you're staying here?" My voice goes up to a weird octave I don't recognize, and I point at the floor as if there is some question about where "here" is. It is probably rude of me to blurt that out, but I'm tired and want a bath and bed, in that order, and now, well, Aiden's standing here looking like an underwear model. It's distracting.

"Yeah, Mom asked Lucy about it Saturday. I've been here since then."

Lucy is my mom, and now I'm even more worried about her dementia because she clearly forgot she gave the key to Aiden last weekend. And how the hell did Charlotte not see this coming from a mile away? She should have known the second key was missing from the front desk. There are two keys to every room. There always have been.

"Don't tell me," Aiden says, biting his lip in a way that makes me envious of a lip for the first time in my life. It's a sort of half tug, half nip with two of his perfectly white, straight teeth showing. "You were planning to stay here too."

"I was," I say, which probably makes me Captain Obvious, since I'm standing here with no shoes and a suitcase and the key still dangling from my hand. I am also nodding way too hard. As if an excessive amount of nodding will dispel the awkwardness. I feel it. I know it. But I cannot stop.

"Did Miss Guin get you?" Aiden asks next, eyeing my legs, his brow arched.

I glance down at my muddy jeans and have to stop myself from audibly groaning.

"She did" is my next obvious statement, and I am not proud of it.

"She's pretty stealthy," Aiden says.

"The stealthiest. The stealthiest of goats," I pronounce. Okay, that was dumb. And there is more nodding. Though it seems more polite than "Are you planning to leave soon, because I'm not really looking for a roommate?" I mean, he can go to his parents' house, right? They have a big place at the far end of the property with lots of bedrooms. I can't stay downstairs. Mom turned my room into a craft room years ago. It's full of yarn. Like, a hoarder amount of yarn and sewing machines and crochet hooks and probably some quilting stuff and a not-uncreepy collection of dolls on one wall. I think there may be some teddy bears too. The point is, I'm not staying down there. Even if I managed to find a blow-up mattress, I can't sleep with dolls staring at me. Besides, this is my parents' inn, and this is *my* apartment to use whenever I come home, and just because I never come home—*sigh*. Okay, I can totally see why the Parkers would have thought it was completely fine for Aiden to stay up here. They couldn't have known I would unceremoniously arrive after being dumped and fired on a random Wednesday, when I haven't been here in years.

"How long will you be here?" Aiden asks next. The towel has dropped to one bare shoulder, and he's looking at me intently. This time he's clearly the one trying to sound casual, and *his* voice goes up an octave. I can tell he's hoping I'll just say *one night*. It's written all over his face. His chiseled, handsome face. I have always been a sucker for tall, dark, good-looking men. And he's quintessential. Like, textbook.

But Aiden's hotness is not going to help the who-gets-this-apartment issue, so I purse my lips and answer his question. "I'm not really sure. A couple of weeks, probably." I kinda shrug and splay my hands wide to soften the blow.

His eyes widen as if I've just told him I quit my job to become a bounty hunter or something. "A couple of weeks?" The incredulity in his voice slightly offends me. I know I haven't been home in years, but is it really *that* unbelievable that I'd show up out of the blue for two whole weeks?

Okay, yes, it is.

I'm the one-off here. Not Aiden.

"So, uh, is there anywhere else for you to stay?" Aiden asks. He's let go of his bottom lip, and now he's kinda wincing. But it's a truly sympathetic wince, totally unlike Steve's fake winces from this morning. Aiden's is more like a we-have-a-problem-and-I-know-it's-probably-going-to-end-with-my-eviction type of wince.

"Mom turned my old bedroom into a sewing room," I announce with an overly dramatic shrug as if that explains everything. I tap my chin as if my next idea has just come to me. "What about your parents' house?" There. Happily tossing the ball back into his court.

"I can't stay there." He snort-laughs and pulls the towel around his shoulders to tug on both ends. His chest flexes. And it is still bare. I checked. No status update there.

"I tried staying with them once, the summer after my first year of college. It's pretty much an established fact that Dad and I will kill each other after one night under the same roof."

I nod. I mean, fair enough. I get it. Aiden doesn't have to explain to me how hard it is to go back home, let alone stay in the same living space as your parents as an adult. I'm not sure if the Parkers own any dolls, but I made sure I had internships in the city every summer during college. I had to stay in a fifth-floor walk-up in Queens with five other roommates once, but anything was better than the dolls.

I hook my thumb over my shoulder to point back toward the door. "I guess I can go ask Charlotte if there are any free rooms or—" At this point, I'm fully being passive-aggressive. If anyone should have to go ask Charlotte for a room, it's Aiden. And he should know it. And stop me from making such a selfless choice.

I'm waiting for him to interject when instead he says, "Look. There are two rooms up here. No reason we can't share the common spaces."

Share? I blink at him. *Share?* I'm an only child. We don't share. Well, not unless we are trying to squeeze into a Queens walk-up, but that was a necessity. And I was nineteen. I'm twenty-nine now. But where can I go if I don't stay here?

"I've got my stuff in the bigger room, but I can move to the smaller one," Aiden adds, already turning toward the bedroom like it's settled.

He really thinks we can share. Like it's no big deal to him.

I cock my head to the side and watch him leave like I'm a confused puppy. I mean, obviously I've been sharing with Geoff the last two years. We have separate drawers in the bathroom for our tooth-brushes and separate shelves for our other stuff, all pre-decided before I hired the movers. But Geoff was my boyfriend. The only man I've ever lived with. Staying here with Aiden feels strange. Intimate.

"Do you truly want to stay here with me?" I call after him because I can't think of a better way to say what I'm thinking.

He stops and turns on his heel. "Why not, Ellie Belly?"

The shock of the nickname takes me back. My mom gave it to me so long ago that I don't even remember when it started, and *no one* calls me that. Not even Mom anymore. It's from a hundred years ago, and I never would have thought Aiden of all people would remember it. Though he did used to call me that to tease me. It started when we were out decorating the barn for the autumn season one year, after he heard my mother calling me the cutesy nickname. He found it *hilarious*. I tried in vain to come up with equally embarrassing nicknames for him, but it was no contest. Despite the teasing, he redeemed himself by volunteering to hang all the stuff that needed to go up high so I wouldn't have to climb up on the ladder, because I don't like heights.

We must have been about twelve and thirteen then. Aiden hung the high decorations, and I placed the low ones. Teamwork, really. Quite efficient. We'd done it that way ever since.

Well, until I left.

"You remember my nickname?" I ask, feeling the tiniest little bit of wistfulness.

"Sure, I do." His answering smile makes my belly swoop. "You were cute back then. You had freckles." Aiden pads back over to me and leans down to study my face. "A few of them are still there, I see." He taps the end of my nose with a finger.

I swat his hand away, an almost-too-familiar reflex, and my belly swoops again. This time it's like a whole three-sixty. "Can we stay on topic, please?" I say.

I swallow and shake my head to clear it. What had he been saying before the subject of my freckles came up? Oh yeah. Aiden asked me "why not?" about the roommates thing.

"I mean, it's kind of tight quarters, isn't it?" I ask the sentence like a question, but there isn't really a doubt. The entire apartment is pretty small. There's a little galley kitchen; a dining space with a table and two chairs; a tiny living room with a tiny sofa and a tiny coffee table; one hall bathroom with the claw-foot tub, a sink, and a toilet; and two bedrooms. It's not big.

I'm quite aware of the fact that, as a New Yorker, it is pretty ridiculous of me to question the tightness of *any* living quarters, but out here in Harvest Hollow, square feet do not have the significance they do in Brooklyn.

"It's only temporary," Aiden says, and shrugs, still obviously committed to the it's-no-big-deal energy. "Unless your boyfriend would mind," he adds in a sentence that comes from so far in left field my head swivels.

"What?" The word comes out like a croak. Super attractive. But *Aiden knows I have a boyfriend?*

"Your mom told me you have a boyfriend. You live with him, right?"

"Right." Oh God. The overly ambitious nodding has returned. "Yep. That's right." I can't tell him the truth and risk it getting back to Mom before I'm ready. I need time to figure out how to frame my story in the best possible light. Otherwise, she'll worry about me. Yep, it's about the worry. Definitely *not* about the humiliation or the fact that the entire tale will be spread through town in minutes once Mom finds out. Lucy Lawson doesn't have a subtle nor secretive bone in her body.

"So, will your boyfriend have a problem with us rooming together for a couple of weeks?" Aiden asks, his brows both lifted.

"No! I mean, no." I say the second no much more casually, rolling my wrist in the air as if my nonexistent boyfriend is super chill and would *never* be the jealous type.

But two can play this game.

"What about your girlfriend?" I tuck a strand of hair behind my ear casually, as if I'm not low-key holding my breath waiting to hear his answer.

"I don't have a girlfriend." His grin is wide, and it occurs to me that of course he doesn't have a girlfriend, or he'd be at her house while his pipe is burst. Either that, or she'd be here with him if they lived together. Which would be a hundred times more awkward.

"Got it," I stammer. Okay, not a particularly eloquent reply, but it's all I have at the moment. Because I am remembering him in the towel, and it has rendered me speechless. Or at least speech poor.

"It's really no big deal, Ellie. I'll move my stuff. It'll just take a sec." He turns and disappears into the bigger bedroom.

I briefly consider telling him not to bother switching rooms. It seems petty. But the bigger bedroom *is* nicer. It has a cute little dormer window and a corner desk, and the big oak tree out back provides shade in the afternoon. Plus, it's sweet of Aiden to offer me the bigger room. He always was a nice kid, I think as I hear him thumping around in the bedroom.

"Thank you." I raise my voice, so he'll hear me. "It'll be nice to have the desk to use while I plan the Autumn Harvest Festival."

The thumping stops, and seconds later he appears in the doorway, his suitcase half zipped and stuffed with clothes that are sticking out haphazardly. I can't help but think that Geoff would die before he treated his clothing that way. "What's that?" Aiden's frowning.

"That's why I'm here," I tell him. "Mom asked me to plan the inn and orchard's Autumn Harvest Festival to go along with the parade. Didn't your parents tell you about it?" I make my way over to the fridge, open it, and look in, hoping for a bottled water. Mom and Dad usually leave some up here. *Yes.* It's there. Though I miss my tumbler that's trapped in Manhattan.

"Uh, yeah. I know about it," Aiden says. "It was my idea." His voice is flat.

I grab the bottle of water and clutch it to my chest, then I spin on my sock-covered feet to look at him. "Oh, I . . . You do know that I'm an event planner, don't you?" I give him the biggest smile I can muster. "It's kinda my thing."

"Yeah, I know." His voice hasn't changed. "But I'm a one-third owner of the orchard now. And unlike you, I never left. *This place* is kinda *my* thing."

Uh. *Ouch.*

Our conversation has taken an unexpected turn. Now I vaguely remember Mom telling me that Aiden had bought into the ownership of the orchard with his parents. But that comment about him never leaving smarts more than I would've guessed it would. It wiggles its way under my skin and lodges there like an apple seed in my teeth. "So, what?" I plunk my free hand on my hip. "I don't have the right to come help when I'm asked, because I moved to the city?"

I really want to hear his answer. He's clearly got a problem with me being gone.

His brow lowers, and he blows out a long breath. "Your parents have missed you," he tells me. "You couldn't come home for Christmas?"

Okay, extra ouch. The guilt that's been slowly rising through me all day is now about to drown me. But I'm not going to admit to Aiden that my jerk of an ex-boyfriend never wanted to come to my parents' house for Christmas. I'm not even ready to admit he's my ex yet. Still, I could've come home without Geoff. I know that. "I . . ." Ugh. I have no comeback. And I get it. Family means a lot to Aiden. He always planned to stay here and work with his parents. I just never realized he thought worse of me for not making the same decision.

The agonized look on my face must be obvious, because Aiden's features soften. "Look, you can help with the festival, but I already have plans." He drags his suitcase across the living room toward the smaller bedroom.

This time *my* brows shoot up. *He has plans?* After the day I've had, the last thing I want to do is fight with another man about my event-planning credentials. Though this one at least appears to have his own ideas. He's not trying to steal mine. An improvement from this morning.

"Understood," I say out loud to keep the peace for the moment. But in my mind, I'm thinking something more like, "we'll see." Because there's no way Mr. Apple Farmer's event ideas are going to be better than *mine*. I'd already sketched out a half dozen great plans on the train ride out here. Scarecrow-dressing contest, anyone? With, like, super-cute clothes.

Aiden nods once as if he's sure he's won the argument. Poor man. He has no idea that that was merely the first shot across the bow.

And I've got a nuclear submarine in *my* arsenal.

"Good, then. Goodnight." He steps into the smaller bedroom and closes the door behind him. "I'll see you in the morning, and we can get started" comes floating out to me.

"Goodnight," I call after him, shaking my head. I tip my suitcase and pull it toward the bigger bedroom. Thank God, this night is almost over. It's been a total cluster today.

The minute the bedroom door closes behind me, I expel my breath. First, Aiden has already changed the sheets on the bed. (I worked in hospitality for eighteen years. I know fresh sheets when I see them.) That was nice of him. Second, I force myself to remember that there is no need to argue about the Autumn Harvest Festival with him tonight.

Because I'm done being walked over by men. Mom asked me to plan this event with Aiden's mom's blessing. And that's what I'm going to do. Aiden's hotness and his status as my temporary roommate have nothing to do with anything. I am a professional. A professional who has just recently recommitted to the notion of *never* mixing business with pleasure again. And while I look for a new job to get back to the city as fast as humanly possible, I intend to plan the best little event Harvest Hollow has ever seen.

Whether Mr. Apple Farmer likes it or not.

Chapter 4

I wake up the next morning to the smell of coffee. Oh, glorious scent! In the city I never wake to coffee because Geoff and I pick up Starbucks on the corner by our office after ordering on the app.

I push myself up on my palms and breathe in another scent. This one less familiar. Bacon? Does that mean . . . ?

I climb out of bed and pull on my cozy black faux-fur robe. I unpacked last night after my bath so my clothes wouldn't be wrinkled. I'd pulled them out of Geoff's closet with the black velvet hangers still attached, so it didn't take long to empty the suitcase. I slide my cell phone into the robe pocket. I'm still tying the belt around my waist when I pad into the kitchen, yawning.

Aiden is standing in front of the stove frying bacon and scrambling eggs in a skillet. He's wearing jeans and an ice-blue cable-knit sweater. And it's official. He's even good-looking in the morning. And he's definitely hot. It was not some trick of the light last night or me being too tired and overcome by nostalgia for home. Meanwhile, I'm pretty sure I'm redefining the term *bed head*. I start frantically pulling my fingers through my hair.

Aiden glances at his watch. "Wow. You sleep late."

I frown and pull out my phone. "It's only seven," I point out.

"I've been up since four."

"Four what?" I narrow my eyes and cock my head to the side. What he's saying makes no sense to me.

"Four o'clock, a.m.," he clarifies. "I just came back from the orchards for breakfast."

I rub the tip of my nose with my palm. Normally, I would make a joke about being a farmer at a time like this, but then I realize he *is* a farmer, and the joke is not gonna land the way I would like it to. I remain silent.

"Would you like some coffee?" he asks next.

"Would I!" My fingers emerge from the long sleeves of my robe, and I do grabby hands. "I can't think or function or do much of anything before coffee."

Aiden pulls a white mug from one of the cabinets and fills it with coffee from a silver carafe. Then turns and hands it to me.

I stare down at the mug as if I don't know what the brown liquid is.

"What?" he says, nodding to the cup. "It's coffee."

"Black?" I don't know what kind of coffee I'd expected, but not black. I blink at the mug as if it's filled with an unknown substance. It might as well be. I don't drink black coffee. I drink coffee with flavors and special milk and anything else my heart desires. "Do you have any creamer? Or sugar?"

"What? You can't drink black coffee?"

"It's not that I *can't*," I explain. "It's that I don't want to. No problem, though. I . . . I'll stop by Starbucks later." I place the mug on the countertop.

Aiden rolls his eyes.

I post a fist to my hip. "You're thinking I'm too picky, aren't you?"

"I didn't say that."

My eyes narrow. "But you're *thinking* it."

"Maybe."

I lift my prim little nose in the air, because I will die on this hill. "I'll have you know that I don't care," I say. "If being picky means not drinking black coffee that tastes like a foot, then picky as charged. As a species we've evolved beyond black coffee. And I, for one, take full, unashamed advantage of that."

"Would you like some eggs and bacon?" he asks next, completely ignoring my little coffee speech.

"I don't eat breakfast," I admit. Fully expecting more judgment.

On cue, he rolls his eyes.

"Breakfast makes me nauseated." I shrug. "I suppose *you* think it's the most important meal of the day." Now I roll *my* eyes because, in an eye roll–off, I'm *gonna* win.

"What's your order?" he asks instead, surprising me.

I frown. "Order?"

He lifts his chin and contemplates me. "At Starbucks, what do you order?"

"What do you think I order?" I'm truly interested in his answer. This should be fun.

"Something complicated."

Okay. I take pity on him. "A hazelnut latte with oat milk."

"Oat milk!"

"And two pumps," I add, to further scandalize him.

"Two pumps of what?"

"Hazelnut syrup. They make coffee that actually tastes good in places like Starbucks. They've figured it out."

"You don't know if my coffee tastes good. You didn't try it." He seems smug.

"Have you tried Starbucks?" I counter.

He shakes his head. "I'm not paying five dollars for a cup of coffee. That's ridiculous."

I frown because the man makes a good point. I am unemployed at the moment. I probably shouldn't be paying for coffee either. Aren't financial-advisor types always saying something like that? Until this moment, I have chosen to ignore them. I lift the mug again and take a tentative sip of the black coffee before squeezing my eyes shut. *Glug* is the approximate sound I make.

Aiden pulls a box of sugar packets from a cabinet and tosses me two. "Try it with these."

"You couldn't give me these when I asked?" I rip the two packets open and dump them into the mug. I turn to find a spoon. He is already holding one aloft.

"I had to give you a little bit of a hard time, Ellie Belly," he says softly.

My mouth twists into an unwilling smile before I pluck the spoon from his fingers and begin stirring. After a couple of minutes (and two more packets of sugar), I am able to consume the coffee. Slowly. Reluctantly.

But I remain partially indignant. This is why people have jobs. So they can afford coffee that doesn't taste like glug. Which reminds me. I need to get online ASAP and start connecting with my network to find a new job. Only, I can't do that where anyone can see me, and my priority is the festival. I'll have to wait until I have a little alone time later.

"So, hazelnut syrup?" Aiden says, shaking his head.

"Or pumpkin spice this time of year."

I watch in fascination as Aiden pushes the eggs and bacon onto a plate with a spatula. He then grabs a fork, sits at the table, and places a napkin on his lap. It's the most domestic thing I've seen in a minute. I wonder if Geoff even knows how to make eggs. He never attempted such a thing in my presence. We were more of the order-in type of couple.

"You left some stuff in the bathroom," Aiden says casually as he spears a big clump of eggs with his fork.

Oh crap.

I quickly turn on my heel and rush into the bathroom. My panties and bra are hanging over the shower curtain. Ugh. I was exhausted last night. Ready for bed. I'd tossed them on the floor and—

Oh, great. This means Aiden has touched my underwear. And it's my wear-under-a-power-suit underwear too. Meant for business. They're not quite granny panties, but they're hardly sexy. And my bra is just a boring nude underwire. It is the workhorse of bras. Not that any sort of underwear would be good for leaving around, but this is just not my best presentation.

"Uh, sorry," I call, feeling a blush heat my cheeks.

"No problem," Aiden calls back.

I don't have long to be embarrassed, because my phone buzzes, and I pull it out of my robe pocket to see a text from Maria.

> where r u? why didn't u pick up last night? r u dead?

Maria and I listen to too many true crime podcasts. We are both a little quick to jump to murder as the cause for either of us not replying. Looking at my phone, I realize Maria texted late last night and I hadn't seen it till just now. The coffee smell distracted me. No wonder she's worried.

> i'm fine. i came out to my parents' inn for a bit. be back in the city soon.

> your parents' place?? is this really you, El? text me something only u would know.

I smile. Maria knows me too well.

> i once snorted espresso martini out of my nose at that party at the Gansevoort.

> hmm 1 more thing

Suspicion runs deep in Maria. It's an excellent quality in someone who is looking out for you.

> i owe you $50 bc Taylor Swift and Travis Kelce made it past the year mark. though I still say I'm surprised.

> hey! you do owe me $50. i forgot about that. pay up!

Yeah, well, I don't have a job, so she's gonna have to wait a little longer. I don't text it, but I think it. you know I'm good for it, I type instead.

I bite my lip. What else can I say without lying?

> i'll explain why i'm out here later. catch up soon?

> sure. but how did your presentation go?

> tltt

tltt = Too Long to Text. Not a lie, but not exactly the truth either. Ugh. I'm not looking forward to telling Maria what happened. I'm not looking forward to telling anyone what happened.

k talk later and a smooch emoji is Maria's trusting reply.

More guilt. I bite my lip.

After tossing my boring work underwear onto my bed, I make my way back to the kitchen and sit down across from Aiden. I take another tentative sip of the sugar coffee. "So . . . the festival. Do you want to tell me what you've already planned so I can take over?" I try to keep my voice as bright and helpful as possible.

Aiden's fork drops to his plate with a clatter, and his brows shoot up. "Take over?" he repeats. "I don't think so."

Ugh. I inwardly sigh. I don't want to fight with this guy over the festival, but he needs to back off and let me do my thing. "My mom and your mom asked me to," I inform him.

"They asked you to take over? Or help?" He eyes me with clear suspicion.

"I got the impression they want me to run it." There. Might as well get down to it. I'm kinda all out of giving any effs about hurting a man's feelings at the moment.

"Look," Aiden says, standing and washing his plate with honest-to-goodness dishwashing liquid and a sponge. I stare at him like he is an actor in an old-timey movie.

"There's a dishwasher," I say, pointing to the little appliance I'd insisted Mom and Dad install up here.

"I know." He stares back at me as if *I'm* from the future. "But it's only one plate and one fork."

"And a frying pan, two coffee mugs, and a spoon!" I add, holding up the spoon.

"I'll wash the spoon too if you can't manage." He has a lopsided grin on his face, but it's still a little patronizing. Why is this guy giving me so much shit?

"I can manage," I say, indignant. "But, I mean, this is what dishwashers are for." There. He can't argue with that.

"I don't have a dishwasher at my house."

Wow. No dishwasher *and* a burst pipe? Where's he living? "That's a shame," I say. I vaguely recall him being like this when we were kids, though. Old-fashioned. Capable. The kind of boy who learned how to do things like fix cars and use a hammer. I think I even saw him with a chainsaw once. There are two types of guys. The type who can change a flat tire in five minutes, and the type with the auto club on speed dial. Geoff is definitely the latter.

Geoff. Thinking about him compared to Aiden is almost laughable. Aiden is flannel shirts and ripped jeans. Geoff is Brooks Brothers and an expensive watch collection. Honestly, being here makes me question what Geoff and I had in common. He grew up in a mansion in Greenwich, and its impressive size only added to the hollow and empty feeling it held. It was nothing like the cozy warmth that the Honeycrisp Orchard Inn exudes.

The only thing Geoff and I connected over outside of our jobs was travel. Geoff loves to travel, and he taught me to love it too. We went so many places together. Places I never would have seen without him. Italy and Vancouver and the Maldives. I didn't even know what the Maldives were until I met him. We'd been planning a trip to Bhutan next. I guess that's not happening now. Meanwhile, Aiden probably doesn't know where Bhutan is. The guy has barely left Long Island.

Aiden leans back against the sink, capturing my attention again, and all thoughts of Geoff scatter from my mind. I can't help but think of how good Aiden looks with a scruffy jawline. It's like he shaves but not daily, and I want to run my fingers over it and—wow. I am being *so* inappropriate right now.

"You can *help* with the festival, but I've already got a lot of plans," Aiden announces.

Okay. Forget the scruff. I shake my head, clear my throat, and fold my hands together in front of me. I then place them on the tabletop as if it's a conference room table in the city. I may be in a robe, but I'm also in a business meeting, technically. "Like what plans?" I ask.

Aiden crosses his arms over his chest, which really makes the width of his shoulders more noticeable. I glance away. It's the professional thing to do.

"You really plan to stay out here and help with the festival?" he asks. The words are sort of a half whisper, half incredulous question.

I lift my chin. "Yes. Mom called me yesterday and asked me to come and plan the festival, and here I am."

His dark eyes narrow on me. "You don't have *anything* better to do in the city?"

My shoulders draw up. "My schedule is open at the moment," I begin. But then it hits me. I finally understand. He thinks I'm not invested. That's why he's giving me shit. He thinks I won't stay here and see this through. "And I'm fully committed to this project," I finish.

I still refuse to look directly at him. Mostly because of the shoulders.

"I just . . ." His voice trails off.

"What? Say it," I prod. He might as well let it rip. *Let's go, farmer. Let's have this out.*

"I just figured you weren't into this place. The inn or the orchard, you know?" He scratches the back of his neck and shrugs a little. "You left and never looked back."

Wow. Okay. Well, I'm not about to apologize for my life choices, but I do get why he's wary of me. If the shoe was on the other foot, I might give him heavy side-eye too, honestly. "Look, I wanted to be an event planner and live in the city," I say. "But just because I didn't choose to stay out here, that doesn't mean I don't care."

This whole conversation makes me a little sad. Is this what they've all thought about me all these years? That I don't care about this place? About them? I should have visited more. I know. "I'm here to help now," I say.

Aiden straightens to his full height, shakes his head, and expels his breath. His energy has shifted. I hope it means he's giving me a chance. "Okay, then. Stop by the work barn when you're ready this morning, and I'll show you what I've got so far."

Great. Perfect. Wait . . . "The work barn?" I'm trying to remember how many barns there are.

He shakes his head again, and the hint of a smile touches his lips. "There's the livestock barn, the food barn, the hay and apple barn, and the work barn. The work barn is the one in the far back. Past most of the fields."

"Ah, yes, the *work* barn," I say, nodding as if I know precisely what he means. I don't remember us calling the farthest barn the work barn, but I'm not about to admit it to him. He may be a one-third owner of the orchard now, but I'm a part of this business too. At least, I am for the next two weeks. And I'm not backing down.

Aiden makes quick work of cleaning the other dishes, including the frying pan and my spoon, before grabbing an apple-themed dish towel and drying everything and then putting it all back in the cabinets. I wrinkle my nose. I cannot recall ever seeing Geoff wash a dish. Not even at his mom's house for Thanksgiving.

Ugh. No more thinking about Geoff.

Or Aiden's shoulders, which still looked good as he washed dishes, if you're wondering.

"I'm just gonna go get dressed," I say, pointing toward the bathroom. "Unless you need . . ."

"Nope. All yours," he replies, giving me a wink that does something funny to my middle. A wide grin spreads across his face. "Roomie."

Chapter 5

"Mom, Pumpkin doesn't *need* doggie day care." I am sitting behind the front desk with Mom, Charlotte, and Pumpkin. It's about nine a.m. Only one couple has stopped by the desk to ask about the pick-your-own apples-and-pumpkins situation. Which is weird. It's usually busier than this. Mom already told me about bingo last night. Donny won like he always does, and the plumbers stayed to play.

"How do you know Pumpkin doesn't need day care?" Mom says, blinking down at Pumpkin. The pug is ensconced in a floofy round cuddle bed that is, of course, bright orange. Because, according to Mom, orange is Pumpkin's favorite color, for obvious reasons. She insists it's not true that dogs are color-blind. She watched a documentary about it.

"Are you bored here behind the front desk all day, Pumpkin?" Mom asks the dog in a completely un-cutesy voice. It's as if she's talking to a human son. "Do you need friends? Do you need structure to your day?"

Pumpkin just blinks up at her with his big bulgy eyes and snorts a little. It's cute that Mom is thinking of sending Pumpkin to day care for his well-being, but it's also because a new doggie day care just opened down the road and Mom loves to support Harvest Hollow's other local businesses. She's friends with most of the other business owners through the Chamber of Commerce that meets at Layla's Diner once a month.

Mom scans the doggie day care flyer that was at the door this morning. "It says here that Pumpkin will be exposed to all sorts of other breeds. Diversity. I like that."

"Yeah," I quip. "Maybe he'll meet a schnauzer and learn German."

Charlotte laughs. I like Charlotte. Good sense of humor on that girl. She is cutting orange ribbon into pieces to make something for the bakery. I am assisting her by tying the ribbons into small bows. It's keeping me busy and keeping my mind off both Geoff and my former job.

I'm wearing a loose pair of jeans and a chunky orange sweater. It's nice to be comfortably dressed. I was getting more and more formal at GMJ. Out here I can plan an event in a normal outfit.

My dad comes out of the apartment, shutting the door behind him. "How much does doggie day care cost?" he asks. "Maybe Pumpkin can get a job there and save us a few bucks." Dad has a dry wit and sunny disposition. He's handy, generous, and loving. He treats my mother like a queen and treats me as if he's the luckiest dad in the world to have me. I love both my parents. I really should have made time to see them more often.

"Hi, sweetie. Glad you made it okay," Dad says, dropping a kiss on top of my head.

"Hi, Dad," I say as he breezes past us out the wooden half door and into the lobby. He has a hundred little tasks to see to each day, and he's off and running. Today I need to follow him real quick, though.

"Dad," I call, catching up to him as he's headed down the hallway to the enormous dining room. "Can I talk to you for a sec?"

Dad is wearing dark-gray pants and an emerald button-up shirt. He dresses like an innkeeper even though he's more like a handyman. He has dark-brown hair and hazel eyes just like me.

"Sure, honey, what is it?"

I spent too much time before I drifted off to sleep last night thinking of how to bring this up tactfully, and I finally decided that I would just have to be blunt. "Is Mom okay? Has she been showing any signs of dementia?"

Dad's eyes widen. "Dementia?"

"Yeah. I mean, apparently, she forgot that Aiden Parker is staying up in the attic apartment right now."

Dad gets a funny look on his face. I know that look. It's the same look he got when he forgot to pick up the clay mold I needed for the science fair in the fifth grade. My project was something I can't even remember about rock formations. I chose it because it seemed easy. And science was *not* my thing. Besides, I may as well have not entered, anyway. Aiden always won the science fair at our elementary school. One year he did something involving the germination of seeds that garnered interest from *actual* scientists.

"Uh-oh," Dad says. The funny look is still firmly planted on his face.

"What?" I give him full side-eye.

He scratches his head. "Now that I think of it, I gave the key to Aiden last weekend. I forgot to tell your mom."

"So, Mom *doesn't* have dementia?"

Dad chuckles. "Not that I know of. But I guess *I* might." He winks at me. "But pleeease don't send me an online test to check."

I roll my eyes. He's kidding, of course, but I also fully intend to send him an online test to check.

I give him a hug, and he's off to putter around the inn all day while I go back to where Mom and Charlotte are sitting. "So, apparently, Dad gave Aiden the key to the attic apartment last weekend."

Mom frowns. "Aiden? Why would Aiden need the key?"

"A pipe burst at his house," I reply. I have not mentioned Aiden yet because I was waiting to talk to Dad about our strategy to get Mom tested for dementia.

Charlotte's eyes nearly pop from her skull. She slaps a hand on the counter. "Wait. Was Aiden up there last night?"

"Yep." I pop the P and nod.

"You both stayed up there?" Mom's voice rises, and I shush her. Not that anyone is around to hear or care, but for some reason, the louder she says it the more wrong it sounds.

Charlotte looks as if she may laugh herself off her stool. "Oh boy."

I'm not about to tell either of these two that Aiden was nearly naked when I tried to get in the door last night. That would ignite a firestorm of questions I'm not prepared to answer. "Yeah, it was . . . a surprise. But we've decided to share the apartment until his place is fixed."

Charlotte's response to this is raised eyebrows, a smirk, and renewed interest in the orange ribbons she is cutting on the countertop in front of her.

"There are two rooms!" I remind her defensively.

Mom shakes her head. "Don't be silly, dear, you can just use one of the inn's rooms."

I furrow my brow. "Won't I have to move every night for special reservations? This is the busiest time of year, isn't it?" Besides, the rooms are nice, but they are just bedrooms. They don't have kitchens and couches. They're smaller than the apartment.

Mom purses her lips. "Oh yes." She averts her eyes and nods. "Yes, yes."

Is it my imagination, or did Mom and Charlotte just exchange a look?

"You can stay in the sewing room if you like," Mom offers next.

"You mean the Doll Room? Pass. I'd rather have a boy for a roommate."

"Don't you live with a boy now?" Charlotte asks, cocking her head to the side. Wow. How much has my mom told the Parkers about me? Oh, wait. Everything. She's told them everything. Mom doesn't have a mute button.

"Yes, yes I do," I reply, and I'm 100 percent sure we've all just lied to each other. But we're even Steven, so we might as well move on.

"How *is* Greg, dear?" Mom asks, not pausing in her perusal of the mail.

"Geoff," I correct her.

"Oh, right, Geoff." Mom knows his name perfectly well. This is her passive-aggressive way of indicating that she doesn't like him. She's right not to. But I'm not ready to admit it. I don't want her asking a hundred questions and worrying about me. Or so I tell myself.

And speaking of worrying. I'm starting to get the idea that the inn maybe isn't doing so great. I've been trying to get ahold of the reservations system all morning, but Mom keeps acting as if she can't remember her password. Earlier, I was still worried that it was another sign of her dementia. Now I know better. The online system is one of the only nods to technology the inn has. It took my parents forever to get used to it. Now, when I'm wishing there was just a big book with names written in it, I'm thwarted.

But there's more than one way to be nosy.

"So, how's business?" I ask, keeping my eyes trained on the orange bows I'm tying.

"Business?" Mom says the word as if it's new, something not in her vocabulary. Or foreign, perhaps.

Charlotte keeps her head steadfastly bent over the ribbons and her scissors. She does not look up.

"Yes, how is the occupancy lately?" I press.

Mom steps back and tosses the mail she's sorted into the recycling bin beneath the counter. "Oh, you don't care about any of that, do you, sweetie?"

I frown. "Of course I do." Not that my absence over the last *four years* would have indicated it. But I'm here now, and if the inn is in trouble, I should know. Shouldn't I? I'm still a part of this family.

Mom flips a hand back and forth in the air. "Pish posh."

Pish posh is my mother's way of saying she wants the subject changed. I've tried many a time to circumvent a *pish posh* with nary a success to show for it. "We're so glad to have you planning the festival for us," Mom says next.

Well, at least she's changed the subject to another one that's near the top of my list. "Yeah, about the festival. Aiden sounds like he has it under control."

"What?" Mom moves over to the computer and logs in to the reservation system. So, she remembers her password after all? I need to sidle over.

"Yeah, he says I can help but he's already got plans," I add. I nonchalantly stand.

"Lyn and I both agreed that we need *your* help," Mom says quite forcefully, tossing the words over her shoulder as she pecks at the keyboard. "We've been doing it our way for a long time. It's time to try some new ideas."

"Okay, but you might want to tell Aiden that," I say as I ease my way behind my mother for Operation: Look at the Reservation System over Her Shoulder.

"Aiden's just bossy," Charlotte offers from behind her pile of ribbon.

Bossy and hot. But I'm not about to say that to his sister.

"And he doesn't like change," Charlotte adds.

I mean, who does?

The minute I get close enough to see the computer screen, Mom hits a key, and it goes to screensaver. Thwarted again!

"That's the last of the ribbon," Charlotte announces. "Want to help me deliver the bows to Sara? I'll introduce you," she says to me.

Sara? Who is Sara? Did Mom tell me about Sara? "Sure," I reply, not wanting to admit I have no idea who she's talking about. I hurry back over and tie the last few ribbon pieces into bows.

"Oh, introduce her to Jesse too," Mom says, waving her hand back and forth again.

Jesse? Now *that* name sounds familiar. They hired him a year or so ago to do . . . something. God. Do *I* have dementia?

Charlotte grabs a big fabric bag from a hook behind the counter and sweeps all the orange bows into it. "Let's go," she says. "Be back in a little while, Lucy," she tells Mom.

I follow Charlotte out the front door. I'm glad to have a few minutes alone with her, because I have questions.

We step onto the porch, and a crisp autumn breeze hits my face. I breathe in the leaves and wood smoke. Charlotte and I make our way down the porch steps to walk along the stone pathway between the house and the food barn. After last night's rain, there are a few puddles here and there, but the grass is a bright, shiny green and the leaves have just begun to turn. Only a few have fallen, but they are obviously preparing themselves. The color is just about to pop. That rain helped. The air is crisp but not yet cold. I love fall *so much*. I'd actually forgotten how much I love it. In the city I would venture to the park if I had time, but here the whole world feels like the season has changed. You can smell it in the air. You can feel it. I close my eyes and breathe it in. It catapults me back to my childhood. I've definitely been away too long. And I don't know why, exactly. All my important reasons seem pretty lame now. The thought brings unexpected tears to my eyes. I make a promise to myself to come out here every fall. At least once. That way, maybe I won't be treated like the prodigal daughter when I show up. And I won't have to *pretend* I know everyone's name.

"I hope you don't mind," Charlotte says, pulling me from my thoughts. "I took your boots, coat, and hat into your parents' place and cleaned them this morning. I can bring them up later if you want."

My face heats. I'd honestly totally forgotten about my dirty coat and boots. I shouldn't have left them out here all night for guests to see. Between that and the underwear, I guess I'm kind of a slob. It used to drive Geoff nuts. "You cleaned them?"

"Yep, well, the boots are suede, so I just brushed them. But they've dried, and they look really good. I hope you don't mind," she repeats.

"Mind? No. Not at all. Thank you. I'm sorry I left them for you to deal with. I forgot they were there."

"It's no bother." Charlotte gives me a big, bright smile.

I blink. I'm overwhelmed by some emotion I can't define. When was the last time someone did me a favor like that? I honestly can't remember. I've been used to taking care of myself for so long. It actually feels good to be taken care of even the tiniest bit. I mean, Maria and I take care of each other, but we're both super independent. For example, one time I was home with a cold, and she sent me some chicken soup from a delivery app. That was nice.

But the mention of my muddy clothes reminds me of Miss Guinevere, and now I glance in every direction, scouring the area like I'm in the Hunger Games. "Are the goats out?"

"Nope," Charlotte says with a laugh. "They're always in the barn in the morning."

Despite Charlotte's promise, I remain vigilant, because frankly, I think that's where Miss Guin was supposed to be last night when she knocked me over like a bowling pin.

"Donny's in charge of making sure they're penned. He was at bingo last night," Charlotte continues.

"Ah, I see." I am finally able to relax a little. "So, which one is the food barn?" I ask, slightly chagrined because I don't know. It used to be the big one in the middle, but now I'm not completely sure.

"The big one in the middle," Charlotte replies, giving me a sideways smile. "You haven't been gone *that* long, Ellie."

I return her smile. That's nice of her to say. And it's almost as if she can read my mind. Because between wondering if the inn is in trouble and whether either or both of my parents have dementia, I've been feeling pretty awful.

And it really is nice here. I lift my face toward the sun. The wind blows through the leaves on the trees, making them rustle. The orchards spread out on the other side of the winding road that leads from the highway. There is a pumpkin patch squared off with a rough-hewn log fence, and apple barrels line the drive up to the inn. Why *don't* I come out here more often? I've been ignoring this place because of my job and my boyfriend. Both of which just let me down.

I sigh. Why are mistakes only obvious *after* you make them? It'd be so much more helpful if the Universe could give you a big ol' heads-up *before* you do something stupid. I guess that's what intuition is. Mine told me not to get romantically involved with a coworker. But did I listen? I did not.

"So, how was it rooming with Aiden last night?" Charlotte asks, thankfully distracting me from my guilty thoughts again.

"It's . . ." How shall I put this? Especially to his *sister*? "He looks a lot different than I remember." The moment I say the words, I regret them. What is Charlotte supposed to do with that? I need to save comments about Aiden's looks for my next long talk with Maria, where they belong.

"When's the last time you saw him?" Charlotte asks next, hitching the bag on her shoulder.

I shrug and wrinkle my nose. Honestly, I spent way too much time after I climbed in bed last night trying to remember the answer to this very question. "Must be at least four or five years." And even then, I think I just saw him from afar in passing. Which is no doubt why I didn't notice how hot he is. Clearly, I need to pay better attention to detail.

"Yeah, there've been some changes around here since you've been gone," Charlotte says. It's a tone completely unlike her brother's, which was decidedly judgy. She was always a nice little girl. I remember her playing dress-up a lot and begging for a pony. She finally got a horse. It lives in the barn with the goats. Persistence pays off.

I want to ask Charlotte what she means exactly about the changes around here. I want to ask her how the inn is doing. If everything is okay out here. If she's noticed any signs of dementia in anyone. I open my mouth to begin the interrogation.

"Do you remember Sawyer?" she asks instead. The question throws me, because there's something about the way she says his name that makes my ears perk up a little.

"Sawyer?" I rack my brain, but that name isn't ringing any bells either.

"He's one of the farmhands who works at the orchard. Dad hired him about six years ago."

"You friends with him?" I ask, glancing at Charlotte to see if I can get any more Sawyer information from her very telling face.

She promptly blushes. "Yeah, we're friends." A shy smile spreads across her lips.

I would *love* to ask more, but we've made it to the entrance of the food barn, and Charlotte swings one of the big brown wooden doors open. "Here we are," she announces.

The moment we step inside the giant space, a familiar scent hits my nostrils. All sugary sweet and cinnamony and delightful. "Apple cider donuts!" I shout. Is there any better smell in the world? I close my eyes and breathe it in. "I haven't had one in years." I feel as if I'm lifted off my feet and am floating in the air toward the scent like a cartoon character.

"Oh, that's just wrong," Charlotte says, laughing. "And Sara's donuts are *the best*, so you're in for a real treat."

So, Sara must be the new baker. I swear I don't remember Mom talking about anyone named Sara.

The barn is huge and filled with picnic tables with black-and-white checkered tablecloths. To the right is the brewery area with a long wood-hewn bar and high-top stools in front.

The left side of the barn is the bakery area, and that is where Charlotte is headed, so I follow. Last I knew, a lady named Susie worked out here and made some pumpkin-flavored cookies and sold the donuts Mom made in her kitchen in the inn. Now I can already see that the operation has greatly changed. The entire barn has changed, really. It looks great. But I can't help but wonder if all these big changes and new employees like Sara and Jesse are why the business may be struggling. Did Mom and Dad and the Parkers overspend?

Barrels line the walls, and hay is not only scattered nearby, but there are bales every few feet too. Big silver stars hang from glittery ropes from the ceiling. They fall at different heights above the tables. There are apples and pumpkins and gourds on nearly every surface. There are dried cornstalks and mums and artfully scattered fake leaves. Despite the size of the barn, it is homey and cozy and smells like a dream in here.

The bakery itself is a countertop-high wall of glass shelving filled with every single delicious-looking fall treat you could imagine. There are apple scones and apple pies, pumpkin bread and pumpkin-shape cookies covered with thick icing. There are apple-filled croissants and fat slices of carrot cake dripping with cream cheese frosting, and chocolate chip muffins as big as my hand. There is zucchini bread and cranberry cobbler and cinnamon cake. And the donuts. Oh, the donuts. Sweet, puffy, hoops of yum! They are piled next to each other in a row, and the sugar glistens atop them, beckoning me. I cannot stop staring. Or salivating. Mostly salivating.

I'm still eyeing everything in a baked-goods-fueled daze when the door to the back of the bakery swings open and a young woman comes out. She looks to be about my age.

"This is Serafina," Charlotte announces with a twirl of her hand.

Serafina? Oh yes. I *have* heard this name before. Mom *did* mention her. Only, when I heard her name, I remembered thinking it sounded super unique. This is *Sera*.

"Hi." Serafina looks up, and the first thing I see is her bright, orange-dyed hair. Otherwise, she is wearing all black, including a long-sleeved T, leggings, Crocs, and an open sweater that hits her calves. She has a mess of thin gold chains around her neck and a moon-shape gold pin in her hair. Her fingers are covered with rings, and the skin I can see, including a bit of her neck and her wrists and forearms, is covered in astrological-looking tats. She's giving total woo-woo vibes but in the best possible way. Almost witchy. Super cool. I have the urge to ask her to read my tarot cards, but then I immediately think it's probably presumptuous of me to assume she does that.

"Nice to meet you," I say. Okay, I admit I also wonder if she is going to ask me what my sign is. And I'll totally tell her. It's Libra, btw.

"Sera, this is Ellie," Charlotte says next.

"*You're* Ellie!" Sera exclaims, clapping her hands and making all her jewelry jingle. She gives me a huge smile. "My energy healer told me there was gonna be a big change around here this month. Now I know why. And please, just call me Sera."

"Hi. I'm not sure what my energy is up to, but here I am." I grin sheepishly.

"Oh, your energy is great. I can feel it," Sera replies.

"Really?" I want to pull up a chair and talk to her for the rest of the day while eating donuts. Also, now I'm feeling like the tarot card question may not have been out of order, but I will save that for later.

"Definitely," Sera replies with a firm nod. And I can't help but wish she'd been around when I'd first started dating Geoff. Maybe she could have told me he had steal-your-ideas energy.

"Sera's food is magic," Charlotte says next. "Here are the ribbons for the cookie bags." She hands the bag of ribbons to Sera and goes around the counter, where she pulls a donut off the glass shelf with a napkin and hands it to me. "Ellie was just saying she hasn't had an apple cider donut in years."

"Are you serious?" Sera blinks at me. Her eyes are clear light green. A really unusual color. Kinda like a cat. And now I'm wondering if she's like Sabrina the Teenage Witch. I want to keep staring at her, but I realize she's just asked me a question and that I have a donut in my hand that's not gonna eat itself.

"Yeah, I used to love these. I can't remember how long it's been,"

I say, truly wondering why I've never managed to get ahold of an apple cider donut in the city all these years. It seems so obviously wrong now.

"Well, eat up," Sera says. "There are plenty. I have two more batches baking in the back."

Without further ado I take a big bite of the donut. And HOLY! Charlotte wasn't kidding. It's the best donut I've ever tasted. And that includes Mom's. It's soft and fresh and sugary and cakey and hits my taste buds in the exact right spots. It then proceeds to essentially melt in my mouth. I close my eyes. Pure bliss.

"This donut is perfection," I announce, reopening my eyes and staring at it as if I've fallen in love, and honestly, I kinda have.

"I'm serious," Charlotte continues, nodding. "Sera's food is truly magical. Like legit infused with *magic*. She's a karmic baker."

Wait. What's this now? I cock my head to the side and stare at them both. "Karmic baker?" I'm sure I would've remembered it if Mom had mentioned a "karmic baker."

Sera laughs. "Yeah, I don't really tell everyone that, but everything is energy. So, I just infuse the food with good energy. I'll explain it to you sometime if you're interested."

Uh, hell *yes*. I *am* interested. She can explain it to me at the same time she reads my tarot. I take another bite of the donut and close my eyes. I don't know anything about energy healing, but the vibe I am getting off the donut feels sooo good. And hey, I don't judge anyone's woo. Just because I can't read energy and make karmic donuts doesn't mean there aren't others in the world with these much-needed skills. I'm here for it.

"Magic energy," Charlotte adds, taking a bite of her own donut. "Sera's apple cider is actually a love potion too."

"Like a real, live love potion?" I ask. I add this to the mental list of topics that Mom has buried the lede on during our phone conversations. Aiden's hot. We're selling love potions now. I mean, *come on*, Mom.

Sera waves a ring-filled hand in the air. "Yep. It's a whole process, of course, and there are rules, but people *have* been known to fall in love after drinking it."

"Really?" Okay, now I'm even more interested, but honestly, I don't care what Sera claims about her apple cider, if it tastes half as good as this donut, it's two thumbs up. Would recommend.

"Sometimes she sneaks good energy into Jesse's brews too," Charlotte says in a whisper.

"Ah, yes. Jesse. He's the new cider brewer, right?" When I saw the bar, I finally remembered where I'd heard that name before. I vaguely remember Mom telling me they hired a guy who was really into brewing. Before that, it had mostly been Dad and Mr. Parker doing the best they could.

"Yeah. He's the brewer. But he's been here nearly two years," Sera says.

"He's *a lot*," Charlotte adds with an eye roll.

"Capricorn," Sera says in a stage whisper. She shakes her head as if that one word is self-explanatory.

I give her my best blank stare, and she must feel my ignorant energy because she adds, "*Intense.*"

I want to ask them both more about Jesse, but the doors to the back of the bar flap open just then, and a tall guy who also looks about my age comes out carrying a big plastic tray filled with upside-down glass beer mugs.

"That's him," Charlotte whispers.

My brows shoot up. Well, now. Jesse is hot too. If you like fit blond dudes with heavenly blue eyes who wear ball caps and flannel shirts. It's not actually my jam, but I know someone who is *very* into it. Though she'll never admit it. Maria. Too bad she's not here right now.

"Introduce me," I say, turning toward the bar.

"Hey, Jesse. Come meet Ellie," Charlotte calls.

Jesse immediately frowns. He puts down the big plastic tray on the far side of the bar, turns, wipes his hands on a bar towel, and then jogs over. "Ellie?" he asks, still frowning.

"I'm Lucy and Mark's daughter," I explain. Why is he frowning?

"Oh yeah," he says, and I get the distinct impression that he's heard something about me that makes him a little wary. Hmm. Now I want to know what.

"You live in the city, right?" he asks.

"Yep," I say, not about to expound upon anything in my life at the moment. I live in the city. That's enough for Jesse to know about me in addition to whatever he also knows that's making him look at me like that. "The brewery looks great," I add.

And it really does. The entire back wall is filled with two neat rows of beer taps. Most of them with long pulls in the shapes of apples or trees or leaves. There are black-and-white pictures of beer steins and beer mugs and growlers along the back wall, and the sleek bar top is the same dark-brown wood as the tops of the stools. The entire space is punctuated by pristine stainless steel sinks and counters, and there are tiny white pumpkins and gourds set in small clusters along the bar.

"Thanks," Jesse replies, finally smiling. "I've been working hard on it. I've got big plans. I actually want to turn this place into a full-service bar someday. Instead of serving mostly cider. That's my real dream. And—"

I listen to Jesse talk about IPAs, and the price of hops, and the difference in a drink's taste based on filtered water, for the better part of ten minutes before Charlotte interrupts him. "Well, we'd better get going," she says. "Ellie's supposed to meet Aiden out at the work barn. They're planning the festival together."

Jesse arches a brow. "*You're* planning the festival?" He points at me. "With *Aiden*?"

"Yeah," I say, narrowing my eyes and letting him see, because I'm kinda hoping he'll elaborate on the words he has tellingly emphasized.

"Wow, okay," is all he provides before he tosses the bar towel over his shoulder. "Nice meeting you, Ellie." He immediately turns and gets back to work while I'm left pondering what the hell "wow, okay" means.

Charlotte tugs me back over to the bakery counter. "Sorry," she whispers. "Jesse can be a little . . . much. Especially when you get him talking about beer."

"I like a man who knows what he wants in life."

"I guess that's one way to put it," Charlotte replies with a sigh.

I glance at my watch. Charlotte was right. It's nearly ten. Half the day gone if you're meeting a farmer. I need to find Aiden. "Can you show me where the work barn is?" I totally plan to ask her what Jesse meant by "wow, okay" during our walk to the next barn. This time I won't dawdle.

"Oh yeah, come on," Charlotte says, ushering me along.

Before I say goodbye to Sera, I point to one more donut. "Can I just?"

Sera nods. "Of course." She grabs another donut from the glass shelf with a napkin and hands it to me over the countertop. I promptly stuff it in the pocket of the jacket I'm wearing. And then I'm off following Charlotte out the door in search of her cranky brother.

Chapter 6

A seven-minute walk later (I timed it), we near the big barn at the back of the property. Aka the work barn. All of the other barns are painted white and have pumpkins and gourds and planters with mums piled up in front of the smoky brown/gray doors. But this one doesn't, since it's a working barn. Not a part of the property where guests go, and of course this is where Aiden is.

"So, what did Jesse mean when he said, 'wow, okay' about me working with Aiden?" I ask Charlotte as we crunch through the smattering of leaves.

"Like I said," Charlotte replies, "Aiden can be bossy. He likes to work alone."

My memory of Aiden from childhood was that he was always ready with an idea. He never seemed bossy to me, but then again, I'm not his kid sister. I do remember that he likes to work alone. At least, most of the time. Whenever I went looking for him when we were kids, he was usually by himself.

"Got it," is all I reply. Aiden is welcome to continue his solitary work. I'll happily take the event off his hands.

We're almost to the doors when a movement in the trees behind the barn catches my eye. "Is that Aiden?" I ask, pointing.

Charlotte narrows her eyes. "Yeah, it is. What's he doing back there?"

"I don't know. But I'll go find out. Thanks for showing me around," I tell her.

"Sure thing. And don't let him boss you. He needs to give a little," Charlotte warns before taking off back toward the inn.

I change direction and stroll under the apple trees toward Aiden. Leaves are burning somewhere, and the wood-smoke smell is even stronger here. The narrow green leaves are turning yellow, and the apples are bright red. The harvest has already begun, but it's not finished yet, and the Parkers always leave some trees to ripen even more. The apple trees back here are the ones for sale to large buyers. The trees in the front near the inn are the pick-your-own orchard meant for guests.

I pull an apple from one of the trees and toss it in the air. Just feeling its cool, smooth skin brings back so many memories from childhood. Me and Aiden helping with the harvest. Me and Aiden playing baseball in the fallow field with an apple as a ball and a stick as a bat. Me and Aiden dumping out the barrels and sorting through the apples to pick the best ones for pies like our moms taught us.

Aiden was such a large part of my childhood, and the fact we lost touch just seems very wrong now. I slip the apple in my non-donut-filled pocket and make my way closer to Aiden.

He doesn't see me approach. He's half facing me, but he's distracted. He's digging a hole with a shovel. When he stops to pull up the bottom of his white T-shirt to wipe his face, I get another view of his blistering abs. I swallow. Hard. Seriously. Mom could've given me a heads-up on his newfound hotness. Maybe she does have dementia, after all.

I'm about twenty feet away from him, crunching through a smattering of fallen leaves, when his head jerks up. "Ellie? What are you doing here?"

"You asked me to meet you out here," I remind him, my forehead wrinkling.

He tosses the shovel to the ground and makes his way toward me quickly. "The barn. I asked you to meet me in the barn."

Wow. Maybe he is bossy, after all. Before I know it, he's got his hand on the small of my back and is hustling me quickly back toward the barn. I let him, but only because I'm amused by how obvious it is that he doesn't want me to see whatever he was up to. Which only makes me more curious. "What were you doing back there? Burying a dead body?" I joke.

"No" is his only answer, and I make a mental note to come back later to see how big the hole was. I don't *truly* think he's burying a body, but I've seen a lot of *Dateline*. Ya never know.

Minutes later, we're inside the dark coolness of the barn. When Aiden hits the lights, the first thing I see is a big flatbed trailer covered with apples and hay bales.

"What's that?" I ask, pointing at it.

"That's our float for the Autumn Harvest parade."

I can't help my frown. Did I mention that I was born without a poker face?

His hands immediately land on his hips. "What? You don't like it?"

I shrug. "Apples and hay bales are cute and all, but they're a little basic, no?"

"Basic?" Now he's frowning.

"Yeah, you know, *obvious*?"

He pokes out his cheek with his tongue and cocks one hip. "Fine. What would you do, Miss Event Planner?"

"Well." I cross my arms over my chest and take a slow walk around the float. My mind is racing with ideas. "I'd probably add white mums and a cozy chair with a furry throw blanket and a chandelier and—"

"A chandelier?" He says the word in the same way one might say a less beautiful word. Something like *smallpox*, for instance.

"Yeah, a chandelier. Why not?" I tap my cheek with my finger, still envisioning the amazing float I'm going to make. "The inn has that great chandelier in the main dining room. It's evocative. A real showpiece. The cozy chair will represent the inn, and I'd also use another corner to advertise the brewery and the bakery. Big fake donuts and beer growlers."

Aiden's brows shoot up. Both of them. "You gonna get Jesse to cough up his precious beer growlers for the float?"

"Heck yes, I am." I am warming to the subject now.

"Who am I kidding? You're hot. He'll probably do whatever you ask," Aiden mumbles.

Wait. I am stunned into silence for approximately 2.5 seconds. And then, "What was that?" I cup my hand behind my ear. "You think I'm hot?"

Aiden blushes, and it's the cutest thing ever. I don't think I've seen him blush before. "I'm sorry, Ellie. I didn't mean to sound sexist. It's just that—"

"Just *what*?" I prod. I cannot help myself. I do not even want to help myself. Plus, him calling himself out for being sexist is, well, sexy.

Aiden dips his hands into his jean pockets and rocks back and forth on the heels of his brown work boots. "Come on. You have to know you're hot?" He gives me a look like it's the most obvious thing in the world.

I don't have to know any such thing, but I do the only sane thing to do when attempting to keep things professional with a business partner, which Aiden obviously is, despite his own hotness, and I say, "Thank you." For some bad reason, it's on the tip of my tongue to inform him that he is also hot, but I decide against it. No more mixing business with pleasure. Not after Geoff. Never again! We need to get back to discussing the float. *Stat.*

"Okay, so beer growlers and donuts, and the chandelier," I say.

"How are we going to make a chandelier?" Aiden asks, skepticism dripping from his voice.

"Papier-mâché, of course. Just like the homecoming parades in high school." Wait. Does the world at-large not know about papier-mâché?

"Yeah, I didn't really participate in the homecoming parades."

Oh . . . right. I bite my lip. "No worries. Leave it to me," I say, because not only do I know how to make a fake chandelier and hang it from a fake sky over a float, but also I don't want to remind him that I was on the homecoming court and student council and was in charge of stuff like this throughout high school. And I enjoyed it.

"I think we should stick with the traditional apples and hay bales," he informs me.

Okay, is *this* what Charlotte meant by "bossy"? Because he's sounding like he's stuck on his ideas and not interested in using any of mine.

"I really think it needs more," I reiterate.

Aiden makes a sort of growling noise. "I know this place. It's my home. People around here like traditional things."

Wow. His words hit me like arrows to the chest. I lift my chin. It's my home too. He really can't let go of the fact that I didn't choose to stay here, can he? "Everyone or *you*?" I ask with more than a little attitude.

I am met by silence and a sort of disgruntled snort. But I'm not backing down. This is my wheelhouse. Making beautiful, wonderful, fun things out of nothing. Coming up with grand ideas and executing them. Putting on a show. I will not put my name on basic-bitch apples and hay bales.

Our standoff is interrupted when a big yellow Lab comes flying through the propped-open barn door headed directly toward Aiden.

Just before the dog is about to jump him, Aiden says, "Sit," in a deep, commanding voice, and amazingly, the dog obeys.

I stare at the pooch in awe. What sort of dog is this? An obedient one? Pumpkin wouldn't sit if you offered him money. Or the car keys. I've seen him on enough FaceTime calls with Mom to know how disobedient that little chunk is.

Aiden pets this remarkable dog's head and says, "Good boy." It's pretty cute. The dog's tongue is hanging out, and he looks like he's smiling at us.

"Who's this?" I ask, smiling back at the Lab.

"This is my dog, Argos. He's staying with my parents until my house is livable again."

I say hello to Argos, who offers his paw to me to shake. Wow. Pumpkin would sooner skip a meal than shake. I take Argos's sturdy paw and think about how much I've missed spending time with dogs due to Geoff's allergies.

I am still regretting how many dog-paw shakes I've probably missed over the last four years when the barn door opens wider and an older man steps in. It takes me two seconds to realize it's Mr. Parker. Aiden's dad, Kevin, has a little more gray in his dark hair than I remember, but otherwise, he looks great. He's not as funny as my dad, but he's a good guy. Very dependable.

"Ellie!" Kevin says. "I heard you were here."

I slide my fingers into my jean pockets and nod. "Yep. Just helping out with the Autumn Harvest Festival," I say. "In fact, that's what Aiden and I were just discussing." I see my chance and take it. "Give us your opinion," I say. "Aiden wants to keep the parade float hay bales and apples, and I think we should add beer growlers and donuts."

"And a chandelier," Aiden mumbles.

"A chandelier?" Mr. Parker says, scratching behind one ear. "Like the one in the inn? That sounds like a great idea. I say you combine all of that."

"Compromise?" I say as if it's a novel idea, making my eyes wide and turning to look at Aiden. "I like the sound of that."

Aiden narrows his eyes on me. I can tell he hates the thought of compromising. He finally blows out a breath and says, "Fine. Apples and hay bales *and* beer growlers and chandeliers."

"Only one chandelier," I say cheerily.

"Good," Mr. Parker says, clapping his hands. "Well, I just came to drop off Argos for the day. I'm meeting the seed distributor at the entrance in a few minutes. I'll see you later."

"Thanks, Dad," Aiden replies, but he sounds a little grouchy. Probably because his dad sided with me.

After giving Argos a pat on the head and telling him to have a good day, Mr. Parker leaves the barn.

"So, you named your dog Argos?" I say after the barn door closes behind Kevin. "As in Odysseus?"

"Yep," Aiden replies, nodding.

My brow rises. "Very academic."

"What?" He laughs. "Surprised to learn I read the classics? I went to college, you know."

"I know," I shoot back probably too quickly. But I'm glad he brought it up. I've been dying to find out more about him, because I apparently never listened to a word my mom said. "Where did you go, again?" I ask, trying my best to be nonchalant as I grab the tape measure that's lying on the side of the flatbed and begin measuring the space for the float. Now that I'm getting my way, I'm ready to get going.

"Not Columbia," he says quickly.

Oh, so he fully remembers where I went? Great. That makes me feel like even more of an ass.

"SUNY Edwardsville?" I ask.

He immediately rolls his eyes. "Wow. You really think highly of me, don't you?"

"What? I had friends who went to SUNY Edwardsville."

"Yeah, the ones who couldn't get in anywhere else. SUNY Edwardsville is the biggest party school in the state."

"Okay, then, where did you go?" I ask.

"Cornell."

The tape measure snaps closed on the tip of my thumb. "Ouch." I wave my hand in the air. "Ouch. Ouch. Ouch."

"You okay?" he asks, stepping closer as if he's going to take a look at my thumb.

"Yep." I stick my thumb in my mouth. "I'm fine," I mumble around my thumb. I don't want to admit that he's just shocked me with his alma mater. Do I remember him getting good grades? He wasn't in any of the honors classes with me. He did have legit scientists interested in his science projects, though. "What was your major?" I ask after I pull my thumb out of my mouth.

"Agricultural sciences."

Of course it was.

"Got my master's there too."

Wait. What? Mr. Farmer here has a bachelor's *and* a master's from Cornell? How did I miss that? So, he's more like Professor Farmer than a mere mister.

"Ithaca," I say, nodding like an idiot again. At least I'm not still sucking my thumb. "Another nod to Odysseus."

"Yep, and a great place to learn about farming."

Aiden picks up a stuffed toy in the shape of an apple that Argos brought in with him and tosses it far across the barn. The dog speeds off after it, clearly in heaven.

"Look," I say, reminding myself yet again to stick to business. "We have a lot to plan. Do you want to go over my list?" I grab my cell phone from my back pocket. My notes app is filled with all the ideas I jotted down on the train ride out here.

Aiden rocks back and forth on his heels. "Uh, not yet. I was just going to show you the float for now. My list is in the apartment."

Of course it is, because Professor Farmer wrote it on a *piece of paper*. "Okay, fine. Later, then?"

He nods. "Sounds good."

"Great," I say, giving him a smile. Thank goodness we've managed a truce. Aiden seems willing to work with me now. And I have plenty of experience showing other people how good my ideas are. I'm not worried about that part. Debacle with Geoff notwithstanding. I hook my thumb over my shoulder. "I'll just head back to the apartment, then. I have some, uh, things to do for work." That's not untrue. I need to do a lot of things . . . to get a job. "See you later?"

"Yep." He does a little finger-salute thing near his temple.

I am about to turn on my heel when I notice that Argos is at my side, and he has his nose in my pocket. The next thing I know, my apple cider donut and the napkin have disappeared down his throat.

Uh-oh.

"What was that?" Aiden asks.

I wrinkle up my nose and wince. Are dogs allowed to eat donuts? Or napkins? "Uh, an apple cider donut from the bakery."

"Bad dog, Argos," Aiden says, frowning at the Lab.

Argos looks slightly chagrined. Which, frankly, is more than Pumpkin would do. Pumpkin would either look entirely unconcerned or proud.

"No. It's my fault," I say. "I shouldn't be walking around all short with baked goods in my pocket." I am embarrassed to have been caught hoarding a donut. But not so embarrassed that I won't stop by the food barn and get another one on my way back to the inn.

I make my way to the door, and Argos and his stuffed apple come to see me off. I pet the dog on the head and say, "I'll see you later too. Don't tell Pumpkin you got a donut, or I'll never hear the end of it." I'm already planning to put an apple costume on this dog and have him on the parade float next to Pumpkin, who will be wearing a pumpkin costume, over his orange jumper, of course.

* * *

Fifteen minutes later, new donut in hand, I'm back in the apartment. I glance down at a yellow Post-it note on the kitchen counter. I can barely make out the scratchy words written there.

Float
Maze
Bobbing for apples
Archery

It's obviously Aiden's festival list. Hmm. This guy needs help, and he doesn't even know it. First of all, no one's bobbing for apples. That's just gross. And I'm not sure what archery has to do with a fall fest. I think he's confusing it with a Ren Faire.

All the signs are pointing to the fact that the inn and orchard may well be in some financial trouble. It might have taken me four years, but I'm here now, and I intend to help them all.

But the apartment is empty at the moment, so it's the perfect time to jump on my laptop to connect with some former colleagues and get my résumé up to snuff. I've always had a CV ready just in case, but I need to update it a little before I send it anywhere, because getting fired wasn't on my bingo card for the year.

First, I do a search for an online dementia test and send it to Dad. *Can't hurt to have Mom take it too*, I write before forwarding the link. Then I spend the next two hours emailing former work associates and scouring job listings as well as the websites of the other big event-planning firms in the city. I am hopeful. With my experience and connections, I'm sure to get some interviews soon and will be back in the city living my real life in no time. Not arguing with Professor Apple about the contents of a parade float.

And apple bobbing? No. Just no.

Chapter 7

Aiden and I aren't back in the apartment together until after dinner. I ate downstairs while Pumpkin sat snorting in one of his many beds and Mom and Dad talked to each other *through* Pumpkin. It works like this: Mom asks, "Does Pumpkin want dessert?" And Dad replies, "I think Pumpkin would *love* some apple cobbler."

Which, same, apple cobbler sounds great, but it can't be healthy to have entire conversations through a dog, can it? But what do I know about marriage? I was just dumped and betrayed by the guy I was in my longest relationship with. Maybe Pumpkin is the linchpin in Mom and Dad's successful marriage. Who am I to question it?

I'm sitting on the little couch in the living room of the attic apartment. My pink laptop is propped on my legs, and I'm wearing my pajamas. The pants are butter soft, and the button-up top is dotted with little fall orange-leaved trees and apples. Mom sent them to me because she knows how much I love fall. Now that I'm wearing them here at the inn it's even more poignant.

I have a facial mask on because it's Thursday, which is mask night, and even though Aiden is hot, I have no intention of flirting with him, so he's gotta deal with my green-tea face mask if we're going to be roomies.

He comes out of the bathroom, where he's just taken a shower, wearing nothing but shorts again, which is patently ridiculous. I mean, if my abs looked like that, and I was a guy, I would probably go around shirtless a lot too, but it's downright distracting.

He stops when he sees me and cracks a smile. "What's that on your face?"

"Green-tea mask," I reply, refusing to look up from my laptop. I've seen enough of his abs for the time being, and I'm already restless and achy and feel as if I could totally pull him down on top of me if the opportunity arose. Which is another reason I slathered on the face mask. Nobody is getting laid with a face mask on.

"Does Starbucks sell that?" Aiden asks.

It takes me a moment to realize he isn't joking. Wow. Dude really has never been in a Starbucks before, has he? I would think he was possibly a Russian spy, but I'm pretty sure a Russian spy would have been to a Starbucks. I tilt my head to the side, seriously considering his question for a minute. "Honestly, I wish they did sell it. It'd be easier than going to the beauty store to pick it up. Anyway, do you want to go over the list of ideas for the festival now?"

After I worked on finding a job this morning, I spent the better part of the afternoon ordering things for the festival. My plan is an age-old one. Ask for forgiveness, not permission. Otherwise, I'd spend too long arguing with Professor Apple here, and that would just waste time. We only have two weeks to prep for the festival. This is going to be a rush job as it is. But I'm not worried. I have a lot of experience with rush jobs. When I first began at GMJ, I got all the last-minute parties. All the new hires do. It's sort of like a rite of passage. They test your mettle by seeing how quickly you can put together a decent event. I thrived on it. So, this is fun for me. And this particular event is even more fun because I don't have to run any of my ideas past the partners at GMJ. It's a freakin' pleasure, actually.

"Sure," Aiden replies, glancing around. "Let me get my list."

He darts into his bedroom and spends several moments shuffling around before I take pity on him and call out, "If you're looking for your Post-it note, it's on the counter."

"Ah," he calls, jogging out of the bedroom. Still shirtless.

He grabs the little slip of paper from the countertop and makes his way over to sit next to me on the tiny couch. It's more of a love seat, really. Which means we're close. Real close. I can feel the heat radiating off his body. I can smell his fresh soapy scent. I shift on my cushion. I turn, pointing my knee toward him, and reopen my laptop, determined not to spend one more second staring at him.

"What are those?" he says, sounding incredulous.

I glance up to see him staring at my hands. I'd just put on some new press-ons tonight along with the face mask. "My . . . fingernails?" I reply. He may be a farmer, but he's got to know what press-ons are.

His eyes are wide. "They're so . . ."

"Fabulous?" I supply as my eyes narrow even further. My claws are bright orange with a little leaf on two of them. I know they're adorable. He'd better not say one word against them.

"Can you type with those things?"

My brows shoot up. "I can do anything with these things." I pat the top edge of my laptop. "Don't worry about me."

"I definitely couldn't work with those."

"It's a good thing you don't wear them, then." I give him a tight smile.

"You're right. You're right. I'm sorry. They're just so . . . orange."

"Orange nails, green face mask. And you're not wearing a shirt. Are we all caught up?" Okay, that probably came out a little more bitchy than I meant it to.

"Wait. What?" He blinks at me. "Do you want me to put on a shirt?" He looks shocked, as if the thought never occurred to him.

"Well, it *is* a little distracting," I admit, wrinkling my green-gooped nose.

"Really?" His voice is completely incredulous. "Distracting?"

I shrug. Oh, great. Now I've waded knee-deep into *this* topic. "Um . . . yeah. I mean . . . you're a good-looking guy, and your abs are—"

"Whoa! You think *I'm* good-looking?" His eyes are wide, and he's sitting up straight now.

"Didn't you tell me I was hot earlier?" I say this in an accusatory manner. The whole conversation is already ridiculous. "So what if I say you're the same?"

"Yeah, but I just assumed you knew that," he replies, as if that explains everything.

"Likewise." Okay, now I wish I didn't have on the green face mask, or maybe I wish I had on more of it and it was covering my eyes so I could not even see him. At least the mask is obscuring the red that is probably spreading over my cheeks. "Look, I just . . . We need to plan this festival, that's all." I focus my attention back on my extremely detailed bulleted list.

"Okay, but let me throw on a shirt first. I don't want to *distract* you." He waggles his eyebrows, and I want to hurl one of the couch pillows at him, but I refrain. That would not be professional.

He's back in a minute wearing a red-and-gray Cornell T-shirt, which is the kind of passive aggression that I admire. He resumes his seat on the couch. "Better?"

"Yes. Thank you," I reply. "I have a strict rule about mixing business and pleasure."

His brow crumples. "Isn't the guy you live with your coworker?"

What the hell? How much did Mom tell him? And how closely was he listening? Sheesh. "He, uh, was."

"*Was?*" One of Aiden's dark brows arches.

I sigh. It's time to come clean. "Look, can you keep a secret?"

He crosses his heart. "Promise."

I hadn't wanted to get into this yet, but somehow I believe Aiden won't tell anyone, since I've asked him not to. I trust him. I expel my breath. "My boyfriend and I broke up."

Both of Aiden's brows shoot straight up this time. "*Really?*"

"Yep. It turns out that dating a guy I work with was a horrible idea, and I'm never doing it again." There. How's that for an explanation?

"Noted," says Aiden. "And your parents don't know yet?"

"Right," I say. I quickly explain how Geoff stole my ideas and how I was fired too.

"Oh, wow. Ellie, that's terrible," Aiden says. He's biting his lip and shaking his head.

It does sound pretty bad when I say it out loud. But the truth is the truth. I plow ahead.

"And since I lived with Geoff, I kinda needed a place to stay," I continue. "So when Mom asked for my help, I agreed."

Aiden crosses his arms over his chest and nods. "Oh, *now* it all makes sense," he says slowly, dragging out the words.

I frown. "What do you mean?"

Aiden shrugs. "I wondered why you were suddenly so interested in this place after all these years."

Okay. Now I'm definitely getting even redder beneath my mask but for a completely different reason. I'm pissed. "Are we seriously back on this topic again? What's your problem?"

Aiden plucks at the bottom of his T-shirt. "I don't have a problem. It's fine by me whenever you want to come home."

"Uh, no, it's clearly not. You've done nothing but give me shit about it since I got here."

He's silent for several moments, and I gear up to tell him off for just how unwelcoming he's been. But then—

"You're right, Ellie," he finally says in a low, calm voice. "It's just . . ." He takes a deep breath and meets my gaze. "I could tell how much your parents missed you. But it's not my place to judge you for it. I'm sorry."

In my fired-up state, that was the *last* thing I'd expected him to say. I just blink at him for several more moments, processing the apology. Is it possible to read facial expressions happening beneath face masks? If so, mine has got to be pure surprise. Because it turns out Aiden Parker is a man who can admit he's wrong? *And apologize?* It may be the swoon-worthiest thing ever. Plus, he's right. My parents did miss me.

"Thank you for that. I accept your apology," I say.

Aiden just nods.

A few more silent moments pass before I say, "So, the festival plans?"

"Can I ask you a question first?" Aiden's lodged into one corner of the couch and is hugging a throw pillow to his chest.

"Sure."

He grins at me. "What were you going to say about my abs earlier when I interrupted you?"

I can't help the smile that pops to my lips. "Maybe you shouldn't have interrupted me, and you'd know already." Okay, that sounded flirty, but I couldn't stop myself.

"Ah, come on," he pleads. "Tell me. I told you that you're hot."

I sigh. "Fine. I was going to say that your abs are . . ." I'm searching for the correct word. It's not easy. "Ridiculous," I decide. "Your abs are ridiculous."

His grin spreads across his whole face. "I swear I wasn't trying to show them off."

"I don't believe you, but I also don't blame you. If my abs looked like that, I'd be shirtless too. Now, can I ask *you* a question?" He's given me the perfect opening. I'm going to take it.

"Sure," he says.

"What were you doing out in the orchard this morning?"

"What do you mean?" He swallows, and I can tell he doesn't want to answer the question.

"This morning, when Charlotte and I showed up. What were you doing out there?"

"Just tending to the trees." His gaze is glued to his Post-it note again.

"Really? You weren't doing anything you didn't want me to see?"

"Like what?" he counters. But he still won't look at me.

He's horrible at pretending. And now I'm stuck because I have no idea what anyone could be secretly doing out in the orchards. I don't have a master's in agriculture from Cornell. What does secret apple farming consist of? I should have searched the internet on that question before I began this discussion. Too late now. "It just seemed like you wanted me out of there quickly."

"Nope. No. Nothing to hide," he says in the most I've-got-something-to-hide voice I've ever heard. He's got no future in being a criminal.

After a few moments, it's clear he's not gonna say any more.

"Okay, fine, so, back to business." I clear my throat and review my long list. "Do you want to go first?"

"Sure," he says, clearly relieved that the subject is changing. The Post-it is stuck to the tip of his index finger. He reads from it quickly. "Float, maze, bobbing for apples, archery."

I wait for a few seconds to be sure he isn't going to expound on any of it. Apparently not. "Great ideas!" I say in a voice that's probably too enthusiastic. But I'd had all afternoon to think about his list and had already decided to seemingly agree to all of it and use the word *and* to present my own. *And* is a better word to use than *but*. My therapist taught me that. Plus, as a rookie event planner I learned to always praise my client's bad ideas and then artfully maneuver the conversation toward my better ideas. It's a whole tactic.

"And I was thinking we could do a scarecrow-dressing contest, a pumpkin-carving contest, hayrides, and live music. Oh, and instead of bobbing for apples, a make-your-own caramel or chocolate apple stand would be fun." I want to say, "more hygienic," but I don't. I am not done, however, and by the time I finish rattling off my list, Aiden has a look that I shall describe as "horrified" on his face.

"What do you think?" I ask, smiling brightly.

He scratches the back of his head. I try not to look at how his shoulder stretches the T-shirt tight. Or think about how I would love to squeeze his bicep and run my hand over his arm for absolutely no reason.

I force myself to concentrate on what he's about to say. Like me, the man has no poker face whatsoever. "I mean . . ." He bites his lip and scratches his head some more. "That's . . . *a lot*."

"Yeah, it's a lot," I allow, "but I think these things could be really good for the inn and the orchard."

"How much will all that cost?" he asks next.

And there it is. The opening I've been waiting for *all* day. "Mom and I didn't really discuss a budget yet. Do *you* know how much we can spend?"

He cringes and lets out a resigned breath. "As little as possible."

It's my turn to frown now. I shut my laptop and face him. I intend to be blunt. "Is there something I need to know about the businesses, Aiden?"

He bites his lip, and I can tell he's wrestling with what to say.

"Are they in trouble?" I prod. If I'm going to help them, I need the truth. "I noticed a lot of changes around here. A lot of money's been spent, hasn't it?"

"Yes." He nods. "On changes I didn't think we needed. Mom and Lucy have really been trying to revamp things around here. We've had a lot of competition in recent years with new orchards in the area that are all over social media, and the damn Airbnbs."

Oh, so there *is* trouble in autumn paradise? "And there are financial issues as a result?" I press.

"It's not great," he admits. "But I'm working on fixing it."

Chapter 8

D o you know where I can get an apple costume for a seventy-
pound dog?" I ask Charlotte the next morning as we sit behind
the front desk.

"Yep, Tifton's Pet Supply. Out on Highway 12."

I jot that in my notes app, pleased that Charlotte just answered the
question and didn't ask me why. She gets me.

"We need to start selling apple costumes for dogs," I say. "And
stuffed apples for dog toys like the one Argos has. Pumpkins too."

After my discussion with Aiden, I stayed up half the night brain-
storming ways to make more money at the festival. If Mom and Dad
and the Parkers are in as much trouble as I think they are, we need
to truly monetize this thing. I did some reconnaissance in the parking lot this morning, and there was only a smattering of cars. Sure,
people could have taken the train out here from the city, but a quick
glance at the number of keys on the wall in the back also confirmed
my suspicion that we're nowhere near full occupancy.

It's obvious. This place is hurting financially.

I plan to ask Mom why she never mentioned anything was wrong.
Even though I already know the answer. *You're so busy, dear. We didn't
want to worry you.* There will probably be a lot of pish poshing, and
she'll try to quickly change the subject. But still, I'm going to try.

"Hey, Mom," I call. She looks up from the computer screen she's
standing in front of. "Take a walk with me?"

Charlotte agrees to cover the front desk while we're gone, and I
loop my arm through my mother's and head out the front door with

her. It's the last day of September, and the chill in the air is even more pronounced than yesterday. I breathe it in. I've missed this. Really missed this. The way you miss something and don't even know it until you're back. And not just the chill and the scenery, but walking around the property with Mom. We used to do this all the time. We'd drink apple cider and talk and laugh. It feels like just yesterday, and it feels like years ago. As if space and time have merged, and there is only this happy feeling in my middle telling me how much I enjoy all these things I've been away from for so long.

"How's it going upstairs with Aiden?" Mom asks as we take the little cobblestone path beneath the trees that leads to the back of the inn. A few leaves float down to land on the grass as we go. The wood smoke is in the air again today. It's a perfect fall day.

It's on the tip of my tongue to ask Mom why she never told me that Aiden was hot, but that's a subject I've decided I don't want to broach. The rumor that wedding bells are in the air will spread before lunch.

"It's good. We're working on some great ideas for the festival," I reply. I don't mention that Aiden brought me pumpkin-spice creamer for my coffee this morning. He told me it was to convince me to give homemade coffee another chance. It was truly thoughtful of him, and I had to admit it tasted great and that it was nice to wake up *before* I left the apartment. It's absolutely divine not to have a commute.

Mom sighs. "Oh, good. I'm so glad you're able to help, Ellie." She pats my hand.

"Me too, Mom." I squeeze her arm. I wonder if she already knows there's something wrong in my life or I wouldn't be here. The same way Aiden was suspicious. She's probably just being mom-like and keeping her questions to herself. I appreciate that. Meanwhile, I'm about to let 'er rip with my own questions. "Why didn't you tell me the inn and orchard are in trouble?"

There. Might as well just toss those cards right on the table.

Mom stops and plucks at her ear. It's a telltale sign that she's flustered. "Who says the inn and orchard are in trouble?" Her voice wavers.

I raise my brows and plant a full-on skeptical look on my face.

Mom's face falls. "Okay, the businesses could use a little marketing. We didn't want to worry you. You've been so busy."

"Marketing?" I repeat. That's an interesting way to *not* say they're in trouble. I need to be even more blunt. "Are you planning the festival to save this place?"

We continue to walk again. "Yes," she admits. And honestly, that scares me more than any pish posh ever could, because Mom not trying to downplay it means it's really bad.

"We tried a few new things, and . . . well, it hasn't quite worked out the way we hoped. If it weren't for those darned Airbnbs!" She shakes her fist and then sighs. "The festival is a last-ditch effort. Aiden came up with the idea." Her voice sounds tired.

My stomach tightens. Last-ditch? Not great.

"If we don't make enough from the festival, we may have to sell." Mom's face is pale, and I feel like an ass for not asking more questions and listening more intently all these years. I was in my own little world all about me. I never thought the inn and orchard could be in trouble. This place has just always been here. My whole life. A stalwart. But that's no excuse. Only, I can't change the past. I'm here now, and I can help, and that's what matters.

Plus, I have seven years of high-end event-planning experience under my belt.

I take a deep breath. "I'm glad you told me, Mom. Now that I realize what's at stake, I plan to pull out all the stops."

"What does that mean?" Mom looks a bit hesitant. I'm sure she's worried about the expense just like Aiden was.

"It means I've got a lot of plans, and I'm going to help you." Of course, I don't tell her I'm skeptical that one festival will be enough to save this place. I haven't seen the books, but if both businesses are a festival away from having to sell, it can't be good.

I also have no intention of telling her that selling might actually be the best thing for all of them. I can't help but think that this place is just the sort of property the Bolt Hotel Group would love for their new Barn and Branch brand. It's bucolic. It's homey. It's set in a gorgeous location. Close to the city. It would be perfect. Plus, I happen to know the Bolt Hotel Group is paying top dollar for places like this. Mom and Dad and the Parkers could cash out and retire.

But I know Mom doesn't want to hear that right now. So I say the only thing that is comforting and true. "I'll do my best, Mom."

"I'm glad you're home, Ellie," Mom says. She smiles at me and her eyes crinkle, and for the first time since I've been back, I realize she looks seven years older than when I moved to the city.

"I'm sorry I was gone so long, Mom." I squeeze her arm again. Now would be the perfect time to tell her that Geoff dumped me, stole my ideas, and got me fired. But it's not about me right now. Mom has enough on her plate. She's spent all these years trying not to worry me. Now it's my turn not to worry her.

"This will always be your home, Ellie."

I can't help but think that it won't be, though, if they have to sell. But I know what she means so I blink away the unwanted tears. There's no time to be sad or take a trip down memory lane. If we're going to turn this festival into a moneymaker, I need to get cracking.

* * *

Fifteen minutes later, I'm back inside, firing off orders to Charlotte, who is rapidly taking notes on her own phone. Dad is there, and so is Mom. Aiden and the Parkers come in when I text them.

Lyn hasn't seen me yet. She's a short woman with dark hair shot with gray. Dark eyes and a perpetual smile on her face. It's no mystery why Charlotte is so lovely. Lyn rushes over and gives me a big hug. She smells like cinnamon and home too. They all do. Well, all except Aiden, who smells like hotness. But that's not the point.

"Oh my goodness, Ellie, look how beautiful you are. Isn't she beautiful, Aiden?"

I turn to him expectantly, batting my eyelashes mockingly. Aiden rolls his eyes and says, "Yeah, of course." It's pretty funny, given the fact that we both admired each other's looks last night.

"We've missed you, Ellie," Lyn says next. "Haven't we missed her?" she says this to the whole room, and all of them say yes at the same time.

"I missed all of you too," I say, and I really, really mean it.

But we need to concentrate on the festival, and I refuse to cry, so I clear my throat, pull out my phone, and start reading my list.

"Okay, we need flowers, props, and temporary staff. I'm hiring a sketch artist and a country rock band. I know a fabulous LED artist who can light up the trees."

"Light up the trees?" Aiden echoes.

"Yeah, the pathways under the apple trees will look so romantic if we add twinkling lights." I snap my fingers. "Oh, and we're going to turn the brewery into a full-on German Oktoberfest Biergarten. Jesse will love that!"

Mom and Dad and the Parkers are grinning from ear to ear. Charlotte is still busy typing on her phone. But Aiden has his arms crossed over his chest again and is looking more than a bit skeptical.

"Anything else?" he asks. He's kidding, but he doesn't even know I'm just getting started.

"Yes!" I say. "We're also going to have a Harvest Ball outside in the food barn on the last night of the festival."

Aiden's eyes bulge. "A what, now?"

"Don't worry. It'll be fun. We're going to offer a special to couples getting a room for two nights. To get away from their kids. The kids will be in one of the other barns in tents with childcare provided from the inn."

"Oh, let me run that!" Charlotte exclaims, looking up from her phone for the first time since I began talking. "Two of my best friends are kindergarten teachers. They'll help. I know they will."

"Excellent." I turn to Mom. "The couple's special will include two nights at the inn, dinner, dessert, drinks, and admittance to the dance in the barn. Can you add a code for that to the reservation system?"

"Sounds good to me," Mom replies. She scuttles off toward the computer.

Aiden scrubs the back of his neck and groans. "This all sounds expensive."

"Leave it to me. I have some favors to call in," I tell him.

Mom, Dad, and the Parkers all look at each other as if they're impressed. I feel a surge of energy shoot through me. This is what it feels like to be in your element. I know because I've been here before. But this time it feels even better. This time I'm doing it for my people, my family, my home. And the best part is, I still don't have to run any of this past the bosses at GMJ. Out here, *I'm* the boss. I never realized how tiring it was to make sure the partners were on board with my ideas. I mean, Geoff could usually be counted on to agree with me, but he'd still have to get approval from the other two.

But I don't have time to think about any of that now. I swivel toward Charlotte. "First things first," I say. "We have to begin with the PR. We're going to need to publicize the festival if we're going to get people from the city and the surrounding areas out here to spend money. And it just so happens that I know a PR genius named Maria Agostini."

A few rapid-fire questions to Charlotte uncover the fact that she has already created social media accounts for the inn and orchard. Which is great. I ask her to get started taking pictures of the most homey-looking things around the inn. The mums. The gourds. The cinnamon sticks. The chandelier. And Pumpkin! Because Pumpkin the Pug is about to get famous. "Make him an account," I tell Charlotte. "Stat."

"Sure thing!" Charlotte's fingers fly over her cell phone, while I turn to my laptop to begin designing the flyers. In addition to all the things we'll do online, I'm about to paper this town with the news about the Honeycrisp Orchard Inn's Autumn Harvest Festival. The biggest news this town has seen since the doggie day care opened yesterday.

Then I text Maria. It's time for the big guns.

Chapter 9

How did you make a paper chandelier in one day?" Aiden asks later that afternoon after I come strolling into the barn with said chandelier in tow. Argos is running around chasing his stuffed apple. I have no donuts in my pocket. They are all in my belly.

"I have my ways," I reply. My ways being me and Charlotte frantically creating faux papier-mâché with colored tape and a wing and prayer during lunch. But it looks pretty good, if I do say so myself. I have also brought a length of wire that will hang the chandelier and the stars and the moon I intend to add.

Charlotte comes traipsing in behind me carrying the big white satin bows and the cornucopia horn we also created.

"What's that?" Aiden says, scrubbing his hands through his hair. He looks nervous.

I march straight up to the float and place the chandelier atop it.

"It's the cornucopia!" Charlotte announces. "Isn't it cool?"

Behind her files in a group of men that I've hired from town. Donny is in the lead. He's the one who found them all. They are carrying pumpkins, gourds, mums, and all the other things I bought from the country market out on Highway 12. They also bring in the apples and barrels. Donny is carrying a life-size stuffed goat.

Aiden points to the goat. "What the hell is that?"

"A goat," I reply as if it should be obvious, and without stopping to explain anything else to Aiden, I ask the men to put all the stuff on the ground next to the trailer. The goat is going to be the centerpiece of the float.

"Need help making the float?" Donny asks Aiden eagerly.

"Nope. No." Aiden points to the door. "Just go make sure Miss Guin isn't loose," Aiden instructs the bellhop.

"I'll do that!" Charlotte volunteers. And I know it's because Sawyer works in the livestock barn most of the day. I found that out last night by making a few discreet inquiries to one of the maids. I'm pretty sure Miss Charlotte has a crush on the farmhand. I have to admit it's a little fun to be nosy.

Charlotte is halfway to the door before Aiden's voice rings out. "Charlotte, stay here. We need your opinion."

Charlotte's face falls. Her brother obviously has no idea she has a huge crush on Sawyer. Meanwhile, it only took me two days to suss it out.

"So, white ribbons and a cornucopia?" Aiden says, coming to stand next to me. He cups his chin in his hand. "And a stuffed goat? We didn't talk about these things."

We didn't talk about a lot of the things I'm doing. But I'm not about to pipe up with that. My motto remains: Ask for forgiveness, not permission. "We didn't?" I try to sound innocent.

I am crouching next to the trailer digging through the huge shopping bag I had slung over my shoulder for the green felt that I intend to use to cover the bottom of the trailer floor. I grab the felt square and pull it out.

"What's that?" Aiden asks.

"The grass, of course."

"We agreed to a chandelier and some beer growlers, not—"

I snap my fingers. "Oh, that reminds me. Donny, will you please go ask Jesse for the growlers? We're going to make the papier-mâché donuts later."

"Papier-mâché donuts?" Aiden echoes.

"Yep. I just wanted to get the main parts placed today. The donuts need to be big. *Really* big."

Aiden stares at me. Argos has come to sit at his owner's side, and he's staring at me too, his red stuffed apple firmly lodged in his chompers. "What?" I ask Aiden as if I don't know what. I unfold the felt and whoosh it out with both hands until it lands flat on the bed of the trailer. "There."

"Do we *need* grass?" Aiden asks skeptically.

"Don't worry," I say. "I promise we'll make a profit." I have no idea if this is true, but I've worked with enough panicked clients to know that confidence is key in the event-planning industry. The more confident the planner is, the less worried the client. I do know that the budget is already far greater than anything Aiden and I talked about last night, but I also know that my plans include several ideas to make money. Part of the reason this place is hurting is because they include too much in the stay at the inn. They need to monetize more. And I'm about to help them do that.

"What's the budget at?" Aiden wants to know. He is frowning.

"Let me worry about that," I reply. I would say "pish posh," but I'm not sure that works on Aiden.

"Oh no!" Aiden says, shaking his head. "That's not the answer I'm looking for."

I turn and plant my hands on my hips. "What's the answer you're looking for?"

"I told you the max amount last night. All of these things sound way more expensive than that."

"Have you ever planned an event before?" I ask.

"No."

"Have you ever heard of industry discounts?"

"There are event-industry discounts?" He looks skeptical. His arms are crossed again.

"Yes, and I happen to know how to get all of them. So, like I said, don't worry. Just help me put these barrels up on the float, will you?"

Another age-old tactic . . . distraction. But it works, because the next thing I know, Aiden has pulled off his sweater and is hefting giant apple barrels up onto the trailer bed. And now I am the one who's distracted, because the memory of seeing his muscles flex every time he lifts one is going to be in my dreams later. If I'm lucky . . .

"We need white satin bows around each barrel," I announce, trying to concentrate on my work. I worked with Geoff for three whole years and never glanced at him twice when he was lifting things. That's a bleak (yet interesting) observation. I stick that in the back of my mind to think about later.

"White satin bows?" Aiden groans, but he hasn't stopped lifting. He's on barrel number three. And I'm still watching the show. I wish I had more barrels for him to lift. I'll have to figure something out.

"Yes, bows are super on trend. Charlotte, what do you think of the white satin bows?" I ask.

"I think they're beautiful," Charlotte replies loyally.

Still love that Charlotte.

Her brother scowls at her.

"Don't worry," I say as one of the hired guys comes back in lugging a hay bale. "We're doing hay bales too." Ooh, until this moment, I had forgotten about the hay bales.

Aiden has finished with the barrels, and he turns to grab the next hay bale. And yes, I'm still watching. The arm muscles, the abs that appear when he lifts, the thick muscles in his thighs when he squats. Damn. Farmers are way hotter than I would have seriously ever guessed. And there is nary a Patagonia vest in sight out here.

"Here are the biggest growlers I've got." Jesse enters the barn, and I smile, clap my hands, and run over to him.

"Thank you!" I say. "Please put them over here." I point to the spot I want.

"No, thank *you!*" Jesse replies, grinning at me. "The Oktoberfest idea is great. I've already begun getting the other beers ready. A Biergarten is my dream come true."

"Excellent." I smile and mentally pat myself on the back.

"Too bad no one thought of that before," Jesse says in a grumbly voice, and I'm positive he just gave Aiden a semi-smug look.

"Do you need anything else from me?" Jesse asks. When I assure him I don't, he heads back toward the door, but not before I notice Aiden giving him a narrowed-eyed glare. Ooh, what's that about? Bad blood between Jesse and Aiden? *How* interesting.

I check my list and mark each item off as I take inventory of the items surrounding the float. Once I'm satisfied that the apple barrels, hay bales, goat, and growlers are all present and accounted for, I stuff my head into my giant bag again to ensure the big stack of flyers I printed earlier on light-orange paper are in there.

"I've got to go," I announce to the barn in general, now that I've found my flyers.

"Go where?" Aiden asks, sounding more than a little suspicious.

"I need to put the flyers up around town. Although, if you want to do it instead—"

"Not a chance," he says. "You know, if you go into town, it's gonna be like the Spanish Inquisition for you. You'll never get through handing them all out."

He's not wrong. And I am not looking forward to it.

"I'm coming with you," he says next, surprising me.

"You don't have to come watch," I huff.

His grin is unrepentant. "You need a ride, don't you?"

Chapter 10

Twenty minutes later, Aiden and I drive out the entrance to the inn and orchard. It's a long, twisty road lined with trees and a rough-hewn wooden fence on either side. I have the window down and stick my head out like a golden retriever. When is the last time anything felt this fun? It's the middle of the day, and I'm just cruising along with the wind in my hair.

I spent all morning doing the thing that makes me happy. Making an event come together. And now I'm sucking in the autumn-scented breeze. It's sweater weather, with candles and cozy blankets in my mind's eye. And I feel total freedom.

Back in the city, I might hop on the subway to grab a few things for an event, but my phone would be blowing up with a million questions from Steve. It's almost always him asking about things I've already taken care of. It slows me down to have to keep him informed of every little move I make. But when I'm in charge, I can do *whatever I want*. It's a feeling I'm not used to, but one I could get used to real quick.

Aiden is driving, and his ride is not exactly what I expected. It's not a car. It's a truck. And while one might guess a farmer drives a truck, this particular truck is an old red jalopy that looks like it should be hauling around the characters from *The Grapes of Wrath*. The thing is old. And loud. And smells like diesel.

But far be it from me to judge anyone's whip. I don't even own a car, and I *am* in need of a ride, so old-timey red truck with apple barrels in the back, it is!

We take Highway 12 straight into town and pull up in front of the coffee shop on Main Street. Everything on this street looks exactly like it did the last time I was here. The little library on the corner. The town hall building across the street. Layla's Diner front and center. The general store on the corner opposite the library. And Wilkins's Hardware Store two down from Layla's. It's all here, and because it's fall, everything is wrapped in orange and green and brown and yellow. Every business is flanked by large planters filled with bright mums, and the little trees planted along Main Street are turning orange and yellow and red. There are pumpkins and gourds and hay bales aplenty. The town square across from the library is filled with apple barrels from the Parkers' orchard, and a scarecrow has been erected near the stone podium where the mayor gives speeches on holidays like Groundhog Day and the Fourth of July.

"Nothing in Harvest Hollow ever changes," I say to Aiden. It's a line I've said many times in the past to my parents and to myself, but this time is the first time I realize it's a good thing. Not a bad one. It's comforting here. It's reliable. Unlike jobs and boyfriends in the city.

"It's true," Aiden replies. "You ready?" He's grinning at me, clearly about to enjoy watching me be grilled by every single townsperson on this street. I'll be lucky to be home by dinner. If Aiden leaves me, I may have to take the only rideshare in town, which I'm pretty sure is operated by Donny.

"Ready as I'll ever be." I take a deep breath and steel myself before wrenching open the door of the truck and climbing out. I know precisely what I'm in for, and it's going to be a lot of *welcome backs* laced with pointed questions about my life in the city, especially about why I'm not yet married, and probably not a little judgment for not having been back in a hot minute. I need to be prepared. Mentally.

"Let's go into Layla's first," I say, pulling the flyers from my bag and tucking them in the crook of my arm. If it's clear I'm on a mission, I may have a better chance at escape in a few of these places. We head toward the glass door with the words *Layla's Diner* painted atop a coffee mug.

Layla's is the center of Main Street here in Harvest Hollow. It's where business deals are made, everyone drinks coffee and eats hamburgers, and, perhaps surprisingly, more than one engagement has taken place. It's a hole-in-the-wall, but it's clean and familiar, and frankly, the food is delicious. Like, seriously delicious. Plus, Layla serves tater tots, which are my favorite.

We walk inside, and the minute the bell on the door chimes it's as if a record scratched. Everyone sitting at the 1950s-style soda fountain counter turns to stare at us.

"Hey, Layla," Aiden calls, putting up a hand in the semblance of a wave.

"Who's this?" Layla says. She wipes her hands on her bubblegum-pink apron and comes around the counter. I wait for her to put on the black cat-eye-framed glasses that hang from a shiny gold chain around her neck, and it's as predictable as three, two, one . . .

"Oh my good gracious, it's Ellie!" Layla points at me and then comes rushing over to hug me. "Ellie Lawson, everyone. She's back!"

This is precisely how I knew this would go, but I'm still turning a little red. I can feel my cheeks heat. If for no other reason, I need to come back here more often to avoid embarrassing moments like this made even more awkward by my prolonged absence.

"Ellie Lawson!" says Abe Bennett. "Imagine that." He's chuckling and shaking his head.

"Look what the cat dragged in," says Homer Wilkins. He and his wife are the owners of the only hardware store in town, but he's in Layla's more often than his store.

"Hi, everyone," I say, giving a little wave.

I see a handful of other locals I know. Like Mrs. Lawrence, who owns the drive-in movie theater. Mr. Timmons, who teaches piano out of his house a block down the street. Mr. Culkin, the building inspector, who, along with his friends—Mrs. Sharma, one of the only real estate agents in town, Mr. Higgins, the electrician, and Mr. Wainwright, the plumber—have coffee here every Friday at this time.

Everyone greets me like I've just returned from the war, before Layla grabs my hand and drags me to one of the stools in front of the counter.

"Aiden, where did you find her?" Layla says as I take a seat. "Don't tell me you went into the city and dragged her back here."

"Nope. No. I came of my own accord," I say quickly so Aiden doesn't have to explain my homecoming. "There was no dragging."

"Is that right?" Layla shakes her head. "What can I get you?" She pulls her sparkly silver pen from behind her ear. "Tots?"

Aww. Layla remembers my love of tots. "Absolutely!" I say, licking my lips in anticipation. I am already looking around for ketchup.

"We can't stay," Aiden interjects, pulling the stack of flyers out of my hands and giving me a fully grumpy look. "We're just here to drop off some flyers."

I scowl at him. He's a tot-blocker.

But as much as I want the tots, I have to admit he's right. I need to remember that I'm here for work. I need to get these flyers hung and help my parents and the Parkers make some money.

I point at the stack of flyers cradled in the crook of Aiden's arm and turn to Layla. "Will you help us get the word out about the Autumn Harvest Festival at the inn and orchard?"

"Let me see that," Layla says.

I pull the stack of flyers from Aiden's arms and drop them on the countertop. After Layla takes one, Mr. Wilkins grabs one too, and so does Mrs. Lawrence.

"Autum Harvest Festival, eh?" says Mr. Wilkins. "So, you're not just doing the standard parade float?"

"We thought we'd do something special this year," Aiden tells him.

"Hmm," is Mr. Wilkins's reply. His eyes are narrowed as he reads the flyer.

I stifle a laugh because it's clear to me that, being as predictable and reliable as this town is, they all question change as if it might signal the apocalypse. I hope two weeks is enough for them to get used to the idea of the festival. It might be too much for them.

"Can I leave some of these here, Layla?" I ask, pointing to the flyers.

Layla nods. "Of course, honey. Leave them right here on the counter and I'll make sure everyone takes one when they pay."

Oh, even better than I'd hoped for. "Can I tape one on the front door also?"

"Sure."

Layla lets me borrow some tape, and I have the flyer up in record time before I come back to stand next to Aiden near the counter. I still say we coulda made time for tots.

"We better be going," Aiden says. "Lots of flyers to distribute."

I nod and begin to turn toward the door. But Layla's voice stops me.

"Don't the two of you just look perfect together?" Layla shakes her head, as I blush because all the patrons of the diner turn to stare at Aiden and me again. "Two good-looking kids," Layla adds.

Mrs. Lawrence's brows shoot up in interest, and I inwardly cringe because back in the day when blogs were a thing, Mrs. L had a blog devoted to town gossip. No one was safe. She used a pseudonym, but we all knew it was her. One of the kids from computer class tracked her IP. It was the town's worst-kept secret. I can tell by the look of sheer delight on her face that the town's biggest gossip is going to spread the word that Aiden and I could be a thing, in a matter of hours. Not days.

Why did I agree to get a ride from Aiden and his rickety truck again? I can think of no good reason at the moment.

"Thanks again. We've gotta go," I say, knowing from years of experience that it's futile to argue with gossips about potential gossip. Arguing just gives them more fodder. Far better to cut and run from them.

I head for the door, ready to book it out of there. I don't even stop to ensure Aiden is behind me. He's on his own. He may need pepper spray.

Just as I'm about to escape, I hear Mrs. Lawrence say, "You're coming tonight, aren't you?"

I do not stop. I go. I go until I'm inside the hardware store. A few minutes later, Aiden comes in behind me, laughing. "What?" I prod. "Where are we supposed to go tonight?"

"The drive-in, of course," Aiden replies.

Oh yeah. How could I forget? The biggest social activity of Friday night in Harvest Hollow is going to Mrs. Lawrence's drive-in movie theater. It may be a little old-fashioned, but so is Harvest Hollow. And frankly, during the Covid pandemic I'm sure the drive-in was a solid choice for entertainment. "What did you tell her?"

Aiden doesn't have a chance to answer because a female voice suddenly says, "Is that you, Ellie?" It's Mrs. Wilkins, the co-owner of the hardware store. The older woman is busily knitting behind the counter like she always does when her husband is at the diner.

I turn away from Aiden. "Hi, Mrs. Wilkins. What're you knitting today?"

"A chicken," she tells me. She holds up the white and red yarn in her lap. "Got the idea from YouTube. A woman there sells them after that insane trial in South Carolina."

A person less acquainted with true crime might have no idea what she's talking about. "The Murdaugh case?" I ask.

"That's the one." Mrs. Wilkins points a knitting needle at me. And suddenly, jobless or not, I know I'm gonna need a knitted Murdaugh-trial chicken. I am also impressed that Mrs. W is familiar with YouTube. I mean, good for her.

"Ooh, can I buy one from you?" I ask, nearly clapping with glee.

Aiden is frowning at me. He frowns too much. Maybe owning an orchard that isn't doing well does that to a person, but he's not going to harsh my vibe right now.

Mrs. Wilkins shuffles around under the desk for a few minutes before pulling out a fully formed knitted stuffed chicken. It is about three inches high. I immediately love it. "How much?" I ask, reaching for my bag.

"Your money is no good here," Mrs. Wilkins says, shooing my hands away from my bag.

I spend a few minutes arguing with her before it's clear she's not going to take a dime, so I thank her instead. It really is nice of her to give me a true crime chicken out of the kindness of her heart.

Mrs. Wilkins proceeds to tell us that her next knitting project will be an ear-of-corn costume for her toddler granddaughter's Halloween costume, and we all agree it's going to be adorable. Honestly, I'm gonna need to see a picture.

She allows us to post a flyer in the window and to leave a small stack of them on the counter.

"You know, Homer and I always thought the two of you would get together one day," Mrs. Wilkins says, nodding toward me and Aiden.

I just about swallow my tongue. Why do people say stuff like that? I mean, how are Aiden and I supposed to respond?

"Anything is possible," Aiden says with an exaggerated shrug, and before I have a chance to process *that*, he points to the door. "Let's go to town hall next."

We're back out in the crisp fall air when I say, "Why did you say that?"

"What?" There's that frown again.

"Anything is possible?" I repeat his own words.

He shrugs. "Isn't it?"

He gives me a side-grin and jogs ahead of me to open the door. He's kidding, right? He's got to be kidding.

The Harvest Hollow Town Hall has smelled like janitorial supplies since the dawn of time. It's an ageless mix of lemon wax and floor cleaner that brings me back to childhood because it is the aroma of, like, every public school ever too.

Mrs. Jackson, the receptionist, has worked here my entire life. She's wearing a bright orange sweater. She's always loved to dress for the season. And I do not blame her.

"Ellie!" she exclaims as Aiden and I enter the familiar old building.

"Hi, Mrs. Jackson," I say, smiling. Her son, Max, was one of my good friends in school. He's a high school history teacher now in another town on Long Island, but we keep in touch on social media. He's married with three kids. I'm thrilled to see his mom.

"How are you doing, sweetie?" she asks.

We chat for a few minutes before she busts out pictures of her grandkids on her phone. Aiden and I ooh and ahh over them. They really are cute, and there's seriously nothing more heartwarming than a grandma's pure joy when showing pictures of or talking about her grandkids.

I tell Mrs. Jackson about the festival and the flyers, and she says she'll post one on the door for me and I can leave a stack on her desk.

"Have you met Millie?" she asks.

I blink. "Millie?" Oh crap. Yet another unfamiliar name.

"Millie's the new mayor. She just took office this summer. Just graduated from high school last spring," Mrs. Jackson informs me.

"What? The new mayor is eighteen?" That's interesting. How have I not heard about this from Mom? I need to have a serious chat with Mom about what she finds newsworthy.

"That's right," says Aiden. "And Millie's one of the best mayors we've ever had. She took to civics class her sophomore year, started coming to the town meetings and calling out the previous mayor, and once she turned eighteen and could legally run for office, she did."

"She's fabulous," Mrs. Jackson agrees. "Knows a heck of a lot more than that last idiot did, and she's got the energy of a puppy. It's a great combination. She's taking night classes to get her degree in government. Want to meet her?"

"I'd love to meet her if she has time for me," I say.

"Oh, she'll make time." Mrs. Jackson nods. "She loves to meet citizens. She's going to run New York one day. Maybe even the country. Mark my word."

Mrs. Jackson picks up the phone, and when she hangs up, I'm expecting us to all go into the mayor's office. Instead, a few seconds later, a young blond woman comes barreling into the reception area.

She's wearing jeans, a blazer, pearls, and tennis shoes. Her eyes are bright blue, and her hair is cut in a crisp bob. "Ellie Lawson?" she says as if she's heard of me, though I suspect she just learned about me from Mrs. Jackson's phone call. "I'm Millie Adler, nice to meet you."

"Nice to meet you," I reply, impressed that she didn't immediately inform me that she's the mayor. "Mrs. Jackson tells me you're very impressive."

After greeting Aiden also, Millie hands some paperwork to Mrs. Jackson before turning back to me. "Oh, it's not so impressive to care about your work. I have big plans for this town."

A smile spreads across my face. I immediately adore Millie. First, she's obviously notable as a young mayor, and second, I love her saying she has plans for the town, because that means she'll encourage our ideas for the festival. I rip a flyer off the top of the stack and hand it to her.

Millie studies it for a few moments before exclaiming, "Oh, this sounds great! I'll be sure to let the town council know at the meeting tonight. We'll all make some calls."

Mrs. Jackson winks at me as if to say, "I told you so." And Aiden and I finish our talk with the mayor by inviting her to the Harvest Ball as our guest.

"I'd love to!" she says. "My girlfriend, Kaylie, and I could use a night off."

"Great!" I shoot off a quick text to Mom letting her know to reserve a room for Millie and Kaylie. Mom sends back a heart emoji. "It's all set," I tell her.

After we leave town hall, we make stops at all the other businesses along the street. Mr. Peyton is sitting in the front of the combo firehouse/police station. He's technically the fire chief, but the man does what needs doing, which, more often than not, is getting cats out of trees. He's a real, live animal whisperer. Even Pumpkin acts right when Mr. Peyton comes to the inn. Hmm. I wonder if he can work his skills on Miss Guin.

We tell him about the festival, and he takes a short stack of flyers and tells us something about the fire code and how he'll have to come out and look things over. I thank him and don't mention Miss Guin, but when he shows up, I'll definitely introduce the two.

"Your mom still boiling cinnamon out there?" he asks just before we take our leave.

"You know it," I reply.

He shakes his head and grumbles.

I need to warn Mom that she's about to get another cinnamon lecture.

After the library and the general store, our final stop is the pharmacy, where Mrs. Goldman, the pharmacist, still stands atop a foothigh dais behind her counter. She has exactly two employees: Missy Stanton and Bob Gillingham. Bob is a middle-aged man who was never young, from what I can remember. He's worked here forever. He's working today, and he goes into the back to get Mrs. Goldman for us.

Mrs. Goldman soon emerges from wherever pharmacists go when

they aren't lording over the counter. She has the thickest New York accent ever. It's pure, delicious Long Island at its best.

"Ellie, sweetie," she drawls. "Where ya been? It's been an age. Hasn't it been an age, Aiden?"

"It's been an age," Aiden agrees in an exaggerated tone. I want to kick him, but I don't.

"You need anything, sweetie?" Mrs. Goldman asks. "Allergy medicine? Candy?"

"I'm good, Mrs. Goldman," I say.

"So happy to see ya, sweetie," Mrs. Goldman says, waving. "Tell your ma I said hullo." Before we leave, she hands one of the flyers to Bob and asks him to post it on the front door.

"Thanks, Mrs. Goldman. See you at the festival."

"I wouldn't miss it," she assures us.

We're back on the street, and I glance at my watch. It's nearly five. We've been here all afternoon. "I'm exhausted," I tell Aiden.

"Honestly, I am too," he says. "Let's go home and take a nap. We need to be ready for tonight."

"Wait. What's tonight?" I frown.

"Drive-in night."

"Oh yeah." With all the socializing, I'd totally forgotten about what Mrs. Lawrence said. "What's playing at the drive-in tonight anyway?" I ask.

"It's the *Gilmore Girls* festival." Aiden says this as if I should have already known it.

I step back in surprise. "There's a *Gilmore Girls* night at the drive-in?" This is news to me. Excellent news. But news.

Aiden nods. "It was Charlotte's idea, actually."

"Truly?" It's official. Charlotte is the absolute coolest.

"One of the biggest moneymakers all year, according to Mrs. Lawrence," Aiden continues.

I don't doubt it. "I love *Gilmore Girls,*" I tell him.

"Yeah, well, every Friday night from September through November, the drive-in plays two episodes."

Okay, that totally sounds like my jam. I am in. "I'll have to ask Mom and Dad if I can borrow the car."

"Why do that when you can ride with me?" Aiden says, and I swear he winks at me.

Chapter 11

I still can't believe Aiden wants to go to the drive-in. He was always so quiet back in high school, and pretty uninterested when it came to pop culture. Who knew he had a *Gilmore Girls*–watching side to him? But then I remember how Aiden used to play Barbies with me and Charlotte sometimes when we were kids. He's always had a soft spot for his sister, and he's never been one to turn down a fun time because it's a "girls thing to do." Which is frankly awesome. Overly macho dudes are the *worst*. But regardless of Aiden's reason for going tonight, if he's driving, I'm not passing up the opportunity to see some *Gilmore Girls*. I only wish Maria was here. She would *love* to go.

Charlotte is going too, of course, but it turns out, despite her obvious crush on Sawyer, she has a date with some mystery guy, so her brother and I are on our own. But it's not from lack of me trying to find someone—anyone—who wants to go with us. Mostly because I don't want this to feel anything like a date. Because that would be awkward. And it's *not* a date.

It's just two business partners going to a drive-in movie on a Friday night together.

Okay, it completely sounds like a date.

After getting turned down by Mom, Dad, and Charlotte, I ask both Mr. and Mrs. Parker, and then finally, Donny. Donny promptly informs me that he cannot attend because he has work tonight, both at the drive-in itself and as the local rideshare driver. He tells me he's the busiest driver in town. I joke that he's the only driver in town, and he says he is not. Millie the mayor's girlfriend, Kaylie, is the other rideshare driver, and it's soon clear to me that Donny is not happy about the competition. "You can't be everywhere at once, though, can you?" I ask.

He shakes his head and says, "Do you even know me, Ellie?"

I went to high school with Donny so, yeah, I know him. The dude has had every job in town since he was old enough to work. He even used to deliver the local newspapers as a kid. The only night he's off is bingo night. With his job at the inn too, I have to wonder when he sleeps. It's worrisome. Meanwhile, he could probably buy and sell the entire town.

By the time I come waltzing out of my bedroom wearing jeans, a cozy black cashmere sweater, and my cleaned-up suede boots, I'm resigned to the fact that Aiden and I are going out together on what feels like (but is definitely not) a date.

Only, it feels even more like a date when I see what Aiden's wearing. It's a heather-gray sweater with a white collared shirt underneath and nice (meaning not ripped or faded) jeans. His dark, curly hair is even slicked back a little. He looks datey. And frankly, so do I. I glance down at myself. Are the boots too cute? Should I change into sneakers?

It's too late, though—he sees me. He tosses his keys in the air and catches them. "Ready?"

"Sure." I grab my wool coat—the one Charlotte saved—and follow him to the door.

"Okay if Argos comes too?" he asks.

Argos! Maybe it won't seem like a date if *Argos* is there. "The more the merrier," I say.

Aiden pulls a big bag full of stuff off the kitchen counter, and we walk down the stairs together and out the side door into the leaves. Argos is waiting for us by the back door. I take a quick survey of the land and see no sign of Miss Guin. Perhaps she is intimidated by Argos. Perhaps she is on break. Either way, I'm happy.

It's a little cooler than it was when the sun was out, and the crisp air feels good as I pull it into my lungs. The scent of the leaves is heavy tonight. And the wood smoke lingers. I feel calm. Calm and centered like I haven't . . . probably since I left Harvest Hollow. That is a sobering thought. Today felt like stepping back in time. To a place that was familiar and easy, filled with people who care. Friends who remember that you love tater tots and who give you knitted chickens for free.

When we get to the parking lot, Aiden steps to the passenger door of a dark-gray four-door Toyota Tacoma truck.

"What's this?" I ask.

"My truck."

"I thought the red truck was yours," I admit.

His brows furrow. "That truck is two hundred years old. We just keep it around for the old-fashioned look for the orchard."

"I didn't know that." I shrug. Clearly, I have offended the man. "Why did you take it today?"

"We were on official inn business. I figured we should take the official inn truck."

Which means we're not on official business tonight. We are in Toyota territory. Purely personal. My heart pounds for some unexplained reason.

Aiden opens the truck door for me, and I give him a little side-eye. He's close enough for me to smell his aftershave, which kinda makes my knees weak, honestly. He *smells* like he's on a date too. "What are you doing?"

"What do you mean?" He opens the door to the back seat of the truck and tosses in the bag. Argos jumps back there too, and Aiden fusses around in the seat for a moment.

"You don't have to open the door for me," I tell him when he emerges. "This isn't a date."

He gives me a sarcastic, crooked smile. "Okay, just for the record, if it *was* a date, would you *want* me to open the door for you?"

He's messing with me. I can tell by his tone and the sparkle in his eye. But the question makes me think for a second. Geoff never opened a door for me. I took that as a sign of respect. Women don't need their doors opened. But honestly, if this was a date—and again, it's *not*—I'm not sure that I would mind Aiden opening the door. It just feels like a nice thing to do. But it's not a date, so it doesn't matter. Which is what I promptly tell him.

"Noted," he says, shaking his head and walking around to the driver's side.

Minutes later we're on the highway headed to the drive-in. It's on the opposite side of town from where the inn and orchard sit. From end-to-end it's only about a fifteen-minute drive.

This time I keep my head inside. No hanging out the window tonight. My hair is coiffed. I am wearing lip gloss. Argos, who has every reason to hang his head out the window, instead keeps his snout pointed between the front seats. I realize at some point that he's wearing a dog seat belt, and I find that adorable.

"I can't believe we're going to the drive-in," I say. "I feel like I'm sixteen again." I reach back and pat Argos on the head.

"Been that long, eh?" Aiden is driving with only one hand gripping the top center of the steering wheel. He's a good, steady driver. Not trying to whip around and impress me. Eyes on the road. I feel safe with him. I'm sure Argos does too. He bought him a seat belt, for God's sake.

I think about Aiden's question for a few seconds. When *was* the last time I was at the drive-in? "I honestly can't remember." It was one of the only things to do in our town back in the day, and it seems as if it's still that way. "Are high school kids still making out in the back row?" I ask, waggling my brows suggestively.

"I wouldn't know," Aiden replies. "I don't park in the back row."

"Because all of the sixteen-year-olds get there first," I say, laughing.

"I didn't park there when I was sixteen," he grumbles.

I stifle my laugh. Oh, this is awkward, because me and my dates definitely used to park there. Was Aiden actually watching the movies? I just sort of nod, happy to let that subject peter right out.

"Mrs. Lawrence is going to have us dating, you know?" Aiden says.

My head snaps to the side to face him. "What?" Did he just say what I think he said?

"Her blog is still up."

"No!" I clap my hand over my mouth, completely horrified. Mrs. Lawrence's blog, where she basically served the tea on everyone in town, is still up? How is that even possible? I haven't looked at it in years. "Is it the same site?" I ask, still horrified but also more than a little curious.

"Yeah, Harvest Hollow Hot Sheet," Aiden says with a laugh.

I've already clicked on the site, and it's loading on my phone. Of course, it's not optimized for mobile, but I'm able to see it. "Oh my God! She's already posted about us stopping in the diner today."

"Of course she has."

"Does everyone still pretend they don't know it's her?" I am frowning hard. How can this be?

"Yep," Aiden reports. "Weirdly, to this day no one has confronted her about it. That I know of, at least. She's Harvest Hollow's own Lady Whistledown."

Well, now I'm completely distracted from talk about the blog. "Wait. In addition to *Gilmore Girls*, you watch *Bridgerton* too?"

Aiden rubs the back of his neck with his free hand but keeps his eyes on the road. "Charlotte had it on one night."

"Sure, she did." This is *very* interesting. Aiden, grumpy-farmer-high-school-loner Aiden, likes things like cozy TV shows and Regency romance dramas? Unexpected, to say the least.

I learn even more about Aiden after we park in the third row at the drive-in and he pulls the big bag he brought with him into the front seat. Of course, I'd been dying to know what was in it but figured I'd find out soon enough.

Turns out it's a quilt and a bag of popcorn. He also brought a stack of napkins. And honestly, *my hero*. Slow clap for that.

"It gets cold out here," he says as he unfolds the enormous quilt and pushes half of it toward me. It's big enough to cover the whole truck, so there won't be any awkward fight over the edges.

I stare at the quilt until it finally dawns on me. Barbies. *Gilmore Girls. Bridgerton.* The quilt. Aiden *has a sister.* Aiden grew up around Charlotte . . . and me. I used to get Aiden to do girly stuff with me all the time, now that I think about it. He painted my nails. He participated in more than one tea party. And he even let me borrow his GI Joe dolls to date my Barbie. Of course, that was before high school, back when we used to hang out together all the time. The year I began high school was when it all started to change. I joined several after-school groups and started hanging with a big group of girls my age. And Aiden, well, he was Aiden. Quiet. Reserved. Not into crowds, so he never went to pep rallies or football games or even the homecoming dance. I was a little sad that we grew apart, but after a while we just sort of fell into a friendly wave or two when we passed each other on the orchard. I mean, kids grow up and grow apart, right?

I glance back to see Aiden arranging a smaller quilt for Argos in the back seat. Aww. In addition to not being a testosterone-fueled jerk, Aiden is a caretaker. A grumpy caretaker at times, but still. It's pretty cute to see him wrap his dog in a blanket. And frankly, now that I know what was in the bag, I'm duly impressed that Argos didn't try to eat the popcorn on the way here. Pumpkin would have had his whole sausage-shape body in the popcorn bag by now, chomping it by the mouthful.

"You take drive-in night pretty seriously, huh?" I say, trying to squelch my smile.

"What?" He shrugs. "The town hasn't changed much, okay? This is basically where everyone is on Friday night." He tosses a piece of popcorn to Argos, who catches it in his mouth. It is clear they have done this before, many times. I smile to myself before glancing at Aiden.

Despite it not being a date, the ingredients are here. Aiden picked me up, packed snacks and a blanket for us, and we're surrounded by couples. In this exact moment, I'm aware that I should be missing Geoff. I should have been missing him this whole time. But he wouldn't do anything like this for me. So, honestly, what is there to miss? And Geoff wouldn't be caught dead at a drive-in on a Friday night. He always wanted to go have drinks at uptown bars he thought some of the GMJ partners would be at, to pretend we just ran into them and talk shop all night. It was super annoying, actually. I'd much rather be watching *Gilmore Girls* and eating popcorn with Aiden and Argos.

"You didn't want to park in the back row, did you?" Aiden asks, the hint of a smile on his lips. I have to glance away from him because my thighs heat at his words. *Whoa*. Talk about unexpected. What would he do if I said yes? Part of me wants to, if only to see his reaction.

"You *never* parked in the back row?" I ask instead, shaking my head as if it's a shame.

"Not in high school," he says. "Once as an adult. With a girlfriend. But we ended up on Mrs. L's blog, so we never did it again."

My heart stops. I'm *so* intrigued. "A girlfriend? Do tell."

Aiden sets the popcorn bag on the quilt between us and hands me a few napkins. "There's nothing to tell, really. We went out for two years. We wanted different things. We broke up."

I roll my eyes. That's *such* a dating story from a man's point of view. No juicy details. "How long ago was this?" I ask. I am not *trying* to be nosy, but I am my mother's daughter and a resident of Harvest Hollow, so there's a certain amount of information I'm gonna need here.

Aiden scoops up a handful of popcorn and shrugs. "Maybe two years ago." He tosses another piece to Argos.

"You've been single since then?" This question is for research purposes only.

"Yep."

Of course, the next question on the tip of my tongue is whether I know her, but that seems *too* nosy. So instead, I make a mental note to check the Hot Sheet archives for news of Aiden Parker and his girlfriend making out in the last row of the drive-in two years ago. Because I am not above such a thing.

I am still trying to picture what his ex-girlfriend looks like when a knock on the driver's-side window startles me.

Aiden rolls it down to reveal Mrs. Lawrence grinning at us. "Hi there, kids."

And now I *really* feel like I'm sixteen again, because we've clearly been caught parking together at the drive-in after showing up in town together today. There *will* be gossip. 'Tis inevitable.

"I see you have your own popcorn, Aiden," Mrs. Lawrence says, arching an overly plucked brow.

Aiden reaches behind him, pulls out his wallet, and gives Mrs. Lawrence a twenty-dollar bill. "Here. This is for the popcorn I'm *not* buying from you."

"Thank you." Mrs. Lawrence tucks the money into her shirt like she's a stripper. "Enjoy the show."

"What was that about?" I ask after Aiden rolls up the window. He's tuning the radio to whatever station gets the feed from the drive-in.

"I like my own popcorn. She likes to make money. It's win-win."

I shake my head. Only another business owner would do that. But it's just the sort of quirky arrangement that makes me miss this town. Where else would there be a twenty-dollar exchange over not buying popcorn with a very civil "thank you"?

The giant screen we're parked in front of starts flashing, and I keep my mouth shut. No more talking. *Gilmore Girls* is sacred. The theme song comes on. It's probably my favorite part of the whole experience. I begin to sing along like Maria and I always do when we watch it.

Aiden arches a brow at me. "Really?" he says.

"Sing with me," I say in between verses.

"Nope." He shakes his head.

"Ah, come on. It's a fantastic song. You know you want to!"

I serenade him, poking his arm, and then suddenly, to my delighted surprise, Aiden joins in on the chorus.

"You know the words!" I shout, laughing as I continue to sing. To his credit, Aiden keeps singing too. By the time it's over I'm smiling so big my mouth hurts. "You sang!"

He shrugs. His face gives nothing away. "Yeah, well, it's a catchy song, and I've heard it a lot."

"It's fun to sing, isn't it?" I say, nodding at him. I'm fully determined to make him admit it.

"If you say so." He shakes popcorn into his mouth.

"Admit it!" I push his shoulder lightly, and honestly, I want to touch it again immediately. It made my fingers tingle.

"It's not a bad song," he allows.

Whatever. That was cute. I turn back toward the screen. I'm suddenly glad there is a giant popcorn bag between us. It's a clear delineation. We won't climb over the popcorn bag and make out. That would be awkward. And potentially messy. *Not* that I want to. Of course, we *could* move the bag to the back seat, but—no. Not helpful. The popcorn is the boundary.

The show begins, and it's halfway through the first episode when I stick my hand in the popcorn bag and accidentally brush against Aiden's hand. A jolt of awareness shoots up my arm. I snatch my hand away without any popcorn. "Sorry," I mumble.

"No worries," he says. He goes back to watching, but now I'm daring glances at him. Did he just feel what I felt? Heat? A shudder? Now it's all I can think about, and it feels wrong because *Gilmore Girls* is not exactly steamy material. And there's a dog in the back seat watching us. Though honestly, Argos may be sleeping. It's dark back there.

I am completely distracted. I try to keep watching, but all I can do is wonder if Aiden is as aware of me as I am of him right now. He smells really good. Like soap and tightly stretched cotton T-shirts. We both already admitted we are attracted to each other. He might feel *something*. I shake my head and blow out a breath. I need to get it together.

I am being ridiculous. And unprofessional. Ridiculously unprofessional. *Eat your popcorn and cool your pants, Ellie.*

I pause at the realization: I'm calling myself Ellie in my head now. Distracted by *that* revelation, it takes me a minute to notice that Aiden is watching me. I can see it in my peripheral vision.

I turn to look at him, and my breath catches in my throat. The bright lights from the screen are playing across his face, and our gazes are locked.

He looks at me intently. It's sexy as hell. He leans closer. I can't breathe. He's *across* the popcorn bag. He's beyond it. He's breached the popcorn.

Oh my God.

He's going to kiss me.

And I want him to. I really want him to! His face is inches from mine, I'm breathing heavy, and I'm just about to close my eyes and lean into his kiss when he reaches out and grabs something near the window by my ear. "Got ya," he exclaims.

The next thing I know he's back on his side of the truck, where he opens his door and leans out.

"What was that?" I ask, completely discombobulated. One minute I'm about to get kissed in the third row of the drive-in, and the next I have no idea what just happened.

"I didn't want to scare you," Aiden explains. "It was a . . . a . . ."

He clearly doesn't want to say, which immediately frightens me because there's only one thing it could be if he's acting this way. "A spider?" I ask with a nervous squeak. I am already glancing around the truck to make sure the insect hadn't brought any of its friends.

"Yeah," he says reluctantly. "I just let it out in the grass."

"Did it head off in another direction?" I ask, my voice a little too high.

"It did. I remember how much you hate spiders. And your rule about making sure they're gone."

I close my eyes and breathe a sigh of relief. I am not interested in killing living things, but I need reassurance that a spider is not still in my vicinity, and Aiden knows it. "Thank you," I say. "You always came running when we were kids and I was shrieking about a spider." I smile, remembering more than one occasion when Aiden saved me from spiders. It's beyond sweet that he remembers. I mean, I may be twenty-nine, but I'm still not a fan of the little devils.

Now that the bug is gone, though, all I can think about is how awkward it was that I clearly thought Aiden was going to kiss me. He has to know it. I was staring at him with stars in my eyes like he was my prom date.

It didn't happen, I quickly remind myself. Which is good. It's great. Thank God it didn't happen. We'd surely be all over the *Harvest Hollow Hot Sheet* tomorrow with that sort of behavior. It was a close call.

After the spider incident, I keep my eyes trained to the screen and watch as Rory and Lorelei slog through an awkward dinner with Emily. The whole time, I can't help but think about what Aiden is thinking about.

Did he know I'd been about to lean into a kiss? Was he horrified? It was gentlemanly of him not to mention it.

Now, it's just starting to seem silly. I mean, a *kiss*? That would've been ridiculous. Not only would it be mixing business with pleasure, but it would also have been wrong. I'm only going to be here for two weeks. Just long enough to pull off the festival, get a new job, and get back to town. A kiss would be cruel. Like I was leading Aiden on. Of course, I have no indication that he wanted to kiss me. Other than his admission that he thinks I'm hot. Which, I admitted to feeling the same. But we are not animals. We can have a mutual attraction without kissing or touching or any sort of physical interaction. Can't we?

I am crunching my popcorn and still thinking about this when leaves begin falling on the windshield. And not just a few leaves, like *a lot* of them. It's almost as if . . . someone is on top of the truck showering them on the windshield.

"Donny!" Aiden calls just before he bangs his palm against the truck ceiling.

I press my lips together. Oh my God. This isn't happening.

Aiden rolls down the window and sticks out his head. "Donny, get off of my truck."

"This is part of what you pay for," comes Donny's insistent voice.

"I don't care. Get off."

I look out my window to see Donny jumping out of the back of the truck with a ten-gallon plastic bucket in his hands. Presumably the bucket had been filled with leaves. Now they are on Aiden's windshield, partially blocking our view of the screen.

"Hi, Donny," I say, waving at him through the leaf pile.

"Aiden never lets me do my job," Donny says, clearly perturbed.

"Your job is stupid," Aiden shoots back. "You're literally blocking the screen."

"I'm paid to bring the fall vibes," Donny argues.

"I'll pay you another twenty to never do this again," Aiden tells him.

Donny lifts his chin as if he's affronted. "How dare you, sir. I am a professional. I cannot be bought."

Aiden retrieves another twenty-dollar bill from his wallet and waves it out the window, holding it between his index and middle finger.

Donny comes around slowly and stands there as if in indecision for a few moments before he snatches it.

"For the record," Donny says, holding the front of his coat like he's Washington crossing the Delaware, "I don't appreciate your attitude, Parker. And I—"

Donny's phone beeps, and he immediately stops talking and looks down at it. "I've got to pick someone up from the train station," he says. "Can you take Billy and Amber?" he says to Aiden.

"No, we can't—" Aiden is saying.

But Donny has already opened the back door to his hatchback that is parked next to us. "I've got a call. I'll be back soon. You can sit in Aiden's car while I'm gone," he says to the car's occupants.

A young man and a young woman emerge from the hatchback and without a moment's hesitation climb into Aiden's back seat. Argos promptly rearranges himself to make room for his new friends. He sits in between them, smiling.

Aiden groans and lowers his forehead to his hand.

"What is happening?" I mouth.

"Donny takes people who don't drive to the drive-in, but sometimes he has to leave if he has to do rideshare," Aiden explains. This is all said as if it's perfectly normal. Annoying, but normal.

"You're joking." I am horrified and fascinated.

"I am not," Aiden replies.

"Hey, thanks, Aiden," says the young man, who is already nestled into the back seat. "I got into a fender bender last week, and my car is still in the shop."

"No problem, Billy," Aiden replies.

Okay, of course they know each other. In the city, you can't just climb into anyone's car, but out here, it's fair game. Billy actually looks familiar to me. I think he's the son of one of the teachers at the high school. He was a lot younger last time I saw him. I'm not sure I know the girl, though. She must be from another town.

"Yeah, thanks, Aiden," the young woman says next. She presses a hand to my shoulder. "Hi, I'm Amber. Who are you?"

Again, behavior that is only acceptable in places where people know each other and apparently have no fears. If Maria was here, I can't even imagine her expression. It would be something akin to an anthropologist stumbling upon an unknown civilization.

Because I grew up here, however, I'm gonna roll with this whole kooky thing. "I'm Ellie." I turn and shake Amber's hand. I also nod and wave to Billy, who smiles at me.

"Ellie?" Amber repeats. She points between me and Aiden. "Are you two dating?"

"No! No." I hurry to say. "We work together. My parents own the Honeycrisp Orchard Inn."

"Oh, *that* Ellie," says Amber.

Huh. "You know me?" I can't help but ask.

"I've heard of you. You're the one who left Aiden."

Wait. What? I *left* Aiden?

"She left the *inn*," Aiden says apparently to clarify, but even in the dim light, I can tell his cheeks are turning red.

"Okay," Amber says, but her tone indicates she's not buying it. Apparently she doesn't want to argue with the guy who's letting her sit in his back seat, though.

We all settle in to watch the rest of the show. First, Aiden has to get out and wipe the leaves off the windshield while I stifle a laugh. I'm not about to admit it to him, but I kinda liked the fall-leaves-on-the-windshield touch. Does Donny do that for all the cars? Or is that only for the ones who slip Mrs. Lawrence a twenty?

Billy and Amber help themselves to our big bag of popcorn without asking, and it cracks me up that Aiden doesn't seem to care at all. They shake some out into their hands, so they aren't sticking them in the bag, but it's still pretty surreal to have strangers in the back seat sharing your snacks. They also provide some to Argos without prompting, which I like.

My eyes are trained on the screen, but I am not paying attention. Instead, I am obsessed with wondering what Amber meant when she said I "left Aiden." I mean, that's pretty loaded. I admit I left the inn. I definitely left town. You might even make the argument that I "left" my parents. But Aiden? How did I leave Aiden?

The only good thing about being obsessed with those thoughts is that at least I am no longer obsessively thinking about Aiden's abs. Or the way he was looking at me when I thought he was going to kiss me. Because honestly, that was really the way he was looking at a spider, but somehow it seemed kinda hot to me, and now I'm wondering what's wrong with me.

I am no closer to figuring that out or what Amber meant, when the first episode ends and Donny's hatchback comes rolling back into the spot next to us.

Billy and Amber mutter their thanks. I say a quick, "Nice to meet you," and invite them to the festival. They say they'll come, before scooching out of the back seat and returning to Donny's car. Donny has more leaves and is soon off to shake them over other windshields.

"I take it that happens often?" I ask Aiden when we're alone again, pointing toward the back seat.

"More often than it should," Aiden grumbles. "Hey, I'm sorry about what Amber said. About you leaving. I hope you don't—"

"I guess I never realized that I'm kinda famous for leaving," I say, frowning.

"Only because of the inn," Aiden hastens to explain.

"Plenty of other people leave this town every year," I point out. "Most of us from our high school moved to the city." We've covered this before, but it feels different tonight. Amber's words hover in the air. There is more to say. "Do you *blame me* for leaving, Aiden?" I ask. There. I said it. The question is out there.

"No!" But his answer is far too quick. He groans and expels his breath. "I mean . . . maybe," he admits. He's quiet for several seconds and rubs the back of his head. "Don't you remember when we were kids and we used to talk about running the business together?"

I catch my breath. That was *completely* unexpected. But he's right. We did used to talk about running the businesses together. But . . . "That was a long time ago," I say, but I can already tell that it mattered to him. And obviously still does. I swallow the lump that has formed in my throat.

I am still watching him when he says, "I know. Look. I get it. I do. And like I said last night, I'm sorry if I seemed like I was judging you. I just . . ." He bites the inside of his cheek and looks away. "I don't know. The family business and all." He takes a deep breath. "I kinda always thought we would be partners one day. The way we talked about."

In that moment, the air is sucked from my lungs *and* the cab of the truck. Aiden held on to those talks we had when we were children? "What?" is all I can manage in a loud whisper.

Aiden shakes his head. His forearm is braced on the door. He's looking straight ahead as he speaks. "I just . . . This town . . . The orchard. It's everything to me. I guess I didn't realize you didn't feel the same way until . . ."

A few moments of silence tick past. I know what he was going to say.

"I left?" My whisper is low this time.

"Yeah." He turns to meet my eyes. His are filled with a little hurt and some other emotion I can't quite name. "Look," he says, blowing out a breath. "Let's start over. I'll stop giving you hell about leaving, and you stop . . ."

"Stop what?" I'm giving him side-eye now. *What do I need to stop?*

"Stop sidestepping the question when I ask how much the festival is gonna cost," he finishes, with a sly smile.

Oooh. That. "I can live with that," I say. "But let me show you the overall budget tomorrow." Because I spent some time earlier plugging in all the numbers, and we seriously will make money if all goes according to plan.

"Okay," Aiden agrees.

"Now let's watch some *Gilmore Girls*." I settle back into my seat and grab a handful of popcorn just as the theme song starts again. I sing it loudly with zero regrets. Aiden sings more softly. It's still cute, though. When the song is over, I notice that the occupants of more than one car near us are staring. Oh, right, I forgot they were here. "Hopefully we won't be on the blog tomorrow."

Aiden tosses a piece of popcorn to Argos, then he tosses another piece in the air and catches it in his own mouth. "Don't count on it."

Chapter 12

The next morning, I hide in my bedroom for two reasons. One, I am still shook by how much I wanted to kiss Aiden last night (like, *could barely sleep for imagining it a little too vividly* shook), and two, I am even now scouring the *Harvest Hollow Hot Sheet* to learn more about Aiden's ex-girlfriend.

Of course, the *Hot Sheet* headline is that Aiden and I were at the drive-in together. Which is enough gossip. If we had started making out, I can't even imagine the tumult that would ensue. There would probably be a meeting about us at town hall today.

There is also (surprising) news that one Miss Charlotte Parker was seen in the company of a young man no one recognized. I make a mental note to ask Charlotte about this later, before I continue reading the story about me and Aiden.

> *This blogger has learned that a spider was discovered in Aiden Parker's truck. Note to Mr. Parker: Donald Briggs is employed by the Harvest Hollow Drive-in to provide a seasonal ambience during the shows. Please do not interfere with his work.*

How the heck did Mrs. Lawrence know about the spider? And why is this considered gossip? This town needs more to do.

There's not much else to say because *we didn't kiss*. Just a brief summary of Billy and Amber sharing our truck. A shout-out to Argos for being a good boy. And another story about a Honda Civic that didn't park straight. I move on to the archives.

I'm combing through them when I notice updates pinging on my laptop from the employment networking site I've been using. It's Saturday, and email after email is coming in from my former coworkers. As I read them, I feel worse and worse. Because all of them basically say the same thing. *Wish I could help, but I can't.*

Only one person, a friend named Kennedy, says, "You didn't hear this from me, but Steve's been saying bad things about you. He's essentially warned all the other companies to steer clear."

What?! He can't do that! That's illegal, isn't it? Only I already know that what is legal isn't necessarily the same as what happens in the real world. People talk. And anyone looking to hire me is going to reach out to Steve and ask him what happened. Now I realize too late that I should have stayed and fought harder to keep my job. I let my anger and hurt get the better of me that day.

I text Kennedy. I know she'd rather talk via text then email through the networking site. A few text exchanges later and she's informed me that Geoff has been spreading the word that I stole his idea and tried to use it as my own, and Steve is confirming it.

I audibly groan. *Of course he is.*

For what it's worth, I tell Kennedy the truth.

That sucks, she replies.

I thank her for her honesty. Of course, there is part of me that wants to get on the first train back to the city, find Geoff, and tell him to shut up. I am also tempted to text Steve and try to explain the truth again. But I'm certain neither thing will matter. Perception is reality. Everyone knows that. Which means, even though Geoff stole my ideas and not the other way around, everyone thinks I'm the thief. Ugh. So unfair.

What am I going to do now? The event-planning business in New York is a tight-knit group. You might think in such a big city there would be plenty of opportunities, but everyone knows everyone. If I've been canceled, it's gonna be super difficult to find a job. A good one, at least.

Another email comes in. This one to my personal email account. It's Dad saying he passed the dementia test. Mom did too. At least there's some good news this morning. I'll ask for their scores later. The distraction reminds me that I was on a mission before I realized my entire career was tanked, and at the moment, since there's nothing I can do to about it, I choose to continue my search of the *Harvest Hollow Hot Sheet* for the identity of Aiden's ex-girlfriend.

For an old blog that is probably still hosted by a site from the 1990s, the *Hot Sheet* has a surprisingly good filter, and I'm able to find the posts from two years ago relatively easily. I begin in the summer. Mr. Nelson and Mrs. Early, two English teachers from the high school, both married, left their spouses for each other. Ooh. I remember that scandal. Mom told me about it. It was *très* shocking.

There are many other stories leading into the early fall. Mr. Kemper's son-in-law, a muckety-muck in finance in the city, was arrested for embezzling. Bob at the pharmacy broke his leg when he fell off the ladder when trying to patch his roof. And Mrs. Jackson's youngest grandchild was born.

And finally, there it is, in early September. Aiden Parker and Maryann Gates heat up the drive-in. Maryann Gates? I don't know that name. The thought is somewhat a relief, though I don't know why. Of course, I am expecting a picture like it's *TMZ*, but there isn't one. That would be far too advanced for Mrs. Lawrence, though I do wonder why she doesn't employ Donny to snap pics for the blog. It would really help. And God knows, Donny would be up for it. Maybe she thinks that would reveal her identity. The thought makes me snort-laugh.

There might not be a picture on the blog, but now that I've got a name, I go to work. Internet search engines are a nosy person's jam. I crack my knuckles, blow on them, and begin. Minutes later, I'm staring at a picture of one Maryann Gates. She lives two towns over and is a second-grade teacher. She has dark hair and brown eyes and is pretty with a bright smile. She looks so nice and wholesome. What happened to make her and Aiden break up?

I'm deep into her Instagram account, where she has a lot of pictures of herself with a cat and children and baked goods, when I glance at the time. Crap. It's nearly nine. I'm supposed to meet Aiden at the float in ten minutes. And bring the giant papier-mâché donuts Charlotte and I made late yesterday afternoon.

I close the laptop and hop out of bed. Twenty minutes later, I am striding into the work barn with a giant donut hanging over each shoulder. Argos comes running toward me, clearly ready for whatever I've got going on. I don't see Aiden.

I make my way over to the float and prop both donuts up along the side of the flatbed. Okay, the donuts *might* be a little too big, but we wanted them to be obvious. Now they're kinda take-up-half-the-float obvious. I shrug. So be it.

"*What* are those?" comes Aiden's incredulous voice from behind me.

I swivel to see him standing near the barn door. Argos races toward him. Aiden leans down to pet the dog.

"They're the donuts," I inform him. "Can't you tell?"

"They're as big as wagon wheels," Aiden points out.

He's not wrong. "We wanted them to be a focal point," I explain.

"I think they're going to be seen from space." His mouth curves up in that semblance of a grin that does something to me every single time.

"You're late," I say and honestly, I've been waiting to say that to him, because I'm usually the one who's late. Plus, I want him to stop making fun of my funny-looking donuts.

He folds his arms across his chest and gives me a smug look. "No, I'm not. You weren't here at nine, so I went to check on the greenhouse real quick."

Damn. I should've known he wasn't late. The man is never late. I've decided it must be a farmer thing.

"There's a greenhouse?" I mention this because one, it's news to me, and two, changing the subject is a solid strategy to deflect attention away from being late.

"Yeah." He nods. "I put one up a few years back. It's big enough for the trees to grow inside. I use it for testing during winter."

Testing? Apple trees? My brows shoot up. "Can I see it?"

"No," he says far too quickly, and then his voice softens. "Not right now."

I file that away in the same spot in my memory where I'm keeping the fact that he was digging a hole behind the barn and wouldn't talk about it. Maybe not *Dateline* material yet, but there is definitely *something* he doesn't want me to know about.

"Fine." I sigh. "Then help me with the donuts?" I give him a hopeful smile.

Aiden strolls over and lifts one of the giant light-brown orbs. "Wow. You really made a big paper donut."

"I made two big paper donuts," I reply. "You didn't think I would?"

Aiden shakes his head. "Did you have to do stuff like this for your job in the city?"

I grin at him. "I can't say I've ever made a giant donut before, but there's a first time for everything. I *did* make a pirate ship for our homecoming parade my junior year."

"Oh yeah, Miss School Spirit," Aiden says. "That sounds right."

"Yeah," I echo before realizing now's my chance to ask him something I've been wondering about. "Why didn't you ever join any clubs in school?"

He purses his lips to the side. "I was in Science Club," he points out.

"Oh yeah. How many people were in that club?" I ask, genuinely curious.

"Umm." He scratches the top of his head. "There were . . . three of us."

"Wow. Worse than I thought."

"It was me and the Donovan twins."

"Michael and Henry?" I say.

"Yep. I remember they planned the holiday party senior year and did a raffle to give away a gift basket."

I try not to laugh. "They held a raffle for three people?"

"No," Aiden replies. "Only one. They didn't put their names in because they planned it. They didn't think that would be fair. The only name to pull was mine." I can't help but picture three little science nerds pulling one piece of paper out of a glass beaker or something and acting surprised by the winner.

I laugh. "Science Club sounds fun," I say, but it's time for another question. "Hey, whatever happened with your science project that company wanted to buy?"

Aiden's face darkens. He rubs the back of his neck. "Oh, uh. That didn't work out."

"Why not? I remember Mom and Dad saying they seemed pretty interested. It was a seed company, right? Like, a really big deal."

"I don't remember the details," Aiden says quickly. "It was a long time ago."

I don't believe for a minute that he doesn't remember the details, but he clearly doesn't want to talk about. I'm about to attempt to change the subject yet again, when he lifts one of the donuts over his head and lowers it around himself to hip level. I can tell by the look on his face what he's planning to do.

"Don't!" I insist, widening my eyes at him. "You'll mess it up."

"That's a chance I'm willing to take." His grin is devilish. Without another word, he spins the donut around hips like a Hula-Hoop. It quickly twirls down around his legs and ankles before landing on the scattered-hay-covered floor.

My eyes go wide. "Look what you did!" I bend over to pull the donut from around his feet. "Step over it," I demand. I am affronted.

"What if I don't?" His hands are on his hips now, and he's giving me a defiant look.

I swat at his ankles. "Stop." I laugh. "It took me a long time to make this."

I tug at the donut probably a little too hard, and it hits the back of his legs. It pulls him off balance slightly, and the next thing I know, he stumbles toward me, and we go toppling together onto the pile of hay behind me.

Most of the air whooshes from my lungs when we land, and I immediately realize that Aiden is directly on top of me. Like, face-to-face, hip-to-hip on top of me. I seriously couldn't have planned it any better if I'd done it on purpose. Which I *definitely* didn't do.

I close my eyes. Oh damn, it feels a little too good to have his weight on me. I bite my lip and shudder. Aiden's forearms are braced on either side of my head., and the pressure of his hips on mine, his hardness pressing into my softness . . . It makes me lightheaded. I suck in my breath when he pushes himself up. But he lingers there. His weight balanced on his strong shoulders. He's looking straight down at me, his gaze soft as his throat bobs. His breath is on my cheek. Another shudder runs through my body. All I want to do is wrap my arms and legs around him, pull him back down on top of me, and kiss him.

He's looking at me like he wants to kiss me too. Like a *real* I-want-to-kiss-you look. Not a-spider-is-on-the-door-behind-you one. It's smoldering. Hot. Needy. I see it in his face when he makes the decision—I draw in my breath as his eyes slowly close and he bends his arms the slightest bit, lowering himself to me. His lips come closer, closer—

"Ellie, are you in here?" The shout from outside makes Aiden quickly roll away. He's helping me up off the ground when Donny comes sauntering into the barn.

"I'm here, Donny," I call as I wipe hay from my clothes and pluck it from my hair.

Donny strolls over and stops in front of us, clearly totally oblivious to what he just interrupted.

"Thanks again for letting Billy and Amber sit with you last night," Donny says.

"No problem." I stare at him silently for a few moments.

Aiden is *glaring* at him. Like, daggers-shooting-from-his-eyes glaring at him.

"Did you need anything else?" I ask. I'm pretty sure Donny didn't come all the way out here just to thank us for last night, but with him you never know.

"Oh yeah." He snaps his fingers and points at me. "You have a visitor in the lobby."

* * *

It's over half an hour later before I'm on my way down from the attic apartment to the lobby to see who is here. Of course, I'm obsessed with the idea that it's either Geoff or Steve. Maybe they've both come to beg me to take my job back. Maybe the whole project with the Bolt Hotel Group has been a mess since I've been gone, and they need me. Maybe Geoff realizes what a great girlfriend I was and sees the error of his ways. It would be so satisfying to reject *him* this time.

After rushing back from the barn to the apartment via the outside door, it took me fifteen minutes to pick the correct outfit with which to entertain groveling. (The other fifteen was spent getting my hair and makeup in order.) I am wearing the black cashmere sweater with old-school jeans, black booties, and pearl earrings. I am convinced that it says, "I'm relaxed and enjoying my vacation from assholes," while also remaining classy and ready to lift my nose in the air when they beg me to return.

But the minute I step into the lobby, I realize I have grossly miscalculated the situation. Because it's not Geoff or Steve sitting there. It's Maria . . . standing there, with her arms crossed tightly over her chest.

Oh crap. She looks pissed. "Hi!" I say, waving, and I know that she knows I'm being fake because I feel guilty.

She eyes me up and down before saying, "Based on what you're wearing, I'm going to guess you thought I was Geoff or Steve."

"What?" But Maria knows me too well. There's no use denying it, and it feels good to have a friend who is so close that she can read your clothing.

It's my turn to eye her up and down. Maria has long, black, curly hair and dark brown eyes and the kind of thick black eyelashes people pay tons of money for. She's always dressed in the latest fashion. But I barely notice her clothes today because the look she's giving me tells me that she's here for the truth, and I'm quite aware that it's time I share it with her.

"Come with me?" I say, pointing toward the front door.

"Would love to," she replies with a tight smile.

Within minutes we're behind the inn sitting in two black Adirondack chairs near one of the stone firepits under the wide oak trees. A few leaves meander to the ground around us. Since it's morning, the firepits aren't lit, but it's beautiful out here at night when they are going. The scent of burned wood from last night lingers, and I breathe it in. Maria does too. She knows I'm acting suspiciously, but she is still enjoying the taste of fall that being at the inn provides. She's not a robot.

"It's really pretty here," she allows.

"Isn't it?" I say, grateful for the reprieve from explaining myself, however short-lived.

"I know you didn't just come out here to see your family," she says next.

Maria and I have had many talks about family over the years. To her, family is everything. She flies to southern California multiple times a year to visit hers, while I have a mere train ride to get to my parents. And yet I find excuses to stay away. But because she knows me so well, Maria is quite aware that my acting like I just up and decided to visit my parents on a random Wednesday is completely out of character.

I bite my lip. "You're right."

She crosses her legs and bobs her foot up and down. "Spill it."

It takes me the better part of twenty minutes to explain my situation to Maria. There is starting. There is stopping. There are many *ums* and *uhs*. But somehow, I manage to recount everything, including last night's near-kiss in the truck with Aiden and this morning's shunning by the entire NYC event-planning industry.

To her credit, Maria doesn't say "I told you so" until the end. And when she does, it sounds more like, "Geoff has always been a dick."

I hang my head. "I know. I should have listened to you."

"But honestly, I wouldn't have guessed he'd be *this* big of a dick." She shakes her head. She is pissed, but she's pissed at him, not me. I'm relieved. I thought she would be mad at me for not coming clean via text. I mean, girl had to hightail it all the way out to eastern Long Island to get the truth.

True to her eternally practical, get-things-done nature, Maria says, "We need to figure out what to do. Is there somewhere we can get a drink?"

"It's ten a.m.," I point out, only because I feel I must.

"Is there somewhere we can get a drink at ten a.m.?" she amends, smiling at me. "It's Long Island, not Mars."

I return her smile. "I think I know the perfect place."

Chapter 13

When I pull open the door to the food barn, the smell of cinnamony baked goods fills my nostrils. I suck it in like a drug. If being addicted to the scent of warm apple-y goodness is wrong, I don't want to be right. I've been out here every day since I arrived, and I always leave with my belly (and pockets) full of deliciousness. Maria's gonna love it too.

"What is *in* here?" Maria asks, already closing her eyes and drawing in the scent like me.

"Magic baked goods," I reply, making my way toward the bakery corner. "And lots of alcoholic cider."

"Magic?" Maria echoes, following me.

"That's right," I toss out just before Sera comes out of the back with a tray filled with tarts.

"Hi, Sera." I wave at my new friend. "This is Maria." I haven't asked Sera to read my tarot yet, but I'm working up to it. Yesterday I casually mentioned something about wanting to know the future. She didn't bite, so I'm relatively certain I'm just going to end up blurting it out one day.

Maria waits for Sera to set down the tray before offering her hand. "I'm El's friend, and I have a ridiculous sweet tooth," she declares.

"Ooh, glad to hear it." Sera is wearing all black again and the chains. It's a look I know Maria will also appreciate. Chic. Timeless. Slightly witchy. Besides, Maria respects woo as much as I do. She once told me her grandma is a little clairvoyant. Which seems to me like being a little pregnant, but what do I know?

I nod toward the tarts. "What do you got there?" I rock back and forth on my heels as if I'm not totally trying to nab one.

"Apple strudel tarts. Want some?"

Of course I want some. I want all. "Yes, please."

Sera points at the sheet with her oven-mitt-covered hand. "Take as many as you like. It's a test batch."

I love the sound of that.

"Happy to be of service." Maria picks up a tart with a napkin she pulled from a nearby stack.

I am much more ill-mannered. I just grab a tart with my bare hand and bite right into it. It is eye-crossingly delicious. I moan.

Maria takes a bite too, and we exchange equally heart-eyed glances.

"Hey, did you hear that Charlotte went to the drive-in with a mystery guy last night?" Sera asks. And now I love her even more because the tart and the smell of cinnamony apples made me forget to ask her the same question.

"Yes," I say. "Do you have any idea who he is?"

"Who's Charlotte?" Maria asks, and as soon as I tell her, she's just as invested as we are. Maria can get on board like that. It's one of the many things I love about her. We both stare inquisitively at Sera, ready for additional information.

"I don't know," Sera says. "But it sure sounded like they were on a date. It was just the two of them."

Well, I know from experience that you can be alone with a person at the drive-in and *not* be on a date, but it's not about me right now, so I keep that comment to myself and instead say, "I kinda got the feeling she likes Sawyer."

Sera's crystal-green eyes go wide. "Oh, she *does*. She *does* like Sawyer."

"Who's Sawyer?" Maria asks next.

"Sawyer is one of the farmhands," Sera explains. "And he's really cute. Not my type, but *cute*."

I want to ask Sera what her type is, but instead I say, "Does Sawyer not feel the same about Charlotte?" I am already sad and a little indignant just thinking about that possibility. Charlotte is adorable and helpful and kind and smart. Who wouldn't like her? Sawyer is a fool if he doesn't.

"I think he does," Sera reports. "Only . . ."

"Only *what*?" Maria and I both say this at the same time because we are equally intrigued when someone is obviously struggling to keep from saying something.

Sera removes her oven mitt to pluck at her gold chains. "Only, from what I hear, Sawyer came to work here when he was twenty-two."

"So what?" Maria says before taking another bite of her apple tart.

"Charlotte was eighteen at the time." Sera lets her chains drop with a clink. "Just out of high school."

"Ooooh," I say, wrinkling up my nose. I see where she is going with this. "Yeah, that's a big difference at those ages. So . . . maybe she had a schoolgirl crush that never went away?"

"Yeah, that's the impression I get," Sera continues. "And Sawyer is a really good guy. He would *never* be inappropriate. Especially with his bosses' daughter."

Sera doesn't have to say more. We all get it. No good guy is going to entertain a crush from a younger girl when he works for her parents. It's just a *hard no*.

"How old are they now?" Maria wants to know.

I am trying to do math in my head when Sera says, "I think she's twenty-four, and he's my age, twenty-eight."

"Oh, well, that's perfectly fine now," Maria adds, ever practical.

"Yeah, but I get it," Sera says.

"I get it too." I sigh. But I'm still a little sad for Charlotte. She is the best, and I can't imagine having a crush that lasts, what, six years? I mean . . . kinda adorable, when you think about it.

"Sounds like she's moving on, though," Maria says. "Probably for the best."

"Yeah, but we need to find out who this new guy is." Sera's voice is stern. "We can't have our little Charlotte dating just *anyone*."

I agree with Sera. Charlotte is special. We need to vet this drive-in date. I tell Sera as much. I finish with, "I'll see what I can find out."

"Sounds good," Sera says. "Now, I'd better get back to the ovens. I'm testing a lot of new stuff for the festival."

"Happy to be the testing subjects," I remind her in a singsong voice before glancing over at the brewery. I nearly forgot the reason Maria and I came out here was to talk and drink. "Is Jesse here yet?"

"He's always here," Sera replies, waving her hand. "Hold on. I'll get you some chocolate chip cookies too." She pulls a plate from under the counter and puts it next to the tarts before she disappears into the back.

Chocolate chip cookies? Yes, please.

"Who's Jesse?" Maria asks. So far, she's doing great keeping up with all these new people. Time to add one more.

"Jesse's the brewer. I'll introduce you when he comes out."

I move the apple tarts to the plate and hand it to Maria. "Head over, and I'll wait for the cookies." I nod toward the bar stools on the other side of the barn.

I drum my fingers along the countertop as Maria makes her way to the brewery counter, where she picks a stool in the center of the space.

I'm still happily waiting for the cookies when the door behind the bar opens, and Jesse steps out with his ubiquitous tray of beer growlers. He stops short when he sees Maria sitting there. She immediately starts to place an order, but he cuts her off. "We're not open yet," he informs her. "Can't you read?"

Oh no!

The cookies are forgotten, and I begin to half run, because if there's something I know about my friend Maria, it's that she's not going to take that sort of rudeness in stride. In fact, she's about to—

"I'm sorry," she's saying by the time I make it to her side. "Did you just ask me if I can *read?* Because you're welcome to read my lips when I say that you can go f—"

"Hey! Wait. Wait a minute, here," I nearly shout as I jump up on the bar stool next to Maria. My voice is panicky, and I'm desperately trying to choose my words carefully. "No worries. No worries. This is just a misunderstanding. Jesse, this is my good friend Maria, from the city. Maria, this is Jesse, the brewer here at the orchard."

Did that sound breezy enough? Happy enough? Conciliatory enough? The thing is, you don't want to get on Maria's bad side. There's no getting off of it. And I like Jesse. He gave me the growlers I requested. He seems really good at his job. He was definitely rude, but I don't want to see him murdered.

My head swivels back and forth between their angry faces. Both of them have narrowed their eyes at each other, and it's clear neither one of them has the intention of either apologizing or backing down. *Oh boy.* What we've got here is an old-fashioned standoff.

"Maria is here with me," I explain to Jesse. "That's okay, right? I was hoping we could get a drink a little early. Sorry if I'm wrong."

"Don't you apologize to him," Maria says. She's got one hand on her hip, and she's glaring at him. If looks could kill, guy's dead body would be lying behind the bar right now. "Doesn't he work for your dad?" she adds.

"So what, I'm at your beck and call?" Jesse claps back. "You come into *my* job, where I'm breaking my neck trying to prepare for a major festival, staring at your phone, and just expect me to drop everything to serve you? What sort of spoiled-rich-girl . . ." His voice trails off, but honestly, the damage is done.

I gulp. This is escalating quickly, and it's about to get way uglier because Maria is the polar opposite of a spoiled rich girl. In fact, she's a third-generation Italian American whose grandma barely kept a small restaurant running to send her father and his siblings to school. She's also a next-level PR genius who is on Instagram all the time for work, so in zero minus zero seconds, Jesse is about to get his ass handed to him and honestly there's nothing I can do for him now. He's made his bed. I tried. I resist the urge to cover my head as if real shrapnel is about to fly.

Maria stands up on the footrest of the bar stool so she's taller than Jesse, who is a good six foot two. "Spoiled? Rich girl? *Rich girl!*" She's not even turning red. She's gone straight to purple. *Not good.* I've never witnessed anyone stroke out before, but there's a first time for everything. Is Donny also a paramedic?

I dart behind Maria and do the throat-slashing gesture with my finger to indicate to Jesse that he had better de-escalate or die.

Maria takes a deep breath. "First of all—"

Jesse tugs at the bill of his black cap and expels a breath. "Look, obviously we got off on the wrong foot."

Oh, thank God. Clearly, he's taken my warning. Wise of him. Very wise. He may live to see the end of this day after all.

"Let me get you a cider," he says to Maria.

Ooh. Now I wince. I forgot to tell Maria that cider and beer are kinda all that's on the menu out here. She's not really a cider drinker. She's more of an espresso martini type.

"Cider?" Maria eyes him up and down with distaste. Her face is slightly less purple but still, cobra-like, she remains ready to strike.

"Yeah, *cider.* Or beer. You got a problem with that?" Jesse asks, arching a brow. "It's a brewery."

Uh-oh. Here we go again. I want to plant my face in my hand, but I still need to try to smooth this over a bit more.

Maria rolls her eyes. Her eyelashes make the whole thing look next-level. She opens her mouth to no doubt say something even more snarky, when I jump in. "You don't happen to have wine or champagne or anything like that, do you, Jesse?"

I am watching Maria from the corner of my eye. Until she sits down, this thing is not officially de-escalated.

Jesse's snort answers the question for me. "Princess here too good for cider? Figures."

Ugh. This guy's got a mouth on him like . . . well, exactly like *my good friend Maria*. Their standoff makes me realize how similar they are. Which, in this case, isn't cool.

"It's *principessa*, you punk," Maria informs him. "And I'll take a cider."

Okay, that last part surprises even me. Clearly, Maria doesn't want Jesse to label her a princess. But I've never seen her drink a cider before, so this is gonna be something to watch. I'm here for it. It'll be like seeing Victoria Beckham eat Taco Bell. Along those lines.

"What'd ya like?" He starts a list on his fingers. "I got hard cider, dry cider, sweet cider, ice cider—"

Her eyes narrow before she surprises *me* by saying, "Surprise me." I mean, it's clear she knows nothing about cider, but Maria isn't a "surprise me" sort of person. She's the type who tells the bartender *exactly* how to make her drink.

Jesse is brave enough to turn his back on Maria to pull her drink from the tap. To keep things simple, I tell him I'll have the same, and he returns seconds later with two mugs of cider, which he slides in front of us.

"Thank you," Maria says, but it's clear from her tone that she meant "eff you." She is seated, however, so I breathe a little easier.

I thank Jesse too, and he pushes open the door to the back. "Call if you need a refill, *principessa*," he says as the door swings shut behind him.

I have to clamp my hand on Maria's arm to keep her from standing up and going after him. Her eyes are narrowed to slits.

"Wow," I say. "I don't think I've ever seen mutual disdain form so quickly."

"He's a jerk." Her eyes are alight with flames.

I wince. "Yeah, it wasn't great. He's been cool, though. I promise you." Then I laugh.

"What's funny?" One of Maria's dark eyebrows is arched.

"When I first met him, I actually thought you'd think he was hot." I shrug and laugh again.

Maria is not laughing. She's giving me stink-eye. "Me and Ball Cap? Don't think so. He looks like he'd be the type to go *camping*."

People who enjoy camping are mysteries to Maria. Along with people who collect stuffed animals and adults who love theme parks. She just doesn't get it. It's too far from her aesthetic. Which is why she only leaves Manhattan for trips to SoCal to see her family. She can get with the LA vibe, but small towns aren't her thing. Which makes it even more touching that she's come to Long Island to check on me.

"Thanks for coming out here," I say, and I mean it. Maria may be intense, but she's also super loyal and a good friend. I'm lucky to have her. You want someone like her in your corner. "And thanks for your help promoting the festival."

The minute I'd texted her yesterday, Maria had replied with two words: *on it*. Several hours later, she'd sent me a long list of all the things she'd done or was planning to do to promote the festival, and honestly, it was a dream list. She even got a really big local travel in-fluencer friend of hers to agree to come out and post from the festival the night of the Harvest Ball. It's a big deal.

"Yeah, well, I was always suspicious of your reasons for coming out here, but when I asked you how it was going yesterday and you said you were having fun, I *knew* I had to come. There's no way you're having fun out here in bumblefuck."

I bite my lip. My old friend guilt is back, because the truth is I *did* have fun yesterday. I woke up to pumpkin-spice coffee, ate too many baked goods, made a papier-mâché chandelier, got to plan an event all day, stuck my head out of a truck window in the autumn-scented breeze, and connected with old friends. Plus, I got to meet Mayor Millie, who is honestly a treasure. And I can't forget my knitted chicken. It's currently sitting on the windowsill in my attic bedroom.

I even had fun at the drive-in last night. I mean, only in Harvest Hollow will you get leaves shaken on your windshield while watching *Gilmore Girls*.

But instead of trying to explain all that to Maria, who'll never believe me, I decide to change the subject. "So, Geoff," I say, lifting my mug to my lips and taking a big sip of cider. It's actually pretty good. Way better than I expected.

"I have half a dozen ideas on how to get revenge," Maria replies, obviously warming to the subject.

Of course she does. She lifts her mug and eyes the cider with a fully unimpressed look on her face.

"Revenge? Now *that's* a good friend," I say. "What's the most realistic idea?"

Maria's smile is glowing. "Tie him up, roll him in honey, and pour fire ants on his head."

"Nice. Solid plan. Only I'm not sure where we'd get fire ants."

"Oh, I can get fire ants."

I side-eye her. The girl can be a little scary. Again, I'm glad she's on my side.

Maria takes a sip from her mug, and amazingly, her eyes light up.

"Good, huh?" I ask.

"For cider," she says.

She's not going to admit it. She's not one to admit she's wrong. But I can tell she kinda liked it.

"Geoff can go to hell," I say next. "I don't want him back. But how am I going to get a job if Steve is spreading lies about me?"

"What about your friend Kennedy?" Maria asks.

"Kenn was the one who told me the truth. But she's still at GMJ."

"Can she put in a good word for you anywhere else?"

"Maybe. I'll ask her." I take another hefty sip of the cider. Wow. It's *really* good. Did Jesse make this? Is this one of his in-house brews? He's *talented.* We need to publicize this stuff more. "There is *one* good thing about Geoff betraying me," I continue.

"What?" I *know* Maria is liking her cider because she keeps drinking it. If she hated it, she would have abandoned it already.

"Him dumping me was an excellent reminder for me to *not* date anyone I have a working relationship with," I say with a firm nod.

Maria's brow arches real high. Pure skepticism. "Didn't you say you wanted Aiden to kiss you?"

"Shh." I eye the swinging door to the back of the bar for any sign of Jesse. I'm still not sure what he's been told about me. And I definitely don't want him to hear about my desire to kiss Aiden. After last night, I'm wondering if Jesse also heard the "Ellie left Aiden" version of whatever story is going around. Maybe that's why he was frowning at me the day we met. I haven't told Maria about what Amber said yet either. I'm not sure how to explain it.

"Even if I *wanted* to start something with Aiden, now isn't the time," I insist. "I *just* broke up with Geoff. I still need to figure all that out."

Maria sighs. "Is there anything to figure out? What you and Geoff had wasn't exactly electric."

I take another sip and consider her words. "Okay. You're not wrong," I say. "Geoff was kinda boring. But it was just so . . . easy with him. We both worked at the same place, knew the same people. We even ate the same thing for lunch every day."

Maria shakes her head and takes another sip of cider. "Uh, matching lunch isn't exactly hashtag-couplesgoals, El."

"He loved to travel," I weakly point out. Though we did have to plan a lot around his allergies. "He always praised my work ethic." I think for a few more seconds. "His mom was nice."

"Ooh, sounds passionate," Maria drawls.

Okay. She's *really* not wrong there. Geoff was convenient and safe, but we weren't exactly smoking up the sheets together. And I can't even picture him giving me a sexy look with or without a spider involved. "It's still better if Aiden and I don't kiss," I say. "We're work partners, and I am never mixing business and dating again."

"If you say so," Maria replies, taking another big swig from her mug.

We continue to chat for the better part of an hour. There's lots to catch up on. I've kinda had a busy week, and Maria always has interesting stories to tell from the world of PR. She knows all the celebrity lore. It's *so* fun to listen to.

As we talk, I chug my cider. It doesn't taste alcoholic. It tastes delicious. Turns out morning drinking is fun! *La, la, la.*

I've just finished telling Maria about my smug Patagonia vest comment to Steve when she suddenly grabs my arm. She's staring directly behind me. Her eyes are wide. "Is that him?" she intones.

"Him? Who?" I make a wobbly turn on my stool and follow Maria's gaze toward the barn door, which has just opened. Aiden has stepped inside.

I turn back around.

Maria arches a dark brow and lifts her chin toward him.

"Aiden? Yep," I say, nodding way too hard. Oh crap. Am I drunk?

"Oh yeah," Maria says. "You definitely need to kiss *him*."

"Shh," I say, pressing my index finger to my lips and being far too loud about it. I am the opposite of stealthy when I'm drunk.

"Hey!" Aiden sees us and jogs over. "I was looking for you, Ellie."

"To kiss you?" Maria whispers, and I slap at her hands. She slaps back. By the time we're done with our eleven-year-olds' slap fight, Aiden has his eyes narrowed on both of us.

"Hi, I'm Aiden." He puts out a hand for Maria to shake.

"Yes. You. Are," Maria says, giving him a totally obvious once-over.

"Aiden!" I nearly scream his name because I also get loud when I've been drinking. Or when I'm in an awkward situation. Both are happening at the moment. "This is my friend Maria, from the city."

"Maria?" he echoes. "PR Maria?"

Maria laughs. "That's me."

"Thank you for helping us promote the festival," Aiden says.

"Maria's the best!" I exclaim.

"I hear you're pretty good too," Maria says to Aiden. She's eyeing him like a sushi appetizer at a fancy work function.

Aiden furrows his brow. "Good at what?"

Maria bites her lip. "Catching spiders."

An alarm is going off in my head, but it's dulled by the delicious cider I have been slamming. My huge mug is nearly empty. When did that happen?

Aiden gives me a smile so sexy it makes me gulp and press my thighs together. "What have you been telling your friend Maria about me?"

Honestly, it would be a shorter list to tell him what I *haven't* told her about him, but I'm not drunk enough to say that. Instead, I say, "Would you excuse us for a moment?"

Aiden's still eyeing me and smiling, but he nods. "Sure. I was going to ask you about the budget, but we can do that later. There's something I need to talk to Jesse about, anyway."

Seconds later, Aiden's gone around the counter and disappeared into the back of the brewery. I immediately turn to Maria. "Be cool," I tell her.

"What? I am cool. As Ariana Madix would say, *I was born cool*."

I have to smile at that because Maria really was born cool, but that's not what I mean. "Don't tell Aiden." I am still being too loud, but I can't seem to stop myself.

Maria leans toward me. Is she drunk too? "Don't tell Aiden what?"

"Don't tell Aiden I wanted him to kiss me!" I nearly shout, and then I immediately want to sink through the floor and disappear because at the exact moment I say it, the door to the back opens again and Aiden steps out.

He heard me. I know he did.

Chapter 14

It's nearly ten when I sneak back into the apartment that night. Maria returned to the city after promising to keep me posted on her PR efforts for the festival. Of course, she offered to let me stay with her while I get back on my feet, but I politely declined. After some discussion we both agreed that our collective wardrobes probably wouldn't fit in her tiny apartment. It's chic as hell, but it's the approximate size of a broom closet. Maria went for quality over quantity. I happen to know she pays half of her rent with pictures of her feet in heels on OnlyFans. She's not proud of it, and I'm sworn to secrecy because if her grandma finds out, there will be hell to pay, but it's amazing how much you can make showing nothing but an ankle and the top of your foot. I honestly don't know why her grandma would object, but apparently, it's a Catholic thing. Or an Italian thing. I'm not here to judge.

I may also have to open an OnlyFans foot account if I can't find an event-planning job. My feet aren't as pretty as Maria's, though. It's not a great plan.

Still, I feel much more centered after seeing Maria. She always puts a practical spin on everything. She told me to just concentrate on planning the festival, put it at the top of my new résumé, and look for remote jobs to tide me over until I can make my way back into the New York scene. She made me feel better about everything . . . except my desire to steer clear of Aiden.

"You *sure* you want to stop mixing business with pleasure so hastily?" she asked just before Donny and I dropped her off at the train station earlier. I had gotten out of the car with her to see her off.

"Aiden's my business partner," I had insisted.

"Your *hot* business partner. And you kinda just told him you want to kiss him. He's gonna make a move. Be ready."

The thought makes my stomach feel like tiny hang gliders are winging through it.

Maria left after promising to keep working on the PR for the festival. She's doing it all pro bono, which is so awesome of her. I don't have anything to offer in return other than a comped room for the night of the Harvest Ball. To my surprise, she agreed to come. "I gotta see how this whole thing turns out. I'm invested now," she said before waving goodbye and hopping on the train.

Now I am slinking into the apartment because I'm pretty sure Aiden is inside, and while I am completely sober at the moment, I do not want to run into him after what happened earlier. I'm never drinking cider again. I'm not used to that stuff. If I'd been drinking a martini, I'd have been in control. I know exactly how many martinis I can drink before getting so wasted I blurt out stuff I shouldn't say. It is approximately 1.5 martinis. I had glugged nearly a whole giant thirty-two-ounce cider mug this morning, and apparently that is my tipping point. What the hell was the alcoholic content in that mama, anyway?

I'm pleased to find the apartment dark. Thank God. Aiden's got to be asleep by now. Farmers tuck in early. I lower my purse to the counter, kick off my boots as quietly as I can, and then fumble around in the dark feeling for familiar objects to locate my bedroom. I have no interest in turning on a light. That might wake up Aiden.

I make my way to the far edge of the kitchen counter. The door to my room is about twenty feet to the left, past the kitchen table and just before the tiny sofa. It's open space between me and the bedroom, though, so I just wave my hands out in front of me to ensure I don't hit anything, and I start walking . . . slowly.

I count the steps in my head. I'm to seventeen when I run into the wall. Oops. I step back and rub my nose. Dang. I must have counted wrong. I am about to step again when the wall speaks.

"Trying to sneak past me?"

Gulp.

It's Aiden.

My heart shoots up to my throat. I reach out again, and this time I realize what I thought was the wall was really Aiden's chest. I pat it. I touch it. I run my fingers along it. Oh yeah. I recognize those pecs. He's wearing a T-shirt, but it's definitely Aiden.

Aiden's breathing hitches, and my hand stops. That one little catch in his breath does something to me that I'm not going to be able to recover from.

"Ellie?" His voice is a deep, sexy whisper.

I close my eyes. "Yes?" My fingers have moved to his lower abdomen.

"I wanted to kiss you too."

The admission makes me ache. I press my thighs together. I clench my jaw, my resolve crumbling away.

His hands move to my shoulders. I have no idea how he found them in the dark. Is my lust making me phosphorescent? One hand moves up my neck, slowly skimming the thin skin there with his thumb. When he reaches my jaw, his thumb traces along the bottom edge of it. My head tilts to the side automatically, wanting more.

His index finger skims my lips, and the next thing I know, his mouth is on mine. His tongue barely touches my lips. He's tasting me, finding me. And my hands move up his abdomen, to his chest, then to his shoulders. I've wanted to grab these shoulders for days. Now's my chance.

His mouth slants across mine, and our tongues meet. He tastes like smoky apples and smells like pine needles and maddeningly hot aftershave. He pulls me hard against his body, his large hands cupping my ass as he holds me close. A wave of wanting shoots through my whole body. I feel like I may collapse. But I cling to his shoulders and wrap my arms around his neck. He leans down, kissing me more, harder, closer. I can't get enough. His mouth moves to my cheek, and then my ear, and I feel my heart race. His tongue traces my earlobe, and I nearly buckle. I make a whimpering sound in the back of my throat. He kisses the sensitive spot just beneath my ear. I shudder.

"Ellie," he breathes against my cheek.

"Yes." I want him to scoop me up into his arms and take me into the bedroom. Either bedroom will do. I'm not picky.

I'm waiting. Any minute now. Scoop! Scoop!

"Goodnight," he breathes, and seconds later, I'm still trying to wrap my head around that when I hear his door click shut.

Chapter 15

I am proud of myself. Last night, I did not pound on Aiden's door and attempt to slide into bed with him. I wanted to, but, like a completely calm and rational adult, I felt along the wall in the dark until I found my own bedroom, went inside, closed the door, and then totally obsessed about our kiss all night.

I mean, how could he kiss me like that and just casually go to bed? It makes no sense. Unless . . . he wasn't as physically affected by the kiss as I was. But I know he was. I *felt* it. I was pressed up against him. His body is just as hard and cut as it looked, btw.

At first, I was kinda hoping he'd come to my room and finish what he started. Okay, perhaps "kinda hoping" is inaccurate. It *may* have been more like praying hard with both sweaty hands pressed together, and some grandiose promises made to the Universe.

Then, I spent way too much time contemplating whether I should go to *his* room. But by the time I finally fell asleep, I realized that the kiss was enough. It was plenty. We got it out of our systems. We both clearly wanted to try it. So we did. And now we can move on and work together.

It's great, actually. If we'd done any more, I would feel guilty. I mean, weren't there townsfolk talking about how I supposedly "left Aiden"? Aiden himself had admitted that he'd wanted me to stay. And I have no intention of staying. Not back then and not now. As soon as I get a job, any job, I'll be back in the city. And then what? If we start something, people will say I left Aiden *twice*? No thank you.

So, by the time I woke up this morning I was counting my lucky stars that all we did was kiss. Anything else would have crossed the line. A kiss is no big deal.

It's nearly eight a.m., and I know Aiden is long gone out in the orchards, but I am still hiding in my room because what if he comes back for breakfast? I'm not ready to face him after last night. I need to gather myself. Gather my thoughts. Gather my . . . everything. When I see him again, I need to be casually yet classily dressed, in full professional mode (perhaps even carrying a clipboard, everyone looks busy with a clipboard), and dripping with confidence. Enough confidence to assure him that the kiss meant nothing, and now that we've gone ahead and done it, we can move along with our business relationship.

I'm still in PJs with bedhead, so I shouldn't risk leaving my room. But I do really want my pumpkin-spice coffee, and Aiden's been leaving the coffeepot on warm for me. It's too tempting to resist.

I slide out of my bed, pad over, and press my ear to the door. No noise. The apartment is empty. I know it.

I crack open the door. Still nothing. And it's daylight, so Aiden's definitely not stealthily waiting for me like last night. It's only about twenty feet from my door to the coffeepot. I am being silly. I am a grown adult, and I want some coffee. I should not have to sneak around in my own parents' attic apartment.

I open the door wide and boldly make my way to the kitchen holding my head high. I take out a mug. I get the creamer out of the fridge. I pour the still-warm coffee into the mug. I grab a spoon.

I am fine. This is fine. All is well.

And that's when the door to the apartment opens and Aiden steps inside.

In addition to my bed head and PJs, there is *nary* a bra. I briefly consider sprinting to my room.

No. It's too late for that. Which means there is only one way to handle this. Complete and total denial. "Morning!" I'm too loud again, but it's the least of my issues.

"Hi," Aiden says. He looks like he should be on the cover of *Hot Farmer Weekly*. He's wearing worn jeans, scuffed brown boots, and a blue-and-gray flannel shirt over a tight white T that's clinging to his abs. *The abs I totally fondled in the dark last night.*

I wish it was dark again. I would slink away. Instead, I pour the pumpkin-spice creamer into my coffee mug and stir with aplomb.

Aiden leans his shoulder against the wall next to the cabinets and bites his lip. I cannot look at that. I am still experiencing memories of his hands on my ass last night. Looking at his mouth—or any of him, frankly—may send me into a full-throttled tailspin.

"Do you want to talk about it?" he asks.

"Talk about what?" There have been times in my life when I am acutely unhappy with the fact that I grew up in a family that made passive aggression an art form. My parents argue through a pug, for heaven's sake. But today, today, I have never been so relieved that I am able, with a completely straight face, to pretend as if I have no earthly idea what Aiden is talking about.

"Uh, *our kiss* last night?"

Well, okay. He's just going to blow my passive aggression right out the window, eh? Fine. I can be assertive too. "No. I do not want to talk about it." I raise my coffee mug to my lips and gulp down half of it. I need the caffeine immediately if we're going to keep having this conversation.

"Fair enough," he says.

I nearly melt onto the kitchen floor in a puddle of relief.

"Then can I ask you about the budget for the festival?" he says next.

I am slowly moving back toward my bedroom while running my fingers through my unkempt hair and sucking down more coffee. "I told you." My tone is light. I want to sound breezy. As if I have everything under control. "A well-orchestrated event is not cheap. But the money it'll bring in should cover it."

"Can I see the budget?" he asks.

"Yes." I mostly agree because showing him the budget means I can disappear into my room for a few moments and get myself together. "Just a sec," I say.

I hustle into the bedroom and close the door. I set down my coffee, then, I rip off my PJs, find a suitable bra, and pull-on leggings and a dark-green sweater. I've been bringing my travel kit from the bathroom into the bedroom with me every night so Aiden can't see all the personal stuff inside it, which means I have my brush, and I make quick work of my hair. I toss on some lip gloss and mascara, grab my laptop from the bedside table, and saunter back out into the living room as if I wasn't just frantically trying to make myself look hot in under five minutes.

Aiden is pouring himself another cup of coffee, so his back is toward me when I slide up to the kitchen counter. I set my laptop in front of one of the bar stools and flip it open. Then I find the budget that's in my recent files.

"Here you go," I announce, turning the laptop to face him.

He turns around and sets down his mug, bending at the waist and bracing his forearms on the counter. And if it all wasn't hot enough, he then proceeds to pull out a pair of reading glasses from his front shirt pocket and push them up on his nose. Much to my dismay, he's giving full Clark Kent.

I swallow hard and look away.

He spends a good five minutes staring at the spreadsheet while I gulp coffee and try not to stare at him. Especially when I sidle around the back of him to get more coffee and all I can think about is the moment he pulled me hard against his body last night. *Oof.* That is going in the memory bank forever. I actually need to write it down in case of future dementia. I cannot rely on my brain to keep ahold of that. It's too good to risk losing.

He's sort of grunting every few minutes. I want to ask him what made him grunt, but I decide to keep my mouth shut. The less discussion we have about the budget, the better. I learned that from working with clients at GMJ. Be transparent but don't linger.

"According to this, we'll make thousands of dollars," he finally says.

"Yep." I hug my coffee mug to my chest.

"Are all these numbers accurate?" he asks next.

"Some are estimates, but they are close," I confidently inform him.

He pulls off his glasses and tucks them back in his pocket. "And where is the money coming from to pay the vendors up front?"

"That's the beauty of it," I say. "I got most of them to agree to bill us."

"Bill us?" He looks skeptical.

"Yep. Bill us, and we'll pay in a month when the festival is over and we've made the money."

To my surprise, he nods and says, "It looks good, Ellie. Thank you."

I want to wipe the sweat off my forehead and make a relieved *shoosh* noise, but instead I merely take a little sip of coffee. It's my turn to ask an unwelcome question. "Now that you've seen the budget, will you tell me what you're doing out behind the work barn and maybe in the greenhouse?" Okay, that was a non sequitur delivered with absolutely no finesse, but in my defense, the coffee has barely kicked in and my brain had signaled loudly to change the subject.

Aiden tips his head to the side and narrows his eyes. "Why are you asking?"

"Because I truly want to know. You can't just act all mysterious and not expect a girl to be curious."

He straightens to his full height and says, "Can you keep a secret?"

"You have a couple secrets of mine," I remind him.

"True," he says with a smile and another tug on his bottom lip with his teeth that causes a tremor of lust to roll through my lower half. He takes a deep breath. "I've been working on a hybrid apple."

"A hybrid apple?" It's not a particularly shocking answer, but it's one I wasn't expecting.

"Yeah." He nods. "It's a cross between a Honeycrisp and a Golden Delicious."

"That sounds good," I say. And it really does. "Why didn't you tell me? This could be huge."

He rests his forearm atop his head. "I'm not sure it's ready yet. The ripe ones taste pretty good, but I've just started planting some others. The skin is thicker than a Honeycrisp to make it less susceptible to sunburn and disease. Calcium deficiency is also a concern, but I'm pretty sure I solved that problem."

"Wow, Aiden. That's amazing. How long have you been working on this?"

"Since I was in high school, actually. This is the first time I think I'm really onto something."

My eyes are wide. I've worked around the orchard for long enough to know what a big deal this is. "Are you working with a distributor?"

"No." He shakes his head forcefully. "There's a lot of competition in the orchard business. I can't let just anyone know I'm doing this until I'm sure it's ready."

"Can I taste it?" The words fly out of my mouth. I'm really excited to see what he's come up with.

His brow furrows, and a kinda shy smile pops to his lips. "You want to?"

I can tell he's nervous, and I want to put his mind at ease. I smile back at him. "Yeah. I really do."

* * *

Half an hour later, I'm out behind the work barn with Aiden. He leads me over to a tree that looks a little different from the others. In fact, now that I study them, all of the trees back here look a little different. He's been experimenting in this orchard. This is Aiden's lab. No wonder he didn't want me and Charlotte poking around.

I also realize this must have been what he meant when he said he was working on saving the inn. A tasty new apple that's disease resistant could be extremely lucrative. He knows that better than I do. Why is he so worried about money?

Aiden reaches up and pulls an apple off the tree we're standing under. It is half red and half gold. A really pretty swirl of color I haven't seen before. It's already unique. If it tastes as good as it looks, the orchard could cash in.

He pulls a folded knife from his back pocket because of course an apple farmer has a knife in his back pocket. He cuts the apple open, slices off a piece, and offers it to me. I take the slice and bite into it. It's crunchy, it's light, it's sweet like a Honeycrisp but even lighter, with an almost cinnamon taste. "Wow!" I say, taking another bite. "This is amazing."

"Do you really think so?" He looks both nervous and skeptical.

"Aiden," I say, meeting his eyes so he'll know I'm serious. "This is really, *really* good." I'm not kidding. I've eaten more than anyone's fair share of apples in my day, and I've never tasted anything like this. It's outstanding. It's got the most delicious parts of both the apples it comes from.

He flips the knife closed and slides it back into his pocket. He sucks apple juice off his fingers, and I have to look away. "You really like it?" he asks.

"I *really* do. Have you let anyone else taste this?"

He shakes his head. "Not yet."

"It needs a name," I say. And quickly. Because the moment the big apple distributors find out about this, they are going to want to buy it, and the Parkers are about to be rich. Like, next-level rich.

"Yeah, I was thinking about the name," Aiden says. He looks almost shy again, and it's the cutest thing ever. "I want to name it after my grandmother. My mom's mom. Her name was Rosie."

"OMG. That's perfect!" I say. Could there be a more adorable name? "What was her last name?"

"Darling," he says.

"The Rosie Darling? I don't think I've ever heard of a better name for an apple."

"It's good, isn't it?" He smiles, and his eyes light up.

"It's really good. The apple *and* the name." I grab the rest of the apple from him and take another bite. Yep. Just as good as the first two. A smile covers my face. "Aiden, you did it. Do you know how much this is going to be worth?" I hold up the remaining part of the apple.

He lifts his hands straight up, palms out. "Hold your horses. I need to have other people taste it. There's a lot to do before bringing a new apple to the market."

"Maybe the *national* market, but we can use this for the festival. Come try the Rosie Darling. It's better than a Honeycrisp!" I announce.

He rolls his eyes, looking away, clearly self-conscious. "All right. That's a bold claim."

"It's true!" I tell him. "And I can't believe you've been sitting on this for so long. You don't need to worry about the festival cost. This apple is going to be a huge moneymaker."

At that, he meets my eyes. "Thank you, Ellie . . . for supporting me." His tone is serious, and the look on his face wipes the smile off of mine. He's looking at me as if he wants to kiss me again. Or there's a spider behind me. I'm not sure.

He steps closer to me and pulls me into his arms. And even though I remember that I had many good reasons to not kiss Aiden again, I cannot think of a single one as his mouth lowers to mine.

He tastes like apples and heat and need. My arms slide up his chest to wrap around his neck the same way they did last night. My head tips back, and the little moaning sound I hear is mine.

His hands splay over my lower back, driving me insane. I want him to pull me against him again like he did last night. Instead, he tortures me by tracing little circles just above my ass. He moves his lips to kiss the corner of my mouth, my cheek. He dips his tongue in the shell of my ear, and my body shakes. Then his mouth moves down to my neck, and he sucks there, gently. His tongue dips into the hollow of my collarbone and then nuzzles down the V-neck of my sweater. I'm about to rip the thing off and toss it into the trees when he steps back.

I want to sob. That's it? It's over? I mean, the man can kiss. But I want more. I'm a sweaty mass of hormones. I glance around frantically as if I'll somehow spot a bed. We're out in the middle of an orchard. We probably shouldn't drop to the ground, but I sure wouldn't mind if he backed me up against one of the trees and—

"Sorry," Aiden says quietly. "I'm not sure if you wanted me to do that again. I should have asked first."

"I wanted you to," I assure him, nodding. But reality comes whipping back to slap me across the brain. I can't do this. As much as I want to. I can't. We can't. "But . . ."

He studies my face. "But?"

"I just . . ." I swallow. I want to sink into the ground. How can I say this without sounding like the biggest self-absorbed a-hole on earth? "I don't want to lead you on."

He raises his brows. "Lead me on?"

You're the one who left Aiden." Amber's words echo in my head. Guilt slithers through my veins. I have to be honest with him. "As soon as the festival is over, I'm going back to New York," I say.

"Did you find a job?" He's frowning.

"Not, yet, but—" The look I give him is filled with remorse. "I just want my old life back."

The briefest hint of disappointment flashes across his face. If I hadn't been watching so closely, I wouldn't have seen it.

He dusts off his hands and expels his breath. "No explanation necessary, Ellie. We're planning this festival together. That's it. I get it. No more kissing."

"No more kissing," I echo. But inside, I am burning.

Chapter 16

It's been a long eight days. But it's Sunday. The festival is five days away, and we've all been working our butts off. I skipped the drive-in last Friday night and have no idea if Aiden went, because I hid in the lobby of the inn with my mom like a coward. There was no mention of Aiden on the *Hot Sheet* the next day. But Charlotte apparently made a second appearance with her mystery date. I asked her about him, but she wouldn't say much.

I texted with Kennedy some more, but she wasn't aware of any job leads. She did promise to be a reference for me if I manage to get any interviews. My prospects are bleak, though. I haven't heard back from two of the places I sent my résumé, and the other three have already rejected me. I suspect it's Steve's doing, but how could I ever prove it?

I've spent a little time online looking for apartments in the city, but for some reason I can't get excited about any of them. I can't sign a lease until I have a job. It's not much fun to get worked up about something you know you can't afford.

At least one thing is going well, however, and that's the festival planning. All of the hard work has paid off, because everything is coming together. Charlotte's been working double time on all the social apps. Pumpkin's account has taken off thanks to some signal boosting from Maria and her friends in PR. The brewery has a special IPA in the works and is already mostly transformed into an amazing-looking Biergarten. The bakery has a magical apple cider donut planned and plenty of other apple-y baked goods on the menu.

And one other thing. Word is spreading about the new apple hybrid. I mentioned it to Maria via text last week without thinking, and she took it and ran with it. I didn't know she'd been planning to publicize it until I saw it on social media. But it's definitely my fault that I didn't keep it a secret. I'm just hoping Aiden isn't *too* pissed.

We've already received a ton of calls about it. Turns out, there's nothing Maria can't promote. Including apples. The inn is sold out for the festival weekend, and the parade float, which is now the fanciest thing Harvest Hollow has seen in a *minute*, is nearly complete.

Things have been good between Aiden and me. Ever since our, *ahem*, second kiss, we've managed to keep everything super professional. Of course, we may have also been avoiding each other, but if that's what it takes to stop kissing, so be it.

Because the truth is, I haven't been able to erase the kisses (either one) from my memory. In fact, they pretty much play on a nonstop loop in my head, where they also live rent free. Seriously, not even a security deposit.

I am in the work barn, walking around the float picking at little things here and there, when Charlotte comes running in. "Hey, you two. Come outside. I need some more pictures for the social media account."

I glance up and am surprised to find that Aiden is on the far side of the barn. I hadn't seen him when I walked in and hadn't noticed him since. But it's not too surprising. We've both sort of perfected the art of being near each other and not making any noise. I've made it my part-time job to sneak into the apartment at night long after I know he's in bed.

Charlotte is staring at us both expectantly, her cell phone in her hand, while Aiden and I exchange looks that clearly say, *Are we going to do this?*

"Come on." Charlotte huffs, rolling her eyes. "It's just a few pictures." She turns and leaves before we have a chance to argue with her. It soon becomes obvious that neither of us is prepared to call the other's bluff, so we both quietly make our way toward the door. We get there at the same time, which is awkward, and Aiden splays out his hand in a gentlemanly gesture indicating that I should go first.

"Thank you," I say, desperately trying not to sniff his aftershave. It's a scent that haunts my really hot dreams lately. I breathe it in but manage to keep my face blank, as if it's not making my knees wobble. I also manage to walk casually past him and out into the sunlight.

"Over here!" Charlotte calls once we're both outside. She's on her way around the side of the barn, walking toward the experimental orchards in the back.

Aiden shrugs at me and I shrug back, and we both walk side by side until we meet Charlotte under the apple trees.

"Okay, I want a picture of both of you laughing. I'm going to get the trees in too. Maria asked for this."

I begin to make a mental note to choke Maria later, but then I remind myself that she's doing us a favor and the least I can do is fake a few laughs with Aiden for our social media accounts. After all, it's all my fault it's gotten awkward between us. I shouldn't have been so high-handed about telling him I didn't want to lead him on. I wince now every time I think of those three words, *lead you on*. Why did I say that? It's not like he declared his undying love for me or something. The man didn't even try to take me to bed. He just kissed me. Twice. And it was hot. But I immediately jumped to this ridiculous place where I assumed I would be breaking his heart if we did anything else.

Aiden is the one who has good reason to avoid me, and here he is agreeing to this mini photo shoot with his sister. The least I can do is play along.

"Where do you want me?" His voice is deep and slightly growly, and I feel it in my belly.

Charlotte points to the base of a tree. "Ellie, you stand there and grab Aiden's hat." She tosses a hat that looks vaguely cowboy-ish but a little more hip onto the grass.

I gulp. "Grab his hat?" It's a simple instruction but somehow it feels really intimate.

"Yeah, and Aiden, after she grabs it, you go for it like you're trying to get it back."

Aiden bends at the waist to scoop up the hat. He puts it on his head and tips down the brim with his thumb and forefinger. "How do I look?" he asks.

I close my eyes and take a deep breath because he looks like a smoke show, and this is definitely karma kicking my ass. Between this and the jeans riding low at his trim waist and the tight white T-shirt and his bulging arm muscles and the maddening scent of his damn aftershave that I am going to pour down the drain later, I am in trouble. But I deserve this for being such a jerk. "Good," is all I can manage.

Aiden reclines against the trunk of the apple tree with the hat on. There are some more instructions and pointing from Charlotte. I mentally go into a space where I pretend like I am acting. I am a model, and this is a photo shoot. It could be prep for my next career on OnlyFans. I may need this experience. How do my feet look?

I step toward Aiden and peer up at him from beneath my hooded eyes. The look he's giving me is seriously hot. But it's not real. I know it. He's pretending too. It's the only way we're both going to get through this.

I grab at his hat, fake laughing. He catches my wrist, and my knees go weak. I close my eyes. I can't help it. I want him to lay me down right here on the ground and—

"That's great," Charlotte calls, clicking her phone camera at us repeatedly. And thank God for Charlotte. Her presence is the only thing keeping me upright at the moment.

"Just a few more," Charlotte instructs.

When did Charlotte become a professional photographer?

About the time you forced her into being a social media manager.

Aiden has released my wrist, but the feeling of his hand around it lingers as I go for his hat again. This time I'm faster, and I grab it. He lunges for me and catches me around the waist. I laugh. But my body is in a strange state between stiff as a board and molten lava. The outside had stiffened, but inside I'm like hot apple-pie filling.

I straighten, still laughing, or at least attempting to, and Aiden slings me around and backs me up against the tree behind us. Oh damn. This was my fantasy last week. It's still my fantasy. He's smiling, but there is a smolder in his eye that is completely distracting. He pushes me until my back hits the tree, but his hand got there first to soften the blow. His lips are inches from mine. He pulls the hat from my now nearly lifeless fingers and puts it on my head.

I am mesmerized by the look in his eye. I want to kiss him again. So bad. Or I want him to kiss me, or both. Whatever.

"That is great!" Charlotte says. She hasn't stopped taking pictures the whole time this has been going on.

The next thing I know, Aiden reaches out and swipes the end of my nose with his index finger. It would be adorable if we were a couple getting our engagement pictures taken. Instead, it steals the breath from my lungs. I ache for him.

"Perfect!" says Charlotte. She's staring at her phone now. "Okay. I think that's enough."

Aiden quickly steps away, and I am left propped up against an apple tree with a hat on my head and way too much lust coursing through my veins. Whoa. It's gonna take me a minute to recover. I am *melting*.

I know Aiden was just pretending like I was, but man, he's good at that. *He* should have an OnlyFans account. Oh God. I can't think about that. That is not helpful. I need some air-conditioning.

"I'm gonna go send these to Maria," Charlotte announces. She turns and is gone in moments.

Aiden is standing in a clearing a few feet away with his hands on his hips. "How did we do?" he asks me.

"Very convincing." My voice is shaking, and so is my body.

"You like the hat?"

I pull it off my head, walk over, and hand to him. "Yeah. I wonder where she got it."

"Must be Sawyer's," Aiden says. "Looks like something he'd wear. And something Charlotte would like."

I'm about to say something about Charlotte and Sawyer when Aiden adds, "She won't tell me the name of the guy she's been going to the drive-in with. I've got some feelers out."

"Oh, good," I say, forcing myself to step back. "Sera and I were wondering about that." Of course Aiden is on the case. He's not going to let his little sister date a stranger without checking into the guy.

"Sawyer hasn't been happy about it," Aiden says.

Ooh, that's interesting. But I don't say anything, in case Aiden wants to add more. He doesn't, and after a few moments of silence, I point toward the barn. "I guess we should get back to work."

"Yeah." Aiden clears his throat. "We should."

As we begin walking back toward the barn, I text Maria. that photo shoot was ur idea?

She immediately answers. what? i want the place to look sexy. u 2 look good together.

There is a pause before she adds, oh, can u send me a pic of the new apple? you said it looks swirly?

We're about halfway back to the barn when I stop. "Maria wants a picture of the Rosie Darling. Can I grab one off the tree in the back real quick?" I turn to head back to where we just came from.

Aiden curses under his breath. "You know, I really didn't want to let anyone know about it yet."

I wince and turn back around to face him. "I know. I've been meaning to talk to you about it. I told Maria offhand, and I didn't expect her to . . . I'm really sorry."

"I've already had a couple of distributors reach out." He shakes his head. "I knew it was a bad idea to publicize it ahead of the festival."

"I completely understand. I shouldn't have mentioned it to Maria.

I told her it was a secret, but I guess I wasn't clear enough. She sorta took it and went with it." I step toward him and search his face. "But the good news is, if one of the big distributors buys it, you'll be a multimillionaire."

He already knows this, of course. I'm clearly only trying to absolve my guilt.

His features harden. "Yeah, well, not all of us *want* to be multimillionaires. You publicized it without my permission, Ellie." His voice is low, accusatory, but worst of all, *hurt*. "And you didn't even come to me and apologize when it first happened."

Ugh. I'm an even bigger ass than I thought I was. And I thought I was a pretty big one. I feel awful for betraying his trust. He has the right to be angry with me. I screwed up. I should have made it clear to Maria that she couldn't publicize the new apple. "I'm sorry, Aiden," I say, biting my lip and wincing. *"Really sorry."*

A few moments of silence pass before he gives me a jerky nod.

There's one more question I can't help but ask. "Aren't the businesses in trouble, though?" I say. "Don't you need the money?" I get that it's his apple and he may want to keep it and sell it himself instead of selling it to a bigger company but . . .

"I'm not selling *my* apple to a big national chain," he growls.

"Okay," I calmly reply. I get it. I do. "You don't have to. You can just tell the distributors you're not interested in selling it. But . . . isn't this what you meant when you said you were working on helping the orchard?" What am I missing? Why is he *so* angry about making money off of his creation?

Aiden's face turns into a mask of stone, and I immediately know I've said the wrong thing. He turns and stomps away from me. "You stick to event planning," he tosses over his shoulder. "I'll stick to growing apples."

Chapter 17

Later that night, I'm walking under the apple trees. It's after nine, and I have been staying out of the apartment till past ten to make triple sure that Aiden is asleep before I go in. I'm especially wary tonight after our fight about the hybrid apple this afternoon. And I'm the one in the wrong. Completely wrong. He asked me to keep it a secret, and I didn't. I knew the minute I tasted it that the Rosie Darling is a winner. But Aiden never *said* he wanted the apple to be part of the festival. And it's his invention, not mine. There's no excuse for what I've done.

I'm a total jerk.

I told myself a dozen times this afternoon to try to apologize again, but each time I peeked at him from behind the float, he looked more foreboding than he had the last time, a thunderous expression on his face. I finally abandoned the float and went back to the inn.

I wrap my hoodie more tightly around my shoulders. I'm still wearing the sweater and leggings I had on earlier, but now I've added mittens with llama faces on them. I came out here to have some quiet and to think. I used to do the same when I was in high school.

There's nowhere more relaxing than under the apple trees on a crisp fall night. The trees are especially pretty this evening with the twinkling lights that we added for the festival looping through the branches. It's like walking through the Milky Way. I spin in a circle as leaves fall all around me. It's a moment that would be nearly perfect if I didn't have so many worries on my mind.

I still haven't told Mom and Dad about Geoff or my job. I keep telling myself that I'm waiting until I have a new job and a new place. As if those things will make the truth of what happened less awful. But I realize I'm just a coward.

And for more reasons than one.

Not only have I refused to tell my parents the truth about why I'm here, but I've also refused to tell Aiden the truth about how I feel about him. And I'm clear about it now. I'm crushing on him. Hard. I have been since I got here. But after our two kisses, I got scared. Like *really* scared. I kept thinking about how things began with Geoff. Friendly coworkers. An attraction. And then, bam, I'm living with him, getting dumped, and my ideas are stolen.

I won't be able to take it if that ends up happening with Aiden. I mean, I know he's not going to steal my ideas, but the other part. The getting-dumped part. The making-a-mistake part. I'm not good at mistakes. I told Aiden I didn't want to hurt him, but the truth is I don't want him to hurt me. Which is why I'm a coward.

I'm about to take another step, when I hear a noise. My heart pounds.

What was that?

I freeze. A cold sweat breaks out on my back. I'm positive I just heard someone else nearby. It sounded like leaves crunching, and it stopped when I stopped. Which means whoever is there knows I'm here.

I hold my breath and listen. My heart is thumping so hard I can barely hear anything above it.

Maybe it's just Miss Guin. I'll never be happier to see that little tackle goat coming straight at me.

But if it's Miss Guin, she would be bleating. She's not subtle.

"Who's there?" I force myself to say like I'm in a bad horror movie. It's not like an ax murderer is going to provide his name and intentions.

I'm poised to start running back to the road when Aiden steps into the clearing.

My hand immediately shoots up to cover my heart. "You scared me," I say, closing my eyes and breathing a deep sigh of relief.

"You scare me," he says. The words come out funny and kind of jumbled.

"No, I meant you scared me just now. I didn't know you were there," I clarify.

"You scared me now too."

I tilt my head and stare at him as he takes a few stumbly steps toward me. If I'm not mistaken, it seems one Mr. Aiden Parker, Apple Farmer Extraordinaire, is drunk!

I plant my llama-covered fists on my hips. "Did you come looking for me?"

"Yep." He braces a hand against a nearby tree. He's wearing jeans and a gray-and-red Parker Orchard T-shirt tonight. No sweatshirt. No gloves. His hair is mussed, and his eyes are ever-so-slightly red. They are illuminated by the twinkling lights in the trees. Even drunk, he's hot. That seems unfair.

"How drunk are you?" I ask next, unable to hide my smile.

"Not enough," he answers.

"Not enough for what?"

"Not enough to *not* follow you out here."

Ooh, that's an interesting answer. And we're really getting somewhere. I like drunk Aiden. He's willing to talk. "Why did you follow me?" I ask next.

"Because I can't stop." He crosses his arms over his chest and leans back against the tree.

I frown. "Can't stop following me?"

"Can't stop thinking about you."

My breath catches. Did he just say that? Truly say that? Because it made my heart flip. "I can't stop thinking about you either," I say.

Partly because it's true, partly because I need to stop being a coward, and partly because I wonder if he'll even remember I said it tomorrow. I don't know how he reacts when he's drinking. He may not even remember he saw me.

He pushes himself off the tree and stares at me, a kind of half smile on his lips. He dips his fingers into his jean pockets. "Can I ask you something, Ellie?"

"Yes," I say, still kinda pinning my hopes on the fact that whatever I tell him may be forgotten by morning.

"Why did you leave? Like, *really* why did you leave?"

I rub my mittens together and blow into my hands in some sort of weird bid to gain time.

"I don't know exactly," I say. It's true, but I need to elaborate. I need to do my best to explain it. Aiden deserves that much. This is clearly an important subject to him. "I guess, around high school, I just started to realize . . . there was another whole big world out there. I wanted to see it. I wanted to be a part of it."

"You went to college in the city. That wasn't enough?"

I shrug. "I liked it. I like the hustle and the pace and lifestyle."

His arms drop to his sides. "And you still like it?"

I have to think about my answer for a few moments. I've always loved the city, but honestly, being out here the last several days has been the first time in years that I've felt . . . home. Settled. Calm. "I still like it," I answer because that's true. "And I like it here too."

He tips his head up to look at the sky. "Do you remember the night we watched the super blue?"

I blink. The super blue. Wow. That was a long time ago. A super blue moon only comes around once every ten years. I must have been a freshman in high school. "Yeah, I remember. It was pretty cool."

His chin dips, and our gazes meet. "Do you remember what you told me that night?"

Oh God. No. I have no idea. I remember we went out into one of the fields and found a spot with no trees. We lay in the back of a wagon. I think Aiden brought a quilt that night too. It was soon after that we stopped hanging out. "No." I shake my head. There's no use lying to him.

A sad smile shapes his lips. "You told me we'd be business partners one day. That you'd own the inn, and I'd own the orchard. And we'd stay in business just like our parents."

I feel like a hay bale has dropped directly onto my chest. I can't breathe. "I said that?" I ask, but it's really only to buy time, because of course I said that if he says I did.

"Yeah." He nods. His voice is quiet when he adds, "And I know we talked about it a lot when we were kids, but that time . . . that time I thought you meant it."

Oh my God. I did. *I did leave Aiden.* And all these years he's known it. I may have just been a kid when I said that to him, but so was he, and he remembered it. I must have said it thinking that one day I'd inherit the inn and he'd inherit the orchard. I clearly hadn't considered it as significant as he had.

And then I remember what he said at the drive-in that night. He'd tried to tell me. *"I kinda always thought we would be partners one day."* He thought that because I'd *said* that.

I'm not just a jerk. I'm a *huge* jerk. A huge jerk with a bad memory. Aiden turns as if he's going to leave.

"Can I ask you a question?" I ask because I don't want him to go.

He stops and turns halfway around. "What?"

"Why did you stay?" I honestly don't know where that question came from. It just sort of formed on my tongue. But now that it's floating in the air, I want to hear the answer. Like, really want to.

Aiden's brow wrinkles, and then he smiles. I realize his smile is something I've come to look forward to. Covet, almost. It's sexy, but also comforting, like feeling the sun on your face when it's cold outside.

Soon he splays his arms out wide and says, "This land is my home. This orchard is my home. These trees are my *home.*"

I nod slowly. I know that feeling too. "Yeah, I get that."

"You do?" His head is cocked, and he blinks at me.

"Yes, and I'm really sorry we publicized the Rosie Darling without your permission. I have a big mouth, and I thought you knew how good it was just because I told you so and—"

He lifts his head to the sky again. "No. It's not you. I'm afraid of my own success," he mumbles.

My brows shoot up. "What?"

"Jesse says I'm afraid of my own success."

Oh, this is getting more interesting by the second. Maybe those two don't have bad blood after all? Or maybe Jesse telling him he's afraid of his own success is *why* they have bad blood. "Is that where you've been? Drinking with Jesse?"

"Nah." Aiden shakes his head. "Jesse doesn't drink. I've been drinking *next to* Jesse."

First, it's news to me that a brewer doesn't drink. It's an interesting fact to stash away for future reference. Second, I'm completely intrigued by Aiden's "afraid of my own success" comment. "Why are you afraid of succeeding?" I ask.

He is quiet for a few moments before he meets my gaze again. "Because things might change," he says.

His answer hits me like a punch to the gut. That's it, isn't it? That's the truth. That's why anyone is afraid of succeeding.

"That's why I didn't sell my science fair project way back when," he mumbles. "They offered me a lot of money. I said no."

My eyes go wide. "Really?"

He nods. "Yep."

"Your parents didn't try to talk you into it?" Okay, I had to ask.

"They tried," Aiden says, the half smile turning up his lips. "But in the end Dad said it was my decision. I wanted everything to stay the same. I wanted to go to college and come back here. I wanted the life I have right now."

I nod slowly and exhale. As much as I had wanted to go work in

Manhattan, I get why Aiden wanted to stay here. "I understand," I say. And I really do.

His eyes narrow on me. "Why are *you* afraid of success?"

"Oh, I'm not . . ." I'm about to brush off his question as nothing more than the parroting of a drunk person, when I realize it's actually a really profound thing to think about. *Am I* afraid of success? Two weeks ago, I would have immediately answered, *hell no*. But . . . I mean. I had the biggest account at the company. I was poised on the brink of bringing their event home. And I just let them fire me based on a lie. Why? And why did I date someone for years, despite knowing I was settling for less? It's not that I'm blaming myself for Steve and Geoff's sins. It's more like examining my own part in all of it. And I realize in that moment, I've never done that before. And it's about time.

It's so much easier to blame someone else.

Oh damn.

"I don't know why," I whisper in answer to Aiden's question. And that's the truest thing I've said in years, maybe. "I would have told you that one of the reasons I left is because I'm *not* afraid of success, but now I really don't know."

Aiden just nods. I can tell he gets it. I don't have to explain any more. It's one of the many things I like about him. There are so many unspoken things that he just knows. And I'm not sure if it's because we grew up in the same place, or we used to be friends, or we're just kindred souls, but it feels like the most effortless thing in the world to be in his company. It's like he fills in my blanks.

"Why was Jesse mad at you about the Biergarten?" I ask, because I am well aware that this is my opportunity to get answers to all my burning Aiden-related questions.

Aiden smiles. "Because he thought of that idea two years ago, and I shot it down."

"Ah, and now you're reconsidering," I say.

"You're not really one to take no for an answer," he tells me.

Now it's my turn to smile. I walk over to him and slide my arm through his. I try to ignore the shiver that makes its way through my body as his warmth spreads to me. "Let's get you home," I say.

He looks down at me, leering. "You're not going to try to take advantage of my drunken state and kiss me?" He's grinning. I know he's kidding. It's endearing.

I laugh. "No, that would be wrong."

"Are you suuuure?" He draws out the last word loud and long.

I laugh again. "I'm sure. Being skeevy applies to both men and women, you know. I would never take advantage of a drunk person. Even a hot one."

Okay, that last part was prompted by the devil on my shoulder. Hopefully Aiden's drunk enough to forget. He just smiles at me.

I tug his arm, and we begin to walk through the twinkly orchard back to the road. We're silent the entire way. The kind of comfortable silence that is only possible when you're around certain people who get why being silent is preferable sometimes.

Before we get to the door up to the apartment, I think of one more question I want to ask drunk Aiden. "What have you told Jesse about me? Did you tell him that I 'left you'?"

"Nah," Aiden says. "I just told him I've had a crush on you forever."

While I reel from that bit of info, Aiden begins climbing the stairs. I scramble to follow him, and once we make it inside the apartment, I stay silent as I tuck him into bed, fully clothed, though sans boots. Thank God his boots were the only things he removed, because honestly, if he had stripped, I would have been tempted to be a little skeevy.

Once Aiden is settled, I go to my own room, change into my autumn PJs, and snuggle into the big, fluffy feather bed. I try to fall asleep, but I can't help but obsessively think about three things. *I did leave Aiden. He's had a crush on me forever.* And *what exactly is it that I'm afraid of?*

Chapter 18

The next morning, Aiden is in the kitchen when I come out of my bedroom. He's rattling around the cabinets and groaning.

"Good morning, sunshine," I say in a bright voice. "What are ya looking for?"

"Aspirin," he says with another groan.

I wince. "Hangover that bad, huh?"

"Yeah."

"Hang on a sec." I disappear into my bedroom and return a minute later with two aspirin tablets.

"Thank you." He takes them from me and immediately gulps them down with a glass of water before asking, "You travel with aspirin?"

"I travel with a small pharmacy," I tell him. "You can never be too careful."

"Wise."

I take a bow. "Thank you."

I am pouring the pumpkin-spice creamer into my coffee mug when he says, "About last night. Is there anything I need to apologize for?"

"Apologize for?" I'm willing to play dumb forever. I'm committed.

"I was pretty drunk. Did I say anything that offended you?"

"No." I shake my head and pull my mug to my lips. Ah, that first sip is truly divine.

"Good." His smile turns devilish. "And it's nice to know you can't stop thinking about me."

My eyes go wide. I lower the mug to the counter. "Hey, I thought you'd be too drunk to remember that."

"I wasn't." Did he just wink at me?

"You said it first," I point out.

"I know." His face loses all trace of humor, and he looks at me intently. "I meant it."

I can't say anything but the truth. "I meant it too."

I don't point out that he also said he has had a crush on me forever. Even though I spent longer than I should have last night thinking about it. I don't want to embarrass him. I probably shouldn't have taken advantage by asking him questions while he was drunk. I feel a little guilty about that this morning. But I did learn some interesting things.

"Look, Ellie. I know things are complicated, but I like you."

"I like you too," I breathe. My chest is so tight it hurts.

He runs a hand through his hair. "And I don't want to make it any more difficult."

I nearly sigh in relief. "Me either." I mean, it would be really fun to have a no-strings-attached thing with Aiden, but now that I know he's had a crush on me and was hurt when I left, I *cannot* lead this man on. I have a crush on him too now, but I refuse to hurt him anymore. Ever.

"So, just friends?" he says, holding out his hand to me.

"Just friends," I agree.

We shake. But I can't help the shiver that goes through my body when he touches me. I only hope he didn't notice. I also can't help but think this isn't the first time we've agreed to keep things only professional. Second time's the charm? We have to try, at least.

Aiden retreats to his bedroom, and I retreat to mine. We only have six more days to work together on the festival. Then I'll find a job (any job) and get out of here asap. In the meantime, Aiden and I will keep things strictly professional.

How hard could it be?

I'm about to grab my laptop and head down to the lobby, when my phone rings. I glance at it to see that Charlotte is calling. I answer and click speakerphone. "Hey, Charlotte," I say. "What's up?"

"We have a problem," Charlotte announces. "Pumpkin is missing!"

I shake my head. "Wait. What? What do you mean?"

"I mean we can't find Pumpkin anywhere. He's been really popular online, you know? We think he may have been dognapped."

"Dognapped?" Oh damn. I never even *considered* that possibility. I mean, it happens, but usually to French bulldogs, right? Didn't Lady Gaga have to pay a dog ransom or something? We can't afford that. Besides, who would want to steal Pumpkin? He's a pug and a curmudgeonly one at that. "Don't worry," I tell Charlotte. "I'll be right there."

I hang up and rush into the living room. Aiden must have heard my raised voice, because he's standing in his doorway looking at me expectantly.

"Mom and Dad think Pumpkin's been dognapped," I say, grabbing my jacket.

"Let's go," Aiden says, not even bothering to question the word *dognapped*, which I appreciate.

Aiden and I scramble down the staircase and knock on the door that leads to Mom and Dad's apartment. Charlotte rips it open. It's just her and Mom in there.

"Have you found him?" I ask. Because it's more likely that Pumpkin is asleep somewhere than stolen. I'm hoping this will all be over in a few minutes, and we'll just find P-dog snoozing somewhere like the little potato lump that he is.

"I've searched everywhere," Mom says. She looks like she's on the verge of tears.

I squeeze her hands. "We'll find him," I promise.

Charlotte pulls up her phone and hands it to me. It's a picture of Pumpkin on the front porch of the inn with his PJs on. "This is the last picture I took of him. It got over 100K likes."

Wow. Is Pumpkin an influencer? A pupfluencer?

"When's the last time you saw him?" Aiden asks.

Mom is wringing her hands. "He was in his bed behind the front desk with me about a half hour ago. I left to carry a stack of napkins to the dining room, and I can't remember if he was still there when I came back. I think so. But I can't say for sure."

"When did you notice he was missing?" I ask.

"About fifteen minutes ago," Mom replies. "I looked down and realized he wasn't in his bed. But he couldn't have gotten out of the front desk area alone."

"Where's Dad?" I ask.

"He's still looking for Pumpkin on the first floor. You don't think one of the guests took him, do you?" Mom's voice is panicked. I feel awful for her. If Pumpkin was snatched, it's probably my fault. I'm the one who decided making him famous would be a *good* idea.

"Did anyone check out recently?" I ask.

Mom bites her lip. "One couple. I'd say about twenty minutes ago."

I narrow my eyes. "How old were they?"

"They were young. Late twenties, maybe."

I wince. I was hoping she wouldn't say that. An older couple isn't likely to steal a pupfluencer, but a younger one just might.

"Did they bring a car?" Aiden asks. "If so, we need to find out what make and model it is."

"Let me look at their reservation," Mom says. She hurries toward the door to the front desk and Aiden, Charlotte, and I follow.

"I really hope making Pumpkin famous didn't cause someone to steal him," Charlotte says. She looks miserable. Her face is lined with worry. It's clear she feels guilty too.

I pat her shoulder. "It's not your fault. I'm the one who wanted Pumpkin to draw in a crowd. You did a great job with the pictures of him."

Charlotte nods, but she doesn't look any happier. "Yeah, maybe too great," she mumbles.

While Mom is pulling up the couple's registration, I quickly text Maria.

we can't find pumpkin

don't you have more than one? she quickly replies.

the dog.

Oh shit. He's one of the biggest draws for the festival.

Umm, and we love him.

Oh, yeah, that too. She sends an upside-down face emoji.

I shake my head. Maria's always thinking about PR. She's never been much of a pet person. But she's right. Pumpkin is a big draw for the festival, and his fame may have just gotten him stolen. I've *got* to fix this.

"Here it is," Mom announces. "They did have a car." She exhales a sigh of relief. "They're from Connecticut. It's a white SUV."

"White SUV with Connecticut plates, got it," Aiden says. "I'll go look for the car in the parking lot. They may still be here." He rushes from behind the desk and out the front door.

Dad comes hurrying into the lobby from the corridor to the dining room. He's out of breath, and his hair is mussed. Poor Dad. "I didn't find him anywhere on the first floor," he announces.

Mom's face falls.

"Is there any place Pumpkin likes to post up lately?" I ask. "You've checked the laundry room, right?"

"That was the first place I looked," Mom replies. "But his PJs aren't being washed."

"I'll go check outside," Dad says. "Around the perimeter of the inn. Maybe someone left a door open."

He's gone in seconds, but Mom and Charlotte and I are not hopeful. The reason they have a swinging wooden half door on the front desk area is so that Pumpkin can't get out. He normally keeps his chonky self in his little bed behind the front desk or wanders into the apartment if that door is open, but he's rarely allowed to stroll around the inn. And if he does, he stays in the lobby. Puppy is a creature of habit, for real.

see anything? I text to Aiden. But honestly it seems like a long shot that the couple would still be here. Especially if they did steal Pumpkin. Why would they stick around?

We should probably call the police, but what do they even do in a dognapping? Would they put out an APB for the white SUV? And what if they're just an innocent couple who left the inn, and we have them pulled over for suspected dog thievery?

There's one thing I do know, and that is I'm glad that this is happening during an event I am planning on my own. If Steve were involved in this, he'd be losing his *ish*. He'd be blowing up my phone with a hundred dumb questions and bad ideas. I take a deep breath. I can handle this. I have handled a hundred last-minute issues in my tenure as an event planner. This may be my first potential dognapping case, but a crisis is a crisis.

a white SUV with CT plates is in the lot, comes Aiden's text.

it's empty tho, follows soon after.

I narrow my eyes as I repeat the texts to Mom and Charlotte. Hmm. If the couple *is* still here and they have Pumpkin, where are they?

I pull up Pumpkin's social media account on my phone. There's the picture of him on the front porch of the inn. There's a picture of him behind the front desk, snoozing in his bed. There's a picture of him sitting next to an actual pumpkin in the lobby. All adorable, of course. Charlotte's really good at taking pictures. But nothing here is giving me a clue.

Wait. What if . . . ? "What's Pumpkin's most liked photo?" I ask Charlotte.

Charlotte bites her lip, thinking for a few seconds before she snaps her fingers. "The picture of him in his apple sweater in front of the lit-up apple trees."

"Where did you take that picture?"

"The clearing in the middle of the pick-your-own orchard."

It's the same place I was walking last night.

"Let's go," I say to Charlotte. "Mom, you stay here in case someone brings Pumpkin back, or he wanders in on his own." I know it's a long shot, but Pumpkin is a quirky little soul.

Mom still looks super worried, but she nods.

Charlotte and I take off out the front door, across the porch, and down the stairs. I begin jogging toward the road. The pick-your-own orchard is on the other side.

Aiden sees us from the parking lot and dashes over to join us.

"We're going to the clearing," I tell him. "It's where Pumpkin's most popular photo was taken."

Aiden nods silently and follows us.

It doesn't take long to make it to the clearing. As we approach, I hear a voice. It's high-pitched and female. "That is sooo cute! Get another one with me in it."

Charlotte, Aiden, and I pile into the clearing to find a young woman and a young man standing near one of the lit-up apple trees with Pumpkin at their feet. Pumpkin looks entirely unbothered. He barely blinks at us.

"What are you doing?" Charlotte shouts, planting her fists on her hips. "That's our dog." Whoa. I've never seen Charlotte pissed before. It's like watching an angry teddy bear.

The young woman's face falls. "Oh yeah. I'm sorry. No one was at the desk to tell. We just wanted to get our picture with him out here."

I take a deep breath and count to five. I want to yell at these two like Charlotte did, but I can already tell that they are more clueless than nefarious. Still, they scared us and caused us all a lot of unnecessary worry.

Meanwhile, Aiden looks like he's about to punch the young man in the face. "I'll handle this," I whisper to him. His nostrils flare, but he steps back.

"Hi, I'm Ellie Lawson," I inform the couple. "My parents own the inn. And Pumpkin is their dog."

"I'm Tiffany, and this is Landon," the young lady says, pointing first to herself and then to her boyfriend. "And Pumpkin is just sooo cute! We only wanted a few pictures to post on social."

"I get it. He's gotten quite popular," I say evenly, "but my mom was really worried when she couldn't find him."

"Yeah, I wondered where she went. I wanted to ask her if we could borrow his apple sweater." Tiffany says this as if she's the put-upon one in the situation.

Landon isn't saying much. He just looks guilty and is kinda kicking at the grass and leaves near the apple tree.

"It would have been nice if you'd at least left a note," Charlotte points out. "How do we know you weren't trying to steal him!"

"Steal him!" Tiffany's bright-blue eyes are bugging.

"Oh, no, no, no." Landon finally speaks. He's waving his hands in the air. "We *definitely* weren't stealing anything."

"Did you get the pictures you wanted?" I ask calmly. Of course, I want to slap them both, but that's assault, and I'm not going to jail over these two fools. Besides, I'm used to this. Event-planning emergencies often call for a cool demeanor. It's not as if I work in an emergency room, but emotions still get high.

"I wanted one more," Tiffany informs us. Her lower lip pops out in a pout.

Wow. Entitled, huh? I shake my head. "Okay, let's get the picture, and we'll take Pumpkin back." I manage to smile at her. It's fake as hell, but I get the feeling Tiffany is used to fake smiles.

Tiff loves my idea, because she immediately drops to her knee next to Pumpkin, flips her long hair over her shoulder, and produces a mega smile. She's all teeth and way too much mascara. "Let her take it, Landon," she orders. "Get in with me."

Landon hurries over and hands me the phone, and I wait for him to get into the shot with Pumpkin and Miss Photo Op before I click a few pictures for them.

"Thanks," Tiffany finally says as she hops back up to her feet. "My friends are going to be sooo jealous."

I hand the phone back to Landon, and Aiden quickly scoops up Pumpkin. He cradles him under his arm protectively. Pumpkin remains completely unbothered.

"Okay, we're off for home. Ta-ta," Tiffany announces as she scrolls through no doubt dozens of Pumpkin pictures on her phone. She doesn't even look up as she and Landon walk away.

Charlotte, Aiden, and I are left staring at each other shaking our heads.

"I already texted your mom and dad that we found him," Charlotte says.

"Thanks," I reply, glad to know that Mom has already heard the good news.

"Those frickin' idiots," Aiden says. I can tell he would still like to punch someone or something, but he's got Pumpkin now. We got what we came for. That's what matters.

We all start walking back toward the inn.

"I guess we need to keep an eye on P-dog now," I say.

Charlotte lets out a loud sigh. "I didn't even think about it. But it stands to reason that lots of followers equals lots of people wanting pictures with him."

We walk silently for a few minutes.

Wait a minute. *That's right!* I point a finger in the air. "Charlotte, that's brilliant!" I say.

"What?" She frowns.

"We're going to set up a booth at the festival and charge for pictures with Pumpkin!"

Aiden gives me a highly skeptical glance. "Charge for it?"

"Yeah, you heard Tiffany. Her friends will be *sooo jealous*." I bat my eyelashes at him in an exaggerated fashion.

"You can try it, I guess," Aiden says. I can tell he doesn't think it's gonna work.

But I'm already picturing the cute little background Maria and I can set up for his photos. "I bet Pumpkin is going to kill it," I predict. Plus, the dog is the least bothered animal in the world. He will not mind having tons of strangers snap pictures with him.

When we make it back to the lobby, Mom grabs Pumpkin and has a whole discussion with him about where he was and what he was doing, as if Pumpkin will ever be able to give her the details. It also adorable when Dad shuffles over and puts his hand on the top of the dog's head and simply says, "Good to have you back, buddy."

I fold my arms over my chest and take in the scene. It was nice to handle this for Mom and Dad. I mean, if I hadn't been here, no doubt Tiffany and Landon would have brought Pumpkin back eventually, but I'm proud of myself for figuring it out. And I'm relieved that I did it without any interference from a boss who frankly just got in my way. I don't need Steve. I never needed him.

crisis averted, I text Maria. pumpkin has been located.

Thank god, she texts back.

My thumbs fly over the keyboard on my phone. And we need to set up a photo booth ASAP b/c that dog is gonna make us some $$ this weekend!

Chapter 19

It's Wednesday. Two days since Aiden and I solidified our friendship in the kitchen and went searching for Pumpkin in the orchard, and two days away from the start of the festival. I am putting the finishing touches on the float in the late afternoon when I hear the door to the work barn open behind me.

It's gotta be Aiden. We've been extremely civil and accommodating to each other these last two days. He's been teasing me about going overboard on the festival details, and I've refused to change a thing.

"We're *not* removing the stars and moon," I say over my shoulder. He's been trying to convince me to "tone down" the float. I have agreed to no such thing.

"Eleanor?" Both the voice and the name make me freeze.

I turn around slowly to see Geoff standing there.

I blink. What's he doing here? I didn't even realize he knew where my parents' inn was.

He's wearing white pants and a navy-and-white-striped sweater. He looks guilty. He looks conciliatory. He also looks dumb in white pants. He's giving *Where's Waldo?* Why did I date a guy who wears white pants? That's on me. There is no excuse.

"Geoff." I fold my arms tightly across my middle. I have my best resting bitch face popping. He will get no quarter from me. Maria's voice is in my head. Hmm. Is it possible to get some rope and honey and ants around here? Chances are better here than in the city, for sure.

"Can we talk?" he says next.

I glance around. Aiden's been gone for a while. He went to check on something in the hay barn. Argos went with him. This barn is empty except for me. If Geoff wants to talk, we might as well do it here. If we went to the food barn or the inn, we'd have an audience.

"Go ahead," I say.

His shoulders relax slightly, as if he'd been expecting me to send him packing, and maybe I should have, but the truth is I am seriously curious about why he's here. What can he possibly say to explain anything he's done?

He walks toward me and comes to stand in front of me. He's only a few inches taller than I am. I didn't realize how short he was until I spent so much time with Aiden and Jesse.

"First, I want to say I'm sorry." His voice sounds small.

It's a decent start. But hardly forgiveness material. "Okay," I say, knowing Maria would have told him to go eff himself by now.

"I was a real jerk. I did the wrong thing."

"The wrong *things*," I say, because his mistakes are plural.

"Yeah, the wrong things." He stuffs his hands in his pockets and kicks at the hay on the ground. "The fact is, I should have broken up with you months ago."

Wait. What? What kind of an apology is this? I don't have time for nonsense. "Why are you here, exactly?" I ask. "Because I'm really busy." I point to the float.

He shakes his head. "Sorry. Let me start again." He cracks his knuckles. I always hated that. "I think we both know we were not madly in love."

I grudgingly nod because yes, I have deduced this in the last two weeks.

"It just seemed so complicated to unravel all of it," he says next.

I have to agree with that too. Working together and living to-gether made a breakup three times as difficult. "You didn't have to steal my presentation, though."

He nods. "You're right, and that's what I'm really sorry for."

"Okay." I continue to eye him with complete distrust.

"Those were all your ideas, and they were great ones. I just got really excited by the notion that I could finally have a top account."

"You could have waited until you'd *earned* one," I point out.

His face falls. "I don't have ideas like yours, Eleanor. You know that."

"That's not my fault, and call me Ellie." I surprise myself with that last part. But I've realized something since I've been here. Ellie was my name for twenty-one years, and I discarded it to impress people who weren't worth impressing. My real friends, the people here, call me Ellie. Even Maria calls me El. It feels good to have a nickname. Like I belong somewhere. Like I've got people. People who like me enough to abbreviate my name.

Geoff frowns. "I screwed up. I know that. I told Steve the truth. Everything."

My brows shoot up. "Really?" I'm gonna need proof before I believe that, of course.

"The Bolt Group event, all the vendors, it's all messed up. I couldn't keep track of everything. It's going to be a disaster unless you come back."

Oh, so *that's* why he's here. He screwed it all up and he needs me to put it back together again. Wow. And of course, Steve didn't fire him for his deception. Classic.

But at least everything is falling apart without me. I can't help but wonder if I manifested this. The day Maria came out to visit, I'd pretty much envisioned this exact turn of events. Hmm. Maybe I can manifest the honey and ants too.

I think he can tell by the look on my face that I'm not buying what he's selling, because he quickly adds, "You don't have to decide now. Steve is going to call you. He's going to offer you a big raise and a promotion. You'll be on the partner track."

Partner track? I'm listening. I'm still pissed. But I'm listening.

"I'll help you find an apartment if you want. You can stay with me until you do. Platonic, of course. I'll sleep on the couch. Just please say you'll think about coming back and taking over the Bolt Group event again."

I tilt my head to the side and narrow my eyes at him. "The Bolt Group event is a week from Saturday. I can't leave here until Sunday."

"I know. I know," he says. "I've seen the flyers. I saw all the social media that Maria's been doing too. You can come up to Vermont on Sunday. You'll have all week."

"That's not a lot of time to fix a mess," I point out with a loud sigh.

"I know," Geoff says. "But if anyone can do it, you can, Ellie. Steve's gonna offer you a bonus too. A *big* one."

A bonus sounds good. And if I agree to do this, it's gonna *have to* be a big one, because I'm not cleaning up this fool's mess for free. Or cheap. These jerks did me wrong. They can sweat while I *consider* it.

"Please, Eleanor, uh, Ellie. I need you. Steve needs you. GMJ needs you."

I roll my eyes. Bet he thought of that line on the train ride out here.

"I'll *think* about it," I say.

Geoff's shoulders slump in what I guess is relief that I've agreed to do that much.

"Are you going back to Brooklyn?" I ask. More to be polite than because I care.

"No. I'm staying for the festival. It looks like fun. The inn is booked, but I have a room at the motor lodge on the highway."

I squelch my smile. The motor lodge on the highway is sketchy AF, but it's where Geoff belongs. Because karma.

There will come a day. Perhaps months from now. Perhaps years. When I sit down with Geoff (possibly over a pumpkin-spice latte that I order myself) and admit to the things I did wrong, like never listening to his ideas and pretty much barreling over him like a steamroller in most instances. But that day is not today. Today is the day for him to grovel. And I would be lying if I said I didn't enjoy it.

"Okay, I'll give you my answer by Sunday," I tell him, still purposely smug.

"Thank you for considering it . . . Ellie."

Chapter 20

Turns out Argos looks great in an apple costume. His hat is like a little red beret with a green felt stem on it. Pumpkin killed his look too. They are both in the center of the float with me and Charlotte and the stuffed goat. Mom and Dad are on the float too. They're holding the beer growlers and pretending to eat the giant papier-mâché donuts. The Parkers are pulling us in the old-timey red truck, the back of which is overflowing with apples and pumpkins and hay bales. Both vehicles are adorned with huge Honeycrisp Orchard Inn and Parker Orchard signs.

Not to brag, but our float murdered the competition. Even the moose-filled float that the Moose Lodge entered. Though I'm not gonna lie, I want to know who made those mooses playing bingo. They were pretty spectacular. Still, I'm not at all surprised when we are awarded first place after we pull into the town square parking lot after the parade is over. Mayor Millie is on the loudspeaker. She thanks everyone and reminds the crowd to go out to the orchard this weekend for the Autumn Harvest Festival.

I am thrilled. We follow a huge line of traffic back home. Donny is at the front of the lane taking money for admission. It's twenty-five dollars per car, and the line is backed up out onto the highway.

Once we get closer to the inn, I can already tell the place is packed. The big parking lot across the street is near capacity, and one of the farmhands is in the backup lot, prepping it to open.

I want to squeal with excitement. We did it. We really did it. We turned this place out in two weeks!

My phone buzzes, and I look down to see a text from Maria. where r u? we're in the lobby.

Yay! Maria's here. And she brought Ashley Cross, the travel influencer. I need to go say hello.

We park the float near the edge of the corn maze, and I take off toward the inn. It's not hard to find Maria and Ashley, because they are standing on the porch by the time I arrive. Maria quickly introduces Ashley and me, and I thank her for making the trip.

Ashley has adorable cornrows and is wearing a cute orange maxi dress with brown boots. She's stylish and funny and (I quickly learn) always looking for a photo op.

"It's my pleasure," Ashley says, glancing around. "I can't wait to see this place. It's like a New England postcard out here."

"A New England postcard serving the best cider and donuts in the state!" I say.

"Oh, probably in the country," Maria adds. "We honestly need to get a donut critic out here."

I am temporarily distracted by the concept of a donut critic. Does such a job exist, and how might one apply? After all, I may need to change professions soon.

"I'm happy to give my opinion to my followers," Ashley says, pulling me back into the conversation.

"You. Are. Awesome!" I tell Ashley. And I mean it. She usually reviews restaurants and venues in the city. It's a big deal to get her on a train to Long Island.

Ashley fake-primps her hair and says, "Oh, go on."

"And this is only the first day," Maria continues. "There will be even more people from the city out here tomorrow since it's Saturday."

I realize she's right. Today is a weekday, and the locals might be here, but the city folk will show up tomorrow. We'll make even more money. Yes!

"I gotta get pictures near that corn maze," Ashley says. "Though I'm *not* going in that thing. I'm not trying to meet bugs."

I refrain from telling her I don't blame her. That seems disloyal to Aiden, who thought the corn maze was a really good idea. It was kinda his only idea that I green-lighted.

"Is that a real, live scarecrow?" Ashley asks next, pointing down the lane that leads across to the pick-your-own orchard.

"Yes," I tell her. "And there's a tent farther down where you can dress your own. We've got everything from overalls to drag."

"That's so fun!" Ashley exclaims. "I've *got* to do that." She takes off toward the scarecrow. "See you later, Ellie. Nice to meet you."

"I'll catch up with you in a minute," Maria calls after Ashley before turning to me. She waggles her eyebrows. "So . . . where is Aiden?"

"I don't know." Which is the truth. I haven't seen Aiden all day. I assume he's doing something apple related. He doesn't even know our kick-ass float won the parade.

"Mmm-hmmm," is Maria's judgy reply.

I'm about to say more to defend myself when something catches my attention from the corner of my eye. I turn to see a *really* long line snaking around the side of the inn. When did that happen?

"What's that line for?" I wonder.

I'm not really expecting an answer, but Maria says, "It's for people to get their picture taken with Pumpkin."

My jaw drops. "Are you kidding me?" Pumpkin's been on the float all morning, so the line must have started the minute we returned. It's already *that* long?

"Nope, not kidding," Maria replies with a smile. "I brought a posterboard background stand for people to have their picture taken with him. We're charging five dollars per picture."

"People are really paying that?"

Maria types into her phone and then turns it for me to see. "Pumpkin's got like 250K followers now, Ellie."

"Oh my God. He's even more popular than I thought. He's gonna need full-time security."

Maria laughs. "Okay, well, after the scarecrow dressing, I'm going to take Ashley to the food barn for some day drinking and donuts," Maria continues. "If you hear an ambulance, it's probably because I hurt that rude brewer guy."

Oh God. I forgot about the Maria and Jesse situation. Jesse told me later he'd been in a really bad mood the day they got into it. But there's no use trying to explain that to Maria. She isn't one to forgive lightly.

"Please," I beg, pressing both palms together in a prayer stance. "Please don't cause a scene during this festival."

"I'll be civil," Maria says, waving as she takes off down the lane. "If he will."

I don't worry for long about Maria and Jesse killing each other because I have too much to do. The rest of the day passes in a blur of activity. In addition to Pumpkin's enormous popularity, there are lines for the cider, the donuts, and the scarecrow-dressing contest. All of them have fees, so that's even more money coming in. The band is playing. The sketch artist is hard at work. And even the corn maze has a little line because some people heard you can get donuts and cider quicker in there.

Charlotte has been tasked with going around and collecting the money periodically from each station. I checked inside with Mom earlier, and she says we've earned thousands of dollars just in the morning. With so many people who gave their services for free, we've more than made a profit. Papier-mâché isn't expensive.

Pumpkin spends the entire day with his costume on over his pajamas sitting on a padded stool in front of the posterboard depicting apples and cornstalks and pumpkins and gourds while people take their picture with him. There is a big Honeycrisp Orchard Inn sign behind him, so every photo that is posted is great advertising for the businesses. Maria knows her stuff. Meanwhile, Pumpkin is in his element. He likes attention. Doesn't mind noise. And loves to sit all day. In addition to the five-dollar picture fee, we charge people another dollar to buy him a treat. We cannot give him all the treats because he would die, but we collect the treats he cannot eat to donate to the Harvest Hollow Humane Society from whence he came. If P-dog knew we were giving away his treats, he'd probably cut us. It's a good thing he can't speak English. Not fluently, at least.

Miss Guin gets out more than once, and each time it's kind of a fun game for all the kids to chase her around the grounds until Donny catches her. I can tell Miss Guin likes it, and the kids do too. Maybe it'll wear her out, and she'll leave us all alone tomorrow. There was one incident in which Miss Guin got loose and went after Bob from the pharmacy. But turns out he's surprisingly agile for an older man. He outran her until Donny was able to corral her again.

As I walk along the grounds, pride surges through me. I am proud of myself for pulling this off. It was a lot of work, but everything really came together. Charlotte was invaluable, and Mom and Dad and the Parkers were too. Even Aiden. He trusted me enough to allow me to go all out. I appreciate that.

I can't help but glance at my phone, periodically. Geoff said Steve was going to call. Is he? Or was that another one of Geoff's lies? And why do I care? I should tell them both to take a flying leap. Plus, I've really enjoyed planning an event without anyone looking over my shoulder. It's been super freeing, actually.

There's a reason I didn't tell Maria that Geoff showed up. She'd track him down at the motor lodge and beat him or at least issue some frightening threats. I also don't want to admit to her that I've actually been thinking about taking my old job back. I mean, I want to hear the offer. But a raise, a promotion, *and* a bonus? Plus, getting on the partner track? It's what I wanted when I planned the Bolt Hotel Group event in the first place.

I'd essentially be getting my whole life from two weeks ago back. Well, minus Geoff as my boyfriend, but that part is fine by me. He was right when he said we weren't a love match. My stomach never flipped 360 degrees when Geoff was around the way it does when . . .

Oof. When Aiden is near me.

My chest aches with the weight of that thought. I can't get my old life back without sacrificing the life I'm rebuilding here, at home, with my parents, with Aiden.

I start to sweat, the gravity of my choice weighing down on me. I can't think about this now. The festival needs me. I'm going to head to the front and check the parking. If the third lot is open, we're *really* killing it.

I turn but immediately stop short when I see Aiden standing about ten feet in front of me.

He pulls his hand from his jean pocket and waves. "Hi," he says.

"Hi." And there it is. The stomach flip. Plus, I'm feeling shy. I am never shy. Why am I shy right now?

He steps toward me. He rubs the back of his neck. "Congratulations are in order."

"Oh, the float?" I say, letting my wrist go limp in a pshaw sort of way. I will not gloat. Gloating is unattractive. But we both know I was right, and he was wrong. That is enough.

"Not the float. Though I heard you won first place, and I'm not surprised."

"*We* won first place," I say.

"That float was all you, Ellie. I had nothing to do with it. But I'm talking about the festival. The festival is amazing. You made all of this happen. We couldn't have done it without you."

I blush. I can't help myself. I always knew what I could do, but it is pretty great to see it all come together. And how refreshing is it for a man to give me credit for my ideas instead of stealing them? "Thanks," I say.

"And, I hate to admit it," Aiden says next, smiling, "but all of your ideas are the popular ones."

I laugh. "What? I saw plenty of people in the corn maze."

He shakes his head. "Only because you were smart enough to put a table selling cider and donuts in there."

I shrug. "Well, food is always a draw. What can I say?"

"Pretty clever. Mom and Dad are impressed too. I've never seen them so happy."

That makes my smile even wider. "How's the Rosie Darling doing?" I ask.

"We've sold over one hundred barrels so far."

"Shut up!"

"I'm serious. I've already got grocery stores reaching out, plus the farmer's market and even some restaurants in Manhattan."

"It's Maria," I tell him. "She's amazing."

"Yeah, well, you're pretty amazing too." He stuffs his hands in his pockets.

"We make a good team, Aiden."

He bites his lip, and there goes my stomach again. *Flip. Flip. Flip.*

"Wanna go through the corn maze with me later?" he asks. "I hear you can get drunk in there."

"We do have people making sure everyone makes it out okay, don't we?" I ask, slightly concerned.

"Oh, yeah. Donny sends Argos in occasionally to round everyone up."

"That sounds right." I am nodding awkwardly now like the first night I came here. The night I saw Aiden with nothing but a towel around his hips and— "Welp, I better go check on . . ." I hook my thumb over my shoulder to point behind me. "Something."

"Yeah," Aiden says. "I actually need to go to my house to grab some paperwork."

Of course he doesn't have Google Docs. But wait. What's this? "Your house? Like your *house* house?"

"Yeah." He laughs. "Did you think I was making it up when I told you I have a house?"

"No, no. Not at all." I honestly spent too much time imagining Aiden's house. I'm positive it smells like coffee and knee-weakening aftershave. Though hopefully not at the same time. And there's got to be a little garage with tools hung in neat rows, and no doubt it's filled with dozens of stuffed apples for Argos.

"Wanna come with me and see it?" he asks, pulling me from my daydream.

My stomach flips again. I feel like I'm on the edge of something, if I just take one more step. "Yes."

Chapter 21

It takes us awhile to get out to the highway because there are so many cars. We're in Aiden's gray truck and it's stop and go all the way. But it's a really good problem to have.

"I've never seen this place so busy," Aiden says. He's smiling.

"The festival was a great idea," I reply.

He tips his head toward me. "Maybe, but *you* made it amazing."

I wrap my arms over my middle as we fly down the highway. Once again, it's a beautiful October day. The sky is bright blue. The air is crisp, and the trees shake in the breeze as their gorgeous bright leaves sail to the ground. The highway is a kaleidoscope of color as we pass. We drive into town and straight onto Main Street. A couple of blocks past the hardware store, we turn down a cute little side street lined with small houses. The street is adorable, with lots of orange, yellow, and red-leaved trees on either side and mums planted in pots on nearly every front porch. It's as if the entire road got together and agreed to be cute. About halfway down, we pull into the driveway of a little white house with slate-blue shutters and a matching front door.

I stare at it. "This is your house?" The thing's got a picket fence. A *white* picket fence. And the yard is filled with colorful leaves.

"Yeah." He nods. "What do you think?"

I think it looks like a magazine shoot for fall in New England. I mean, a *white picket fence*. "Nice."

"It's a three-two," he says. "About eighteen hundred square feet."

"Eighteen hundred?" This is a mansion compared to most apartments in the city.

I climb out of the truck, and Aiden opens the gate. I follow him along a cute little stone pathway in the grass to the front stoop, which is basically two stone steps with an overhang. He's got mums in a slate-blue wooden planter box, and there is a doorbell, a security camera, and a really cute little bronze knocker in the shape of a Labrador retriever. "Mom bought me that," he tells me.

"It's adorable," I assure him.

"Not really what most grown men are going for, but I'll take it."

He punches a code into a pad near the handle, and the lock buzzes. He opens the door, and I step inside. It smells like apples inside. Because of course Aiden's house smells like apples. It couldn't be more perfect.

It's neat as a pin in here. There are original hardwood floors, and a small wooden table along the wall next to the door. Aiden tosses his keys into a wooden bowl atop the table. There's a decent-size living room to the right with a camel-colored leather couch, a big comfy-looking navy chair, a couple of end tables, and two floor lamps. A big TV is mounted to one wall. And there's a super-cozy-looking brick fireplace with a painting of Argos above it. *The man had his dog painted.* Endearing, much?

"Want the tour?" Aiden asks.

"You bet I do."

We walk beneath a rounded doorway into the kitchen. It's got stainless appliances and butcher-block counters. The floors are also hardwood in here. The cabinets are white with black knobs, and the backsplash looks like Italian tile in a slate blue similar to the door and shutters. There is a small dining room opposite the kitchen with a mid-century-modern table and four chairs.

We walk through the kitchen, and Aiden opens the back door to show me a super cute square of lawn with a grill and four wooden

Adirondack chairs sitting around a paver-stone fire pit. The white picket fence outlines the entire backyard, and there is an honest-to-goodness, Snoopy-looking doghouse. It's made of white wood panels with a dark-gray shingled roof. *Aww. For Argos.*

"Don't worry. He sleeps in the bedroom with me," Aiden says, as if he's read my mind again.

When we step back into the kitchen, I nonchalantly peek into the pantry, because if stuff is organized the way Geoff had it, I've gotta make a run for it.

But, while tidy, the canned goods are mixed with the boxed goods, thank God. I breathe a sigh of relief.

"That's pretty much it," Aiden says, leaning back against his kitchen counter.

I turn my head to face him. "Wait. What about the bedrooms?"

He tilts his head. "You want to see the bedrooms?"

"I mean . . . yeah. I thought I was getting the whole tour," I say.

"This way," he says.

I follow him down a narrow hallway between the kitchen and the living room to the back of the house. The first bedroom is on the right. It's pretty small, and he's turned it into an office. There's a brown wooden desk. An office chair. A patterned rug. And a computer. Everything is neat enough, but something seems off.

"Where is all your paperwork?" I finally ask. Who has an office with no paper?

He walks over to the closet and opens the double doors to reveal an impressive-looking storage system. There are drawers and doors and shelves all perfectly positioned. There's a printer in there and a filing system with typed labels.

"Wow. I'm not going to be able to stop thinking about this," I tell him.

"What? Being organized is a good thing."

"There's organized, and then there's *organized*. It's like a UPS Store up in here."

"That's ridiculous," he informs me. "I don't even have a Styrofoam-peanut dispenser."

"Don't get me wrong," I say. "I'm fully jealous." I could do some damage with this much office space. Seriously.

We leave the office and go to the next room on the right, which is another bedroom. This one has an actual bed in it. "The guest room," Aiden says. "It doesn't get much use. Sometimes Charlotte sleeps over if she drinks too much on game night."

"Game night?"

"Our family has game night once a month. Mom and Dad come over, and we play Trivial Pursuit or whatever."

"Trivial Pursuit?" The fact that his family has game night together is beyond, but I let it go. My mom has a room full of dolls. I am in no position to throw stones.

The queen-size bed is covered in pink sheets and a pink-and-white quilt.

"Did Charlotte pick out the bedding?" I ask. It looks like something she would like. Soft and feminine and homey.

"No," Aiden says. But his voice is oddly clipped.

I turn away from the bed and face him, lifting my brows.

"Maryann picked it out," he admits.

Ah, *Maryann*. His ex-girlfriend. I could pretend I didn't do any recon, but that would be disingenuous of me. Instead, I opt for, "Your ex?"

He nods. "Yep. I just never changed it."

"It's pretty," I tell him, and it really is. "I bet Charlotte loves it." Then I take a deep breath, because he's just given me the perfect opening. It's time. "So, what happened with you and Maryann, exactly?"

He presses his lips together and looks a little pale. "I thought I told you. We wanted different things."

"Pretty standard breakup reason," I say, nodding. "Though I fully admit it's better than being betrayed and fired."

"Yeah, that's pretty bad," Aiden agrees.

"So, like, you wanted kids, and she didn't?" I press. I know I'm being intrusive, but I want to know.

"Kinda the opposite," Aiden says. "She wanted to go a little faster than I did." He steps out of the bedroom and back into the hall. I am forced to follow him.

"Ahh, marriage?" I ask.

"Yeah. I wasn't ready."

I nod. It's a solid reason for a breakup, and yet, I'm somewhat surprised by it. Aiden seems like the marriage, house, and kids type to me.

"Here's my room," he says, pushing open the door to the one bedroom on the left of the hallway. I guess we're done discussing Maryann.

I step inside the room. It's bigger than the others. There's a king-size bed backed against a wood-paneled wall. The bed is covered in a blue-and-white comforter. The far wall is covered floor to ceiling with what looks like a custom-made bookshelf.

"Is that a ladder?" I ask, hurrying over to touch it. I've never actually seen a bookshelf with a ladder in person. I mostly live vicariously through Belle in the *Beauty and the Beast* movie. But here is one staring me in the face. I must approach.

"Yeah, I made it."

"You *made* it?" It's taking too long for this information to filter into my brain. I cock my head like a confused dog. This man *made* this bookshelf. With a ladder. For himself. In his house.

"I like to read," he says.

"Yeah, I like to read too, but I can't make a whole bookshelf."

"I'm a woodworker." He shrugs as if it's no biggie.

Frankly, I could stay here and stare at the bookshelf all day, but there's one thing I *must* do before I go. "Can I climb up it?"

"Go for it," he replies, shrugging.

It's a total scene out of a fairy tale.

I don't wait. I hurry over, grab both sides of the wooden frame, and pull the ladder to the far end of the track. Then I start climbing. Once I'm at the top, I look down. "This is the coolest."

"I'm glad you like it." Aiden chuckles.

"Can you indulge me with one little thing?" I say, wincing and wrinkling up my nose. He may refuse my request, but on behalf of all library-loving women in the world, I gotta ask.

"What?" He's eyeing me with something akin to suspicion.

"Can you pull me across the length of this thing?"

He laughs. "What? What are you, five?"

"I'm serious. Can I just get you to pull me across it? Like in one fell swoop."

He shakes his head as he comes over, a bemused smile on his face. "Okay, hang on."

I grab the sides of the ladder and squeal as he pulls it all the way down the length of the wall as if I weigh nothing. I throw out an arm, Belle-style, as I go, because some things need doing.

Moments later, I'm back on the floor standing next to Aiden, hopping up and down. I am giddy. *Giddy!* "Thank you for doing that," I say, laughing. I can't remember that last time I had such pure fun. Like I was a kid again. And in that moment, I realize that the memories of fun I have from when I *was* a kid are mostly with Aiden.

I glance away from him and clear my throat. I've asked myself a hundred times why I didn't remember that I told him we would be partners one day. I just cannot remember it. And who knows what a fourteen-year-old was thinking one night fifteen years ago? But still, it bothers me. How can it not?

I walk toward the bed. It looks comfy, and there's a big dog bed on the floor next to it. "For Argos?" I ask, moving over to stand near it.

"For Argos," Aiden confirms.

There is a large walk-in closet filled with farmer-like clothing. I sniff in there a little because it smells like him. There is also an en-suite bathroom with a white claw-foot tub and white-tiled shower, dual vanities, and a water closet. It all looks freshly reno'd and really stylish.

"Someone has good taste," I say.

"Thank you." He nods.

We're about to leave his bedroom when I stop. "Wait. Where's the burst pipe?" How have I seen this entire house without asking this question till now?

Aiden scrubs the back of his head. "Well, it *was* in the hall bathroom."

"Was?" I narrow my eyes.

"Yeah, it's kinda . . . fixed."

"Kinda fixed or fixed?" I blink. What's he saying?

"It's fixed," he says. "Definitely fixed." He looks guilty.

"Oh, like they just finished? Today?"

"No. They finished last weekend."

"Wait. What? Your house has been fixed since last weekend, and you've still been staying at the apartment?"

The moment the sentence leaves my mouth, I wish I could grab it out of the air and stuff it back in my big mouth because it's immediately obvious to me why that might be.

Aiden presses his lips together and scrubs a hand through his hair. I've already learned that he does that when he's anxious. Or nervous.

"I wanted to stay there, because you're there." His eyes have darkened. He steps toward me and pulls my hands into his and squeezes them.

I can't breathe. Tears are stinging my eyes. Because that has got to be one of the most romantic things I've ever heard. He lied about his burst pipe to stay near me. He's staring down at me with hope and something that looks a lot like lust in his eyes.

"Really?" I say, and I know it's stupid, but what else am I going to say? I've got no words.

"Really," he whispers back.

I tilt back my head and close my eyes, and I'm not at all embarrassed this time because I know I'm right. There is no spider. Aiden is about to kiss me.

And I want him to.

When his lips brush against mine, my whole body lights up. I shiver.

Aiden pulls back. "I know we decided to just be friends, but—"

"Shut up and kiss me," I say.

"You're so bossy," he says, smiling against my lips.

"You have no idea."

And then there are no words because Aiden's hands are in my hair, and mine are wrapped around his neck, and we are kissing like we can't get enough of each other.

I begin pulling off his clothes and he's pulling off mine and the next thing I know we're lying on his bed together. And my hands are resting on his abs, pressed flat against them.

"Ridiculous?" he asks.

"So very ridiculous," I say.

I am still wearing my bra, and he glances down at my breasts. "You're . . . gorgeous." His hand moves behind my back, and he pops the clasp to my bra. Then he pulls it off my arms. He tosses it away, and his hand reaches up to gently cup my breast. I close my eyes. He plucks at the nipple, and desire shoots directly to my core. When his mouth moves down to suck me, my fingers tangle in his soft hair. I moan.

His teeth graze my nipple, and he bites me softly, enough for me to clinch my thighs. He rolls atop me and pins my hands above my head with one hand. Damn. How does he know I love that? His mouth moves to my other breast, and he sucks that nipple, softly nibbling. He licks me, and I arch my back.

When one of his hands moves between my thighs, I quiver. I'm still wearing my panties, but I want his touch so much I am shaking. One hand slides between my hot skin and the soft fabric. I shudder again. And then a single finger slides deep inside of me, and I cry out. But it's not until he crooks it and touches a spot so perfect that my breath comes out in soft, short pants.

He lets go of my hands so that he can move all the way down between my thighs. He uses both hands to pull my panties off my hips, and when his head dips to lick between my legs, my fingers filter through his hair again. I am mindless. What this man is doing with his tongue is something I've only ever read about in romance novels. I never knew actual men knew about it. I figured it was just a women's fantasy, but here he is. I glance down to see his dark head moving between my thighs while his finger strokes inside of me.

His tongue flicks over my clit. Again and again. And his finger doesn't quit. It doesn't take long before the movement of both simultaneously sends me hurtling over the edge of climax. I call out his name and am left gasping, drenched against the sheets.

Aiden flips onto his back, and by the time I have regained any modicum of strength, I look over to see him smiling proudly up at the ceiling.

"Wow," I say. "I thought the abs were ridiculous. But that . . ."

I move to his side. My hand slides down his flat abdomen. His smile vanishes, and his breath quickens.

"You have no idea," I say, "how much I wanted to see all of you like this that first night I showed up with my suitcase." I push down his boxer briefs and move my hand between his legs and grasp his hard, hot length.

"Really?" He has an almost pained expression on his face. It's the sexiest thing I've seen in *a minute*.

"You in that towel," I whisper in his ear. "I see it in my dreams."

"You don't say." His eyes close, and his jaw clenches. "Ellie," he breathes.

I stroke him up and down while his hands fist in the sheets next to his hips. I want to ride him, but first, *I'm going to blow his mind*. I want to give him the kind of pleasure he just gave me.

I push up to my knees and then move my leg over his far thigh. He opens his eyes and widens them. I lower myself so my belly is touching his. My face is in the crook of his neck. I breathe him in. I lick his neck. I kiss his shoulder. My hand is still working him, so his breath is hitching.

I smile to myself. Having this man at my mercy is the most heady feeling I've had in a long time. And damn, his body does not disappoint. I mean, the abs, the thighs, the long, strong legs. It's like rolling around in bed with Adonis. His cock doesn't disappoint either. I squeeze him, and his breath hitches again.

I kiss my way down his chest. His skin jumps as I nip at the tight skin along his abdomen. When I make it down between his legs, I pull my hand away and let my heavy breath blow on him once, twice.

"Ellie," he groans. His jaw is clenched.

I lower my head and barely kiss his tip. His hips jump. His hands tangle in my hair. "Ellie." My name is almost a sob now. I grin to myself. Then I lick him.

His hips jerk. I press my hands against his thighs. I know he can get away if he wants to, he's twice my size, but I like the illusion of power, holding him down while I suck him.

I open my lips and let him slide into my throat. I cast my glance up to watch the emotions play over his chiseled features. He's watching me, and I know he likes it. His body shudders. I wrap my lips tightly around him and pull up. All of his fingers dive into my hair. He is not holding me to him, but he could if he wanted to. That thought turns me on. He could have me at his mercy, but instead I'm in charge. I slide my lips down his length again and his hips buck once more. His eyes are hooded, his jaw is clenched, and pure bliss is reflected on his face.

He lets me suck him once, twice, three times more before he grabs me under the arms and picks me up as if I weigh nothing.

"I can't take it any longer," he growls into my ear as he flips me over. He lurches toward the side of the bed where he rips open the nightstand drawer. "Condom," he says and wastes no time putting it on.

I nod.

Then he's on top of me again, and his weight presses me into the mattress. I wrap my arms over his killer shoulders and kiss him deeply. Our lips open for each other, and our tongues slide together. And the next thing I know, his cock is pressing between my legs.

"I want you," he breathes. His eyes are open, his forehead is pressed hard to mine, and he's poised at the entrance to my body.

"I want you too," I tell him, and it's all I need to say because then he slides inside of me with one sure thrust.

I gasp. I've never been so filled before. I've never been so turned on before. Usually, sex is pleasant. Like scratching an itch. But this is going to change my soul. I already know it.

When Aiden begins to move, I am transformed. He hitches one of my thighs up over his arm and thrusts into me. I cry out into his ear. His mouth is sucking my neck while his hips rock into me again and again. "Touch yourself," he whispers into my ear. "I want to see your face when you come."

I shudder. I've never had a man say anything like that to me before, and it's like he set my body on fire. My hand moves down between us while he whispers some of the dirtiest things I've ever heard in my ear. Things about touching me, tasting me, fucking me, making me come again and again. And I can't get enough. My fingertip finds my clit, and between his cock sliding in at just the right angle, his dirty words in my ear, and the little circles I'm drawing with my finger, it doesn't take long. I come again, my body shaking with desire, zinging with pleasure.

The minute I'm done, he releases my thigh, grabs both of my hands and pins them above my head again. Then he thrusts into me, groaning, all the while his hot, deep voice is in my ear telling me how good I feel, how much he wants me, how he's going to come, he's going to explode. And I think I could come again just listening to him. I never knew how hot dirty talking could be, but Aiden is setting me on fire with it. I already want him again.

"You're so tight, so wet, so perfect," he tells me. "God, Ellie, I've wanted you for so long."

I am just listening. I feel like I'm being adored and worshipped. Like my body is an instrument and he is a virtuoso. "*Fuck.* I'm gonna come," he whispers in my ear.

My legs wrap around his back, and he slides into me one last time before groaning and shuddering. He calls my name, and we kiss again and it's wet, tangled, and hot. And then, he collapses, a spent heap on top of me.

I am breathing heavy and staring at the ceiling. I have *never* experienced anything like that before. This man has just ruined me for all others.

I wrap my arms around his shoulders and shudder. "Oh my God, Aiden. We've *got* to do that again."

Chapter 22

We drive back to the apartment. Okay, not before having sex two more times. But we decided to go back so we'd be there ahead of the traffic in the morning.

We barely make it in the front door, drop our stuff, and kick off our shoes before Aiden lifts me up on the kitchen counter and pulls off my leggings and panties in one quick maneuver. Moments later, his jeans are down to his knees and he's pulling me hard against his body.

"You have no idea," he whispers hotly into my ear, "how many times I've wanted to fuck you right here on this counter."

"How many times?" I ask, tipping my head to the side so he can kiss my neck.

His answer is thrusting into me. Hard. Oh shit. *What* a good answer.

"So. Many. Times." Each word is another thrust. I can no longer remember the thread of our conversation.

My mouth tangles with his, and my ankles lock around his hips. Somehow, he kicks off his jeans, then he picks me up and carries me to the sofa. He lays me on my back and lowers himself on top of me.

"I've also imagined this too many times to count," he says, thrusting again.

I gasp into his mouth and clutch his shoulders. I've never had sex like this. All consuming, unstoppable. Like I can't get enough no matter how many times we're together.

"Anywhere else?" I manage to ask between gasps. Because honestly, let's do it.

He kisses me deeply and picks me up again. This time he takes me into his bedroom. He lays me on the bed and leaves me momentarily to rip off his shirt. Then he leans down and pulls my sweater over my head. He throws it away too. We are naked now. I spread my legs, and when Aiden comes down on top of me this time, he thrusts into me again. His arms are locked on either side of my head, his hands are sifting through my hair. He's watching my face while his hips are owning me, making me cry out each time he thrusts.

When he lowers a hand between us and touches me, I whimper. Then I hold my breath, wanting to chase the pleasure his finger is giving me. I'm right on the edge when he stops.

"No!" I cry.

His smile is devilish. He kisses the underside of my chin. "Tell me what you want."

"Touch me," I say.

"Why?" He kisses my cheek.

"Make me come. Please."

That's what he wanted to hear. His finger moves back into place, and he plays with me, circling my clit until my thighs clench and my jaw locks and my body explodes with pleasure. Then he thrusts into me one last time and joins me in a soul-shattering climax that leaves us both breathless.

* * *

It's nearly two in the morning when I cautiously trace my fingers up Aiden's chest. We're snuggled together in his bed, but we haven't done much sleeping. Or any sleeping, actually. He looks down at me and gives me a sly smile. "What?" he says. He can tell I'm up to something. And I am.

"I kinda . . ." I stop. I'm positive my face is flaming. I'm glad it's mostly dark in the room.

"Kinda what?" he prods. He kisses my temple.

"Well, you had your fantasies about where we had sex, and . . . I have mine."

His brows shoot straight up. "Really?"

"Yep." I nod.

He nuzzles my ear. "Tell me," he whispers.

I bite my lip. My hand is resting on his ridiculous abs. "I kinda can't stop picturing us doing it against an apple tree."

"Really?" he repeats.

I nod. I'm all in now. I might as well go for it. "Yeah, like you back me up against it and pick me up and—" I shudder.

He's already out of the bed and pulling on his jeans. "Let's go," he says. "Your wish is my command."

Okay, what woman doesn't want to hear *that*? But . . . "It's cold outside," I say, suddenly worried that it might be a bad idea, after all.

"I'll warm you up."

"There are a lot of people here tonight. What if they see us?" is my next halfhearted protest.

He shakes his head slowly and confidently. "I know a place no one will find us."

Well, in that case. I slide out of bed and pull on my clothes.

On the way out of the apartment, I grab my coat. Aiden grabs his, too, but I can't help wondering how this is gonna work, exactly.

We make our way down the stairs and out onto the grounds. The LED lights in the trees illuminate a lot of area. It's really pretty, but far too bright to have sex out here. Anyone looking out the windows of the inn would see us, and then I would have to immediately poison myself like a character in a Shakespeare play.

Aiden takes my hand and leads me down a path toward the work barn. I think we're going inside it, but at the last minute we turn and head to the right. It's a path through the trees I haven't taken before.

It's cold, but my coat and the anticipation of what we're about to do keep me pretty warm. Adrenaline is pumping through my veins. Are we really going to do this? Outside?

Minutes later, I see what we've been walking toward: a giant greenhouse. Well, it's more like a half dome made of plastic, but there are trees inside! It's all fogged up from the humidity. We approach the door, and it's locked. But Aiden has the key. And when we step inside, I realize how just how hot and humid it is. Aiden locks the door behind us.

"Oh my God," I whisper, just before he takes my hand and leads me into a small forest of trees.

"This one looks pretty sturdy," he says, slapping one of the trunks. He backs me up against it, and I quickly suck in my breath. My nipples tingle. I am already aching.

"Is this how you imagined it?" he asks. His hands are braced on either side of my head against the tree. It's completely dark in the greenhouse except for a thin slice of moonlight.

"Yes," I admit. Because this is *exactly* how I imagined it, only better because we are warm and it's getting hotter.

I kick off my boots while Aiden drops to his knees and pulls down my leggings and panties again. Then he leans forward and licks me between my legs. My knees buckle. I grab his shoulders for support. God. I *love* his shoulders. He licks me again.

"Aiden," I gasp. I tug at his T-shirt. This feels good, but I want what we came here for.

He understands. He moves to his feet, drops his jeans, slides on a condom, and picks me up. His arm snakes around my back to shield it from the tree bark. My legs wrap around his hips, and I shudder. He's got to know the exact moment this particular fantasy bloomed in my head . . . when we were taking pictures in the orchard.

"I'm sorry I don't have the hat," he says against my mouth as he positions himself.

"Don't be." I find it hard to care at the moment—my eyes are closed, but this is better than anything I dreamed of because, when Aiden slides into me, it's heaven. One of his hands is on my ass, and the other is shielding my back. My hands are on his shoulders, and he takes me against the tree exactly like every single sexy fantasy I've had since that photo shoot.

And it's good. At some point, mindless, we end up on the ground on top of our clothes. I ride him. His hands are on my hips, and his face is chiseled in stone. I can see glimpses of it in the moonlight that filters through the dome. I slide down him again and again before he rolls me over and thrusts into me, taking control while I touch myself, and an orgasm hurtles through both of us at the same time.

* * *

Sometime later, the moon guides us back through the apple trees. We sneak into the inn and up the stairs to the apartment as quietly as we can. We throw off all our clothes again and snuggle together in his bed. My head is tucked under his chin. His arm is slung around my waist. It feels right. Like two matching puzzle pieces that have found each other.

He kisses my temple again. "So? How was it?" he asks.

I giggle. "Exactly like my fantasies, only better."

"Good," he says, and I can hear the smile in his voice.

I burrow into his side, and minutes later, we finally fall asleep. We've got a big day tomorrow. The both of us.

Chapter 23

There's a lot of traffic this morning. I can hear it from all the way up in the attic. I'm already dressed and gulping down my coffee. Aiden is in the shower. We *may* have had sex one more time this morning . . . in my bed. Might as well cover all the bases, right?

I am still buzzing from the past twenty-four hours. I mean who knew that the sometimes grumpy, kinda quiet Aiden could throw down in bed like that? And the *dirty talking*. Oh my God. In a hundred years I wouldn't have guessed that Aiden Parker was a master at saying superhot things in bed. And that's not the only thing he's the master of. I mean, I had heard tell of a G-spot before, but until he found it like he had a map, I had no idea what my body was capable of. The speed with which I orgasmed—two thumbs up. Would recommend. There really should be a Yelp for sex.

We need to discuss it, of course. The sex. The orgasms. The additional sex. Maybe even the dirty talking. We need to talk about what it means and what it doesn't and just . . . *what*? But one glance at my watch tells me we're already cutting it close. It's nearly eight. There is a large group of people who are going to hunt me with pitchforks if I don't get downstairs ASAP and start answering questions and handling things.

Aiden comes out of the shower with a towel wrapped around his hips, and I am catapulted back to the night I arrived here.

"I've gotta go," I say.

"Yeah, me too. I'm meeting an apple distributor at eight," Aiden says.

I stop. "Wait. You are?"

He shrugs. "I'm going to hear him out, at least."

I smile at him. "That's amazing. I'm proud of you, Aiden."

He grins, bashful, before disappearing into his room. When he comes out, he's dressed, but his hair is still wet and he's rubbing it with the towel in that way that makes me a little insane. I swear, one word from him, and I'll be back in bed with him again.

"Hey." He stops me as I try to pass him to grab my laptop from my room.

"Hey," I repeat. I am watching his bottom lip. The same one I sucked on endlessly last night. The same one that whispered filthy things in my ear while I screamed his name.

After the things we did to each other last night there should be no shyness today, but I can't help but glance down. Looking at him and his mussed hair isn't helping me with concentrating on the work I have to do today. The ache between my thighs can wait. It's going to have to wait.

"We need to talk," he says.

"Yeah, definitely." I nod. "Later?"

"Later."

I move past him, grab my laptop and my bag and hustle over to the door. I promised Maria and Ashley that I'd meet them for coffee in the food barn this morning. I'm still hoping Sera will read my tarot.

* * *

It's late afternoon before I can stop and take a breath. The place has made twice as much money today as it did yesterday, and we haven't even gotten all the income from the Harvest Ball tonight. We are well beyond our expenses and far into profit territory. The bakery is raking it in. The brewery is raking it in. "Pictures with Pumpkin" is honestly still the largest draw, but none of the activities are under-performing.

I am sitting at one of the picnic tables in the food barn when Sera slides onto the bench across from me. It's less busy in here right now but still packed. She has a small team of helpers from town working behind the counter at the moment. It's the first time I've sat down all day.

"Hey!" I say.

"Hi," Sera replies. "You look tired."

I frown. "Thanks?"

"Sorry. I just meant . . . you've done so much. And it's been fantastic, Ellie. I've made more this weekend than the last two seasons combined."

I give her a tired but sincere smile. "I'm really glad to hear that."

"You were right, putting up a sign that says the cider is magic really made sales take off."

"Yeah, well, I could use some magic right now." But what I need is an energy drink, not magic cider.

"Hang on, let me get you some."

"Wait," I say. "You don't happen to have any tarot cards, do you?"

Sera's eyes light up, and she nods. "I sure do. Want me to do a quick reading for you?"

"*Please.*"

She returns with a cup of apple cider and a pack of tarot cards. She hands me the cup and spreads the cards on the picnic table in front of us.

"What is the question you want answered?"

I don't have to think very long. "What does the future hold for me?"

She nods sagely. There is much shuffling and some woo-woo talk before she knocks her knuckles against the cards, spreads them once more, and says, "Choose five."

"Any five?"

"Yep."

I reach out a shaking hand and select five cards from the spread. Sera collects them into a little pile and sets them in front of her. Then she flips over the first card.

"The Hierophant," Sera says. "It means you'll have a long and happy life."

"That's promising." I scooch closer and take a swig of cider.

She flips over another. "The Judgment card. Ooh, that means you have a big choice to make."

"Do I ever," I groan. "What choice should I make?" I am staring at the cards as if they can actually speak to me. Like, stand up and talk. And honestly, I wish they would. Should I take my old job back if Steve offers it to me? Or, better question, *is* Steve going to offer me my old job back?

Sera flips over the next card. "Uh, oh. Two of Swords." She shakes her head.

"What? What does that mean?" Can you have a panic attack over tarot? Seems like the wrong vibe, yet here I am.

"It means confusion lies ahead," Sera tells me.

"Ahead? No. Confusion is in the here and now, believe me."

She flips over the fourth one. "Oh, wow."

"What?" My leg is bobbing up and down beneath the table like a piston.

"Two of Wands. You're faced with a decision that will impact your long-term direction in life." She sets down the card and touches my hand. "Something really big is coming up. It's an important decision. You need to be ready to make a choice, Ellie."

"No kidding," I moan. Okay, I guess this means Steve will be offering me my old job back, right?

"One more," she says.

I take a deep breath. "Hit me."

She turns over the last card. There is a naked man and woman standing in a garden. An angel is hovering over them. It is not unlike

Adam and Eve. Nor is it unlike some of the things I've done recently. The irony is too much. I shift in my seat and clear my throat.

"Oh, the Lovers," she breathes.

"Love?" I ask.

"Yes." She nods. "Love."

I am frantic. Just love? "Love now? Love later? When love? What love? How love?" I fire off these questions in rapid succession, staring at Sera like a deranged person.

Sera laughs and shakes her head. "You've got to relax. Remember, everything in the universe is always in perfect order."

Tell that to my bouncing knee. "Is it? Because at the moment it feels like a helter-skelter mess."

"It is," Sera assures me. "And as for what it means, some say the Lovers card can indicate a spiritual connection with a soulmate," she says. "Or a relationship that teaches you to be true to yourself and make good decisions."

Spiritual connection with a soulmate? Aiden's face pops to mind.

A relationship that teaches you to be true to yourself and make good decisions? Geoff, in a roundabout way.

Sera touches my hand again. "Just remember, Ellie. The answers to every question are already inside of you. You'll know them when you need them."

Okay. Look. I love a good Yoda-like saying as much as the next girl. I really do. But at the moment, Sera's words just make me want to stamp my foot. "Thanks," I say. Because getting angry with Gandalf types is a losing proposition. Everybody knows that. Plus, it was nice of Sera to read my tarot. Now it's up to me to figure it all out.

As I leave the barn, the hired hands from town along with all the farmhands are already stringing up the lights and garlands to turn this barn into the Autumn Harvest Festival showcase tonight.

I stop by the hay barn to check on the makeshift kindergarten set up inside. The space has been divided into sections. Each has its own big tent. Babies and toddlers. Younger kids. And older kids.

Charlotte has organized all of this, and there are at least three adults
for every set of children per the legal guidelines. The kids are engaged
in age-appropriate activities, and all seem to be having the time of
their lives. There are plenty of space heaters and sleeping bags, and
the kids are thrilled they will be camping for the second night in a
row. There is also a plan to take them by the animal barn to meet
the livestock. We've already established that, despite her insurance
policy, Miss Guin will remain in her pen. No point tempting fate. We
want it to be a safe and fun evening for everyone.

"My friends and I are all gonna take turns stopping by the Harvest
Ball," Charlotte informs me. "I'm planning to go first."

"I'm glad you'll get to see it," I tell her. "Thank you for handling
all of this," I say, waving my hand around the barn.

"Are you kidding? This is fun for me," she replies. "I love kids."

I leave Charlotte to chase after some five-year-olds, and head back
to the inn. On my way up to the apartment, I go to the front desk.
Mom is there. I take a deep breath. I need to get this over with. It's
time. "Hey, Mom, can I talk to you for a sec?"

"Of course, dear."

We step into the apartment for some privacy. If anyone comes to
the front desk, there is a little bell for them to ring for service. It's
old-timey and quaint, and at the moment I'm very thankful for it.

We're sitting in the Doll Room when Dad walks by. "Dad, can you
come in for a minute?"

Dad steps into the room. "What's on your mind, dear?"

It's time to come clean. I take a deep breath and slide my hands
down my legs and over my knees. "I should have told you both this
way before now," I begin. My belly feels sick, and my heart is pounding. Why is this hard? I'm an adult, and I have some news about my
life. It shouldn't be difficult to share with my parents. They love me.

"Yes?" Mom prods.

I can't look at the dolls. I feel like they're judging me for taking so long to share this news. "That day you called me and asked me to come help with the festival . . . I had just been fired, and Geoff had dumped me the night before."

Mom's face doesn't move an inch. "We know, dear."

Wait. What? "You knew?"

"Yes, Geoff texted us and told us you would probably need us."

"*Geoff* texted you?" I'm frowning, because how did Geoff even have Mom's number?

"We traded numbers the last time we were in the city," Mom replies. "I don't like to think of you spending time with people I don't know and can't contact, dear."

For his part, Dad looks a little guilty. He shifts on his feet. "We thought about telling you we knew but figured you'd tell us when you were ready."

"I . . . I . . . thought you'd be disappointed in me." Wow. That was more difficult to say than I thought it would be.

"Disappointed?" Mom shakes her head. "I never liked Geoff, dear. I thought you knew that."

"No, not disappointed about Geoff, disappointed that I got fired."

"Yes, how exactly did that happen?" Dad's brow is furrowed.

So, Geoff left out that part, did he? Figures. I spend the next fifteen minutes explaining to Mom and Dad exactly what happened. They are both very displeased at the news that Geoff stole my ideas, lied, and got me fired, but thankfully they don't remind me again that they never liked him. I think everyone is now in agreement that Geoff is a douche.

"All that matters is that you're here now and the festival has been a wonderful success. You can stay as long as you want, dear."

I bite my lip. "Steve hasn't called, but if he does, do you think I should take my old job back?"

"That's got to be your decision," Mom says. But then she sighs. "But your dad and I would sure love you to stay."

Stay? Like stay *here*? *Work* here? Why has that thought never occurred to me until now? I mean, OnlyFans isn't my only option. I could stay and plan events for the inn and orchard.

My heart clenches, and I realize that Mom has never said that she wants me to stay before. I mean, I always guessed it, but she's never been this blunt. I hug her. "I'll think about it, Mom. I promise."

She smiles at me. "You have to follow your heart, Ellie."

I *love* sayings like that. I just wish it was as easy to know how to do it as to say it.

A thought occurs to me.

"Mom, do you think I'm afraid of success?" This question has been plaguing me since Drunk Aiden and I talked about it. And my mom knows me better than anyone. She should be able to answer it.

"No, dear." Mom shakes her head. "But sometimes in life there comes a time when you have to redefine what success means to you."

I expel my breath. Redefine success? I'm about to ask Mom a follow-up question, when the bell rings from the front desk. Mom hops to her feet. She hugs me again quickly. "Don't worry, dear. Everything will be okay."

It's close to what Sera said with the tarot cards but more mom-like. Mom leaves for the front desk, and Dad and I just stare at each other.

"So, what do you think of the festival, Dad?"

"I think Pumpkin's made more money this weekend than I have in the last year," Dad says, an ironic smile on his lips.

"Same," I say. "Social media is a weird, weird place."

"Don't get me wrong." Dad stands, steps over, and kisses me atop the head. "I'm thankful for it. We needed the business. Now. Let's go get ready for the ball," he says. "I can't stay in here with these dolls staring at me."

Agree.

I hug Dad and leave the Doll Room to walk through the living room to the door that leads up to the apartment. I push open the door and begin the long, slow march upstairs. I have to drag myself up the final steps. Sera is right. I am tired. Exhausted, really. I didn't get much sleep, and it's been a long day. I saw nearly everyone from town today, and they all congratulated me on the success of the festival and told me how great it was. It made me feel good. It made me feel useful. They all assured me they'll be at the ball tonight. I am looking forward to it.

Like I told Mom minutes ago, Steve hasn't called. It's probably not happening. Maybe Geoff was just trying to talk him into rehiring me. Who knows? But it's nearly six, and the Harvest Ball starts at seven. I need to get ready and change my clothes.

I take a shower, blow-dry my hair, and toss on the cute little down-homey farm-girl-like dress I ordered off the internet last week for tonight. I'm normally not one to buy clothes online, but when I asked Charlotte where she shops, she recommended a site. I figured, when in Rome . . . The dress I ordered is a red-and-white gingham mini with puff sleeves. I pair it with some cowboy boots. I'm ready for a hootenanny. Or at least a Harvest Ball in a barn.

I'm just walking out of the bathroom when the door to the apartment opens and Aiden steps in. I haven't seen him since this morning, but I've been thinking about him all day. His hair has fallen over one eye, and my chest aches. I want him again. I can't help it.

"Hi there," he says, giving me that smile that makes my knees buckle. He looks me up and down. "You look amazing."

"Hi," I reply. "Thank you."

"Did you hear how much we made today?" he continues. "It's unbelievable."

"Yeah, pretty great. Pumpkin can start his own hedge fund. And don't put it past him." I push my hand through my hair. "How was the meeting with the distributor?"

"He gave me some things to think about."

I nod. "Did he make an offer?" *I must know.*

"Not officially, but he gave me a ballpark."

I lift my brows. "Care to share?"

Aiden sucks in a breath and slowly expels it. "Enough to never have to work another day in my life. Or Charlotte or Mom and Dad either."

"Really?" I say. I am desperately trying to stop thinking about his mouth at my ear last night or his hand on my—

"Yeah, well, that is, if we keep living our simple lives out here. Not buying Park Avenue penthouses for each of us or anything like that."

"I get it," I say. "That's great." I clear my throat and swallow. I am so effed. We can no longer just be partners or friends. All I can think about is rolling around in the sheets with this man.

"Yeah, maybe." He steps toward me and takes my hands. "Can we talk now?"

"Definitely." Though I still have no idea what I'm going to say. I may have thought about him all day, but I came to zero conclusions. I mean, if Aiden *is* my soulmate, how would we ever make it work? Mom wants me to stay, but I don't know if that's what *I* want. I want to hear Steve's offer, honestly. And *if* it happens and *if* I take it, it's complicated. New York City to Long Island may only be a train ride away, but where would Aiden and I live? There is more than one problem with the difference in our lifestyles. Maybe we can have a weekend sex pact? I'm not exactly sure how to bring that up, though. Seems like it might be offensive.

I decide to push those thoughts aside for the time being. I need to hear Aiden out.

He's giving me a knowing, sexy grin, and I can't help but want to kiss him. "I really enjoyed last night," he says. "*And this morning.*"

I blush. "I did too."

"Ellie, listen, I—"

A knock sounds on the door, and it might as well be someone pounding. It's that startling.

"Who is it?" I call, scrunching my eyes closed in agony.

"Maria!"

I give Aiden an apologetic look and mouth the word *sorry*, then I pull away from him and hurry to the door.

The minute I open it, Maria steps in. She's wearing a slay-all-day set of chic overalls (trust me) with wide legs, a big white puffy shirt, designer boots, and a straw hat that somehow looks super expensive. Maria can even make farmer clothes look good.

"I came to get you for the ball," she announces. "You're my date, aren't you?"

She glances between the two of us for a few seconds and then gives me a look that tells me she *knows* we had sex. And I know she knows. And I'm not even going to question how she knows, because I'm positive my alchemy has changed since last night. I'm surprised more people haven't asked me about it today, actually. I might as well be wearing a sign around my neck. *I got laid. Ask me how.*

"Yes! Yes, I am *your* date," I hasten to reply. At this point I want nothing more than to hustle Maria out of the door, because the last time she and I were alone with Aiden I managed to embarrass the crap out of myself. I may be sober right now, but I'm not risking it. "Let's go." I grab my bag. "See you later, Aiden?" And the look I give him implies that I know we still need to talk.

"Yeah," he says. "See ya."

Chapter 24

The Harvest Ball looks like old-timey and postcard-y had a baby. The food barn has been transformed. I hired the best company I knew to turn it into a night under the stars inside. The roof is filled with softly twinkling lights. Votives on each table fill the space with the scent of pumpkin and ginger, and the amount of apple-filled desserts available in the bakery adds a cinnamon touch to the air. The country rock band we hired is set up on a stage against the far wall, and they are playing a steady stream of music that has the dance floor in front of them filled.

The entire town is here. There's Millie and Kaylie, Mr. and Mrs. Wilkins, Mrs. Lawrence, Abe Bennett, Mr. Timmons, Mr. Culkin, Mrs. Sharma, and Mr. Wainwright. Mr. Higgins and Mr. and Mrs. Goldman are here too. Billy and Amber say hello when I walk by. Mrs. Jackson is out there cutting a rug with her husband. They are all looking good in their dresses and boots and jeans and pullover sweaters. Mom and Dad look ten years younger. And the Parkers are already out on the dance floor doing some sort of line dance. Who knew they could move like that?

Mr. Peyton was here, but I asked him to stop by the livestock barn real quick and have a talk with Miss G. We'll see what he can do. I mean, he can't make it *worse*. That's my logic.

I stroll over to the wall nearest the bakery to take it all in. The guests all seem to be having a good time, and I've never seen the barn so full. Maria is standing in front of the Biergarten bar talking to Jesse. They are both alive but obviously arguing. I can tell by the hand gestures. I can't wait to hear what they're saying to each other. Maria spent the entire walk over here trying to get me to admit I had sex with Aiden. When I finally did, she squealed and said, "It's about time."

"But I don't know how I feel about it," I told her. " What if it was a mistake? I'll probably be leaving here soon."

"So what?" Maria promptly replied with a shrug. "Since when is jumping in bed with a hot guy a mistake? You don't need to go pick out wedding venues or anything."

"I can't explain it," I told her. And I really can't. If it had been some guy I met in the city, it would be fine, but it's Aiden and there's history and it's complicated. But I don't have time to get into all of it with Maria tonight.

I decide to sidle over to the Biergarten and stand with my back to a thick, wooden post near the bar, close enough to hear what Maria and Jesse are saying but not to be seen. If this is wrong, I don't care. I tell myself it's my civic duty, because if one of them starts a tussle, I'll be there to break it up.

"Not if you were the last man—*like, literally the last*—on the face of this earth," Maria is saying to Jesse when I start to listen.

I clap my hand over my mouth to keep from laughing out loud, because that's pretty much along the lines of *exactly* what I guessed she'd be saying to him.

"What? You don't dance?" Jesse replies, sounding a little playful and a little perturbed.

"Oh, I dance. Just not with you." Boom. Maria is not one to mince words.

"I don't believe you can dance to country music," Jesse replies.

"What is that, reverse psychology?" Even though I'm not looking, I *know* she just rolled her eyes.

"Prove it, then," Jesse says.

"I don't have to prove anything to you, Ball Cap."

Okay, I admit I take a peek, because I don't remember seeing

Jesse in his ubiquitous ball cap tonight, and when I look, I learn that I'm right. In fact, Jesse looks pretty good. He's wearing jeans and a zip-up dark-blue sweater that makes his eyes pop. His blond hair is slicked back, and his tats are mostly hidden. Not that I mind the tats, but he looks like he really made an effort. It's kind of heartwarming.

"Coward," Jesse says next, and I have to fight the urge to duck for cover because he's *not* going to get away with that.

"What did you just call me?" Maria says through obviously clenched teeth.

It's time to intervene. I swing around the wooden beam and call out, "Hey, there, kids. Having fun?" Of course, I already know they are not, but I'm not about to admit it.

"No," Maria says at the same time that Jesse says, "Principessa here won't dance with me."

Okay. It's cute that he remembers how to say princess in Italian. "Did you ask her nicely?" I say to Jesse before Maria has a chance to flay him with her tongue.

"No, he *did not* ask me nicely."

"There's your trouble," I say to Jesse with a shrug.

He heaves a deep breath. "Ms. Agostini. Will you please do me the honor of dancing with me?"

"No," says Maria. She gives him side-eye.

"See!" Jesse tosses a hand in the air.

"Let's go, El," Maria says. She takes my arm and turns abruptly away from the bar.

"Wait," Jesse says.

Maria stops, turns halfway, and gives him a long-suffering stare. There is much blinking of her fabulous eyelashes. "What?"

"I got you something," he says. He's fumbling under the bar and comes up with a champagne bottle. It's a good brand too. I recognize it. He grabs two champagne flutes from somewhere else under the bar and expertly opens the bottle with a loud pop.

"I do love that sound," Maria whispers to me. She's not about to let Jesse hear her though.

Jesse pours champagne in both glasses. "Ladies," he says as he presents the flutes to us. "These are on the house. Thank you for all you've done for the festival."

Maria stalks over and takes the champagne glass. She's not dumb. I take mine too. Pretty classy of Jesse to get these for us, and it's clear he's trying to get on Maria's good side. Poor guy doesn't even realize it's too late.

"Thank you," I say, nodding to Jesse.

"Thanks," Maria reluctantly concedes.

"Enjoy your evening," Jesse says just before he gets sucked back into a swarm of bar patrons shouting out orders.

Maria and I meander toward the dance floor sipping our champagne.

"That was nice of him," I say.

"I guess." She still looks a little pissed.

"Honestly, the way you two were looking at each other . . ." I purposely let my sentence drift off.

"What?" Maria demands, glaring at me.

"I'm just saying." I wave my hand in the air. "Next time get a room maybe."

Her nostrils flare. "Mr. Plaid Flannel Shirt? No way!"

"Dude's not wearing plaid flannel tonight. In fact, I'd say he cleans up *real* good." I waggle my brows.

"You can't be serious." She rolls her eyes.

"Whatever you say. But I saw what I saw." I also know that, in addition to being a sucker for blond hair and blue eyes, Maria likes dudes she starts off thinking are assholes. But I'm not going to point it out to her tonight.

Maria plants her free hand on her hip. Her eyes shoot swords at me. Not daggers, fully formed swords. "*You're* just trying to keep me from bringing up you and Aiden again."

"Maybe," I admit, taking another sip of champagne.

A sly smile pops to her lips. "Come on, spill it. Was it good?"

"It was *so damn good*!" I groan. "Like, romance novel good."

"Really? Well, you definitely needed that."

I sigh. "I did. I really did."

"So, did you two talk about it this morning?" she asks next in a sing-song voice.

I wrinkle my nose. "We were trying to talk about it when you knocked."

Maria winces. "Oh damn. Sorry."

"It's fine. We'll talk later."

We've made our way to the sidelines of the dance floor. Maria dances in place to the music while I let my gaze wander around the periphery of the room.

Ashley Cross is taking pictures in front of the band. Mrs. Jackson is teaching the Wilkinses how to dance. Or trying to, at least. Mom and Dad are laughing with the Parkers. I don't see Aiden. I'm torn between whether I'm relieved or anxious that we didn't get a chance to finish our conversation earlier. Part of me would like to have heard what he had to say. The other part is glad to have a reprieve. I still don't know what to say to him. I don't regret what happened last night . . . or this morning. But how will that impact us in the long term? I have no idea. If I end up staying here and we get closer, that would be one thing, but . . . if Steve does call and offer me my job back, I'd be a fool not to take it, right?

Who am I asking? My own confused self? Ugh.

Across the way at the far end of the barn where the bakery counter meets the wall, I see Charlotte. She is talking to a very hot guy who I recognize as Sawyer. I finally met him last weekend. And the minute I did, I immediately knew why Charlotte had a crush on him. He has dark-brown hair and emerald-green eyes and an easy smile that lights up his face. When I met him, he was wrapping one of the goat's legs because it had been injured, and I could tell how careful he was not to hurt the poor thing. He spoke to the goat in a soft, calm voice and pet its little head from time to time to reassure it. The goat seemed really happy to have him in his corner. As Sera would say, Sawyer's energy was really good.

Sawyer also tipped his hat to me like we were in Texas, and when he smiled, his dimples popped. It was pretty cute. I know *exactly* why Charlotte is smitten.

I can tell by the serious looks on their faces that Charlotte and Sawyer are having an intense conversation. And judging by their matching frowns, they are not happy. *Interesting.* I turn away to give them their privacy.

I am just about to go say hello to Millie and Kaylie when Aiden steps in front of me. He's wearing khaki chinos and a green sweater and looks like a dream. He smells even better. I want to go up on tip-toes and press my nose into the crook of his neck and breathe him in.

"Hi," he says.

"Hi." I bite my lip.

The band has just started a slow song, and the lights have dimmed like it's homecoming in the gym.

Aiden's gaze never leaves mine. "Will you dance with me?"

I nod and he takes my hand, leading me to the dance floor. There are other couples surrounding us. Millie and Kaylie. The Wilkinses. The Parkers. Mrs. Lawrence and Donny (weird). Mom and Dad. Mr. and Mrs. Jackson. The Sharmas. Charlotte and Sawyer make their way to the floor too. Interesting.

Aiden and I sway back and forth to the music. I have my arms around his shoulders, and there's nowhere else I'd rather be now, honestly. It's as if I can pretend I'm sixteen again. Not a care in the world. Just this cute boy and my cute dress, and this dance and this moment.

I would press my cheek to his chest if I didn't think it would end up on the *Hot Sheet* in the morning. As it is, we'll still probably be there just for dancing. If Mrs. L knew about what happened in the greenhouse, her head would explode. Oh, that makes me smile.

"I'm sorry we got interrupted earlier," I say. "I thought I was meeting Maria out here, but she came looking for me."

"It's okay," Aiden says. "But there's something I need to tell you." The look in his eyes is serious. Intense. It makes me shiver.

The tiniest bit of panic bubbles in my chest. But I have to hear him out. Maybe whatever he says will make what I want to say more obvious, because at the moment, I have no idea what I want to say to him. I'm so confused. And I haven't had much sleep.

"Ellie, I—"

"Ellie!" Someone is calling my name. Loudly. I pull my arms from Aiden's neck and turn toward the crowd. Who said that? I exchange a brief confused look with Aiden.

"Ellie!"

We've stopped dancing. The crowd parts, and Steve Gibbons and Geoff are headed directly for me. Geoff was the one calling my name.

Aiden and I move off the dance floor to meet them.

"Eleanor, there you are," Steve says. He is out of breath. He looks totally disheveled, not at all his usual put-together self. His clothes are wrinkled, and he's got mud on his pants. Did Miss Guin get him? *Ah, karma. Sometimes you come in the form of a goat.* I can't help but smile at that thought as I introduce all three of the men. I also note with some smug satisfaction that Steve is not wearing a Patagonia vest tonight. He's got on some sort of a blazer instead.

Aiden gives Geoff a once-over while Steve puts a hand on my shoulder. I pointedly stare at his hand until he removes it. I take a step back. I can feel Aiden's strong, comforting presence behind me.

"What are you doing here, Steve? I thought you were going to call me," I say, crossing my arms over my middle.

"I decided to drive out here instead. This event," Steve waves his hand in the air to indicate the entire barn, "is the hottest thing on social right now."

I furrow my brow. "Wait. What? The Autumn Harvest Festival?"

"Yes. It's all over my Instagram and TikTok feeds."

I refuse to look surprised. Instead, I shrug one shoulder as if it's totally what I expected. "I'm really good," I say. "Anyway, why did you come out here?"

"Geoff says you're considering coming back, and I thought I'd have a better chance of convincing you in person."

"You're considering going back?" comes Aiden's voice from behind me. I do not miss the surprise in his tone. Or the disappointment.

I turn to him and tell him the truth. "I don't know."

Steve threads his fingers together. "Please, Eleanor," he begs. "Please come back." He reaches behind himself and pulls a piece of paper out of his back pocket. He promptly hands it to me.

"She goes by Ellie now," Geoff informs Steve as I unfold the paper to see the GMJ letterhead. It's a job offer. Twice my previous salary and a bonus as much as half that. There is also a new title on the page. Lead Event Planner. I had been an associate planner. A lead planner is on track for partnership. They get all the biggest accounts.

"What do you say?" Steve asks, staring hopefully at me with big, fake puppy-dog eyes.

I stare back at him as a hundred thoughts fly through my head. If he's offering me double my salary, that means I was paid *way* too little before. Plus, what exactly did Geoff tell him happened? And why was he so quick to believe the worst about me?

"Geoff told me what happened," Steve explains. "He told me all the ideas were yours. He told me he lied."

"If he told you the truth, why is he here with you? Why didn't you fire him like you fired me?"

"What? Well, I . . ." Steve's normally nonstop talking temporarily drifts into silence. "I mean, he admitted what he did."

My voice rises. My nostrils flare. "You didn't even give me the courtesy of an explanation. You wouldn't even let me go back to my desk. You still have my tumbler!"

Steve's mouth keeps opening and closing like a puppet's while I get madder and madder. I may have made some mistakes in my life, but whatever else I do, wherever else I go, I'm *not* going back to a place that wouldn't even let me take my sweater and my tumbler when I left.

"I'm not coming back," I say to Steve. His face falls. So does Geoff's. "And both of you can suck it."

"What?" Steve points at the paper I'm still holding. "Didn't you see the numbers?"

"I sure did. And frankly, if you can pay me that much now, it means you weren't paying me what I was worth before."

"But . . . I . . ." He's at a loss for words, and honestly, it's fun to watch. Finally, he tugs on his lapels. "Take the night. Think about it. Sleep on it."

I am in high dudgeon. My dudgeon is high. My chest is puffed up, and I'm standing up as tall as a five-foot-four lady wearing boots can, and I know my eyes are flashing fire. There's no stopping me now. Once that voice in my head green-lighted all of this, I mentally pulled the rip cord. It feels good. It feels great, actually! "I don't need the night. The answer is no. And if you keep telling other companies lies about me, I'm going to sue you *and* GMJ for everything you're worth."

Steve's face turns red. He clenches his fists. Now he looks angry. "You're going to regret this, Eleanor."

"I don't think I am." I cross my arms over my chest. "And don't make a scene, Steve. You don't want to *burn any bridges*, do you?"

"Look, Eleanor." Steve's hands are on his hips now.

"You heard the lady, Steve. And it's *Ellie*." This comes from Maria, who steps out of the crowd to give Steve her best you-eff-with-my-friend-you-eff-with-me face. "Now get out of here."

Steve and Geoff finally slink away. I'm about to turn to Aiden, when I glance up to see four people dressed in suits looking quite out of place in the barn. They are about ten feet away, and they are all watching me.

One of the members of the group, an older woman with dark hair and a killer black business suit, steps forward.

"Good job, Ellie Lawson," the woman says. She has a bit of gray at the temples, is wearing very expensive heels and jewelry, and looks like she belongs in an executive boardroom, not at this festival. I bet her watch costs more than my old yearly salary.

"You know me?" I say, and then I glance at her companions. I realize they look familiar. They're the three executives from the Bolt Hotel Group. The ones who I'd presented to the day I was fired.

"I know *of* you," the woman informs me.

If those are the executives, then this woman must be . . .

"Laura Bolt, chief executive of Bolt Hotels." She offers a hand for me to shake.

Oh my God. Laura Bolt! She is a legend in the hospitality industry. She built the company from the ground up. I cannot believe she's here. Why is she here? I shake her hand, feeling as if I'm in a dream.

"We've been looking for you," Laura says.

"You've been looking for *me*?" I point at her first and then at myself. That can't be right. I must have heard her wrong.

"Yes," she says. "As soon as I met Geoff, I knew he hadn't planned one minute of our event." She shakes her head.

"I planned it," I tell her.

"I know. My team told me *you* were the one with the original presentation," Laura continues.

"How did you find me?" I ask. Because seriously, *what* is happening?

Laura's similarly well-dressed female associate steps forward. "Your social media account was filled with news about this festival." She waves a hand in the air. "It's beautiful, by the way. *So* well done."

Laura Bolt nods. "Just as beautiful as I want my Barn and Branch event to be next weekend."

I gulp. How is this happening?

"We want to hire you," Laura says. "May I?" She nods at the piece of paper still in my hand. I give it to her. She scans it and hands it back to me. "I'll *triple* your previous salary, and I'd like you to come on as the head of event planning for the new brand. And you're right. They *were* definitely underpaying you." She winks at me.

Have I died? Is this heaven? Or have I fallen asleep and this is a dream I never want to end?

"You want *me* to be the head of event planning for Barn and Branch?" I repeat the words as if they were not originally spoken in my native tongue. As if I need to ensure I understood them correctly.

"Yes, I didn't realize how much of a background you have in the hospitality industry. Until this." She rolls a finger in the air indicating the barn. "Your parents own this place, right?"

I am vaguely aware of Mom and Dad standing off to the side watching all of this unfold. I glance over at them, and they smile at me. They are watching my dream come true. I notice some other townsfolk watching. This is sure to be top of the *Hot Sheet* in the morning.

"In fact," Laura continues, "this inn and the orchard are perfect candidates for the brand. We'll send over an offer first thing Monday morning."

Now I'm about to start hyperventilating. I have never hyperventilated in my life, but don't I always say there is a first time for everything? And it's all starting to hit me. I am being offered my dream job. At triple salary! The exact type of high-end event planning I've always dreamed of. And if Bolt Hotel Group buys the orchard and the inn, Aiden doesn't even need to sell the Rosie Darling. My parents and the Parkers will all be rich.

I want to yell *yes!* and see if Laura Bolt is one for a hug, but instead all I can think about is . . . Aiden. And the look on his face when he thought I might go back to GMJ. I swivel to find him. I don't see him. There are lots of people. But he's not there. He's no longer in the small crowd around me.

He's gone.

I glance around. Maria gives me a sad shrug to indicate she doesn't know where he went.

"Can I . . . Can I think about it?" I ask, turning back to Laura Bolt. She smiles at me. "Of course. Take the night. But if you're going to say yes, we need you first thing in the morning." She hands me her card. "Text my personal cell when you decide."

"I will," I breathe. "Thank you."

A flurry of congratulations and we're-proud-of-yous come from my neighbors and friends. I hug Mom and Dad real quick, but they both see the tears in my eyes. I don't stay long to discuss it with any of them.

"I need some air," I say to Maria. She handles the crowd while I escape.

I don't look back. I rush out the barn doors, through the grass, and across the road into the orchard. It's still lit with all the twinkling lights. The other night it felt like the Milky Way, now it feels like a refuge.

It's quiet here. I can think.

I slow my breathing and wrap my arms around myself because it's colder than I expected. But I like it at the moment, because it's helping me to think. There's no real choice, is there? I may have fallen back in love with my hometown, but can I really stay out here and live a life? I mean, that would be insane, right? You don't *leave* Manhattan. You *go to* Manhattan. And I was already there. At least, I had been.

And even if I was considering it, how foolish would I be if I turned down *my dream job*? It's one thing to tell Steve and Geoff to go eff themselves. This was different. I'd be working for a highly successful woman-owned business. I could learn so much from Laura Bolt. I'd be an idiot to turn down this offer.

There is a rustling in the leaves nearby, and I already know who it is before I look up. Aiden is there. Before saying a word, he pulls off his sweater and hands it to me. He's wearing a white T-shirt underneath.

I pull the sweater over my head, breathing in the scent of him, and then look at him. Tears sting my eyes. "Thanks."

"Big night, huh?" he says. He slides his hands into his pants pockets.

"Lots going on," I say. It's Understatement of the Year Award material. I kick at the leaves with my boot, willing my eyes to stop watering. This is excruciating.

"I heard the job offer with the hotel group," he says.

"It's a pretty big deal," I say, and then I want to kick myself for saying it. He's a pretty big deal too.

He nods. "Yeah. Triple your salary? Pretty great."

"Uh-huh." It feels like a golf ball is lodged in my windpipe.

He points his face toward the sky and expels his breath. "You gonna take it?"

My chest is so tight it aches. My face feels like it could crack into pieces. "It's a really good offer. It's my dream job."

He nods. I see his Adam's apple work as he swallows.

"They want to make an offer for the inn and orchard too," I hurry to add. "This place is perfect for their new line."

He lowers his face again and presses his lips together before he says, "Yeah. I don't think we're gonna sell."

I take a step toward him. "But, Aiden, don't you see? If you all take the Bolt Group money, you'll be rich. You won't have to work another day in your life, *and* you can keep the Rosie Darling." I search his face. He has to understand what an amazing opportunity this is.

The hint of a sad smile touches his lips. He kicks at the leaves too. "But what will we do all day?"

I shake my head. I don't understand. "Whatever you want."

He pokes his tongue into his cheek. "What if what I want is to run this place?"

I frown, then shrug. "I'm sure you can get a job with the Bolt Group here. With your experience—"

He makes a frustrated groan and scrubs both hands over his face. "You don't understand, Ellie. It's not about taking a job. It's about owning something. Loving something. Doing what you love all day every day. Answering to no one but yourself."

My heart is breaking. I understand. But except for answering to someone else, that's what the Bolt job would be for me. He has to understand that this is what I've been waiting for my whole career. "Aiden, I—" What else is there to say?

He steps toward me and takes both of my freezing hands in his. He rubs the tops with his thumbs to warm them up. Our gazes lock. "Look, Ellie. I haven't been able to get the words out, but what I wanted to tell you earlier . . . what I've been trying to tell you . . . is that I love you."

My eyes are no longer watering, now full-on tears are stinging them. "No, Aiden. Don't."

"I have to say it. I realize you may not feel the same, but I have to let you know, or I'll regret it forever. Just like last time."

My breath sticks in my throat. My heart pounds. I swallow. I say nothing.

"I've loved you since we were kids, Ellie, and I always hoped we'd run this place together. When you left, I tried to move on and live my life, and I did . . . for a while. But when you came back . . . it was like I finally had my chance. And I knew I had to take it." He squeezes my hands this time. "I love you and I want you to stay, but I won't be the reason you miss out on your dreams. I want the best for you. I want you to be happy. If you have to go, I understand."

Chapter 25

It's raining the next morning when the big black SUV that the Bolt Hotel Group sent for me pulls out of the winding drive away from the inn. I am in the back seat. I managed to dodge Miss Guin. She got away from Donny when he was loading my suitcase into the back of the car. I did get to pet her, however. To tell her goodbye. I smell a little goat-y now, but I don't mind.

The drive to Vermont is long, but it will give me plenty of time to go over all the plans for the Bolt event again. I never deleted them. I just put them in an archived folder.

This is it. This is what I worked for, the last seven years. I'm going up to Vermont, and I'm going to ensure the Bolt Hotel Group's new brand launch next weekend is the most spectacular thing anyone has ever seen. I spent my entire summer planning it. I deserve this.

And I am *not* afraid of success. Or at least if I am, I am choosing to overcome it right now. And this was obviously what the tarot cards meant when they told me I'd have a big choice to make. It was one of the hardest things I've ever done, to walk away from Aiden last night, but I had to. *I had to.* I'd live the rest of my life with regret if I hadn't taken this job.

I thought about asking Aiden if he wanted to try a long-distance relationship. But that wouldn't be fair to him. He deserves someone who'll be there with him every night in his cute little house with the white picket fence. Argos deserves a full-time dog mom.

Of course, I didn't leave without a scar. A big one. There is an open wound where my heart should be. And I know I won't be the same again. I cried last night. Out in the orchard, Aiden pulled me into his arms, and I cried against his strong shoulder, my body shaking with sobs. And then he walked me to the apartment, where I went to sleep. My brain was too scattered to make any decisions right then.

But when I woke up early this morning, I knew what I had to do.

I have no idea how it'll be with him the next time I visit the inn. The cowardly part of me hopes Mom and Dad will sell their part to the Bolt Hotel Group. They've been talking about taking a Caribbean cruise for years. Now is their chance.

At least I was brave enough to tell Aiden to his face. He was up making coffee when I pulled my suitcase out of the bedroom this morning. I stopped short when I saw him. "I'm sorry," I told him, hugging him like I never wanted to let him go. "I have to do this."

He nodded and squeezed me tight, resting his chin on the top of my head. I tried to memorize the feeling of being in his arms even though I knew I had no right to.

He gave me a to-go cup filled with the pumpkin-spice coffee, and Donny's knock on the door saved us from any further awkwardness. Honestly, it also saved me from bursting into tears again.

It's painful. And it sucks. But this is for the best. I know it. Aiden and I were great together. In more ways than one. But I cannot turn down a once-in-a-lifetime opportunity. I just can't.

My heart will stop hurting . . . someday.

Won't it?

* * *

It's Saturday.

Because I am a magician and damn good at my job, everything has fallen back into place over the last six days. Since Monday, I've

been able to get all the plans I'd made back on track. The Bolt Hotel Group event is going to go off without a hitch today. Just like I
always envisioned it.

I am standing in the two-story glass dining room of the Barn and
Branch Inn in Vermont. The white gourds and small white pumpkins
are artfully arranged on the tables. The farmhouse flowers are perfectly posed in their milk jugs. The pumpkin-and-cinnamon-scented
votives in tiny glass holders have filled the air with the scent of fall.
The thick off-white tablecloths and gold flatware are on point. The
entire dining room feels like a cornucopia from an autumn harvest.
The pesto-encrusted broiled salmon entrées and the apple-crisp
bread pudding topped with semi-melted white chocolate chips are
being prepped in the kitchens as we speak.

Just the way I planned it.

It's all here. It's all pristine. It's all gorgeous.

So why can't I help but think about how there are no old-fashioned
hay bales or rickety apple barrels? Or an old red truck that makes
me nostalgic? There isn't a goat around to knock anyone over or a
chonky little pug sporting orange PJs. And there's definitely not a
yellow Lab wearing a beret.

And despite being given a lot of free rein, I still had to check in
with the executives throughout the week on my progress. I can't help
but miss the feeling of being in charge—well, as in charge as I could
be with Aiden looming over my shoulder.

A sad smile curls my lips.

My phone buzzes, and when I look down, I realize that I was hoping it was Aiden. Just like I've been hoping every text I've gotten
since I left Harvest Hollow would be from Aiden. But this one isn't
from Aiden either. It's from Mom.

*You left your wool coat in the apartment. Aiden found it. I'll ship it to you once
you're settled back in the city.*

I heave a sigh. Those words are perfectly normal. Right, even. It's nice of Mom to offer. But I can't help but think that she didn't say that I can pick it up at Thanksgiving. Or even Christmas. Because she knows I won't be there. Because I haven't been there. I can't even use the excuse that they might sell the inn anymore, because she already told me earlier this week they turned down the Bolt Hotel Group's offer.

"What would we do with all that money?" Mom asked. I was tempted to ask her if she wanted me to write a list, but I knew what she meant. It's the same thing Aiden meant. Money isn't the most important thing to everyone. Some people just want to be happy. I do too.

I honestly haven't thought about the holidays yet this year. With the festival and then this new job, I've been too busy to think about them. But now I am obsessing over them. If I go back, I'll see Aiden. Half of me wants to go early. Half of me wants to make an excuse to stay away.

All of me is picturing Aiden pulling my wool coat out of the closet. I am hoping it will smell even vaguely like his aftershave and am wishing I'd stolen one of his T-shirts.

I glance down at the text again. I think about how Mom asked me to stay. I told her I'd think about it. And I did. But she knew how important this opportunity is to me. She hugged me that last night in the barn. Told me she was proud of me. And the morning I left, she brought me some of Sera's apple cider donuts and hugged me again. Dad kissed me on the top of my head. "Go get 'em," he said.

My eyes water. I shake my head. I need some air.

I push open one set of latticed French doors and make my way around the side of the barnlike building. The grounds are perfectly coiffed. It's peak leaf season here, and the landscape is filled with oranges, reds, and yellows.

I kick through them, smiling a little as I make my way up a small set of stone stairs to a balcony that overlooks the inn's currently covered pool area. I stop in front of the stone balustrade and lean over it. I look across the parklike grounds and can't help but think how much it reminds me of home. Because of the fall-ness of it all.

I sigh. My chest is heavy, and I don't feel right. It's no surprise. I've been under a ton of stress the last two weeks. I got dumped, fired, ostracized, planned one huge event, and then rescued another. It's been *a lot*.

And then there was Aiden . . .

"Tell Henry that if they don't agree to that price, there's no deal," comes a confident female voice from somewhere nearby.

I frown and turn around to see who is talking.

Laura Bolt is just coming around the corner of the inn. As usual, she's dressed in a slay-all-day power suit, and she's pressing a button on her cell phone. Clearly, she just hung up a call. She stops short when she sees me, before giving me a smile. She makes her way to my side and leans on the balustrade next to me.

"Hi, there," she says.

"Hi," I say. I've spoken with her a handful of times this week and she's always been friendly, but she's also the billionaire owner of a major US corporation, so she's clearly not someone to trifle with. She intimidates me a little when she's nearby.

"I hope I didn't bother you with my phone call," she says.

"Oh, no. Not at all." I smile. "I just hope Henry agrees to the price. I can tell you mean it."

Laura Bolt chuckles. "I do mean it."

There are a few moments of companionable silence between us before she says, "The venue looks fantastic, Ellie. I told my people the minute they hired that other guy that it was all going to fall apart. They didn't listen." She sighed. "Sometimes you have to let your people make mistakes."

I nod. "*I'd* listen to you." And I mean it. I'm not just blowing smoke. She's a smart lady who clearly knows her stuff.

She gives me a half smile. "I certainly didn't get to where I am without understanding who the real talent is when I see it."

"Thank you," I say, inordinately pleased with myself for garnering praise from this impressive person.

"And without learning a few hard lessons," she continues. She points her cell phone toward me. "Between you and me . . . sometimes it takes a woman to see another woman's talent."

"Now *that* I know is true," I say. Though I have no intention of expounding any further. Geoff and Steve may have thrown me under the bus, but I won't do the same. I won't stoop to their level. They can have their bro code and their inside frat jokes. I'm taking the high road.

"Hey, where's your boyfriend?" she asks next. "Did he come up with you?"

"Oh, I don't have a boyfriend," I say. If she means Geoff, I don't want to get into all of that. I'm just going to leave it at "I don't have a boyfriend." It's the truth.

"I could've sworn that handsome young man with the dog dressed like an apple was your boyfriend."

Oh God. *She means Aiden.*

I begin shaking my head even before I speak. "No. No. He's not my boyfriend."

"Are you sure? I saw the picture of you two on the inn's social media account. You were wearing a hat, and he bopped your nose. You looked great together."

Charlotte's photo shoot. "Oh, that was just for promo. It was nothing."

Laura crosses her arms over her chest and turns to side-eye me with skepticism practically dripping from her face. "You could've fooled me. I've never seen a smile so big. I know that smile. It's the smile of someone in love."

"Er . . . excuse me?" Is billionaire Laura Bolt seriously telling me I'm in love with Aiden?

She turns and leans back over the balustrade again. "You know what? I was a multimillionaire by the time I turned thirty-five."

Okay? Frankly, she can brag all she wants. I'm just glad she stopped asking about Aiden.

"I was a billionaire a few years ago when I turned fifty," she continues.

I nod. "Impressive," I say.

"I'm not looking for praise." She laughs. "I'm telling you this to also tell you that I'd give up every cent I've ever made if I could go back in time and make things right with the one who got away."

I think I'm frozen to the balustrade, because I'm pretty sure Laura Bolt just told me that I have made the wrong decision taking this job.

"Uh, we . . . we wanted different things," I say, feeling like a fool. I'm pretty sure Laura doesn't want to hear the details, but I also feel as if I need to explain myself.

"Oh, my guy and I also wanted different things," she says. "And not one of them really mattered."

She looks at her phone again and presses a number. I can hear it dialing. She turns and begins walking away. Should I say, *Thank you, have a nice day, I'm sorry you lost the love of your life?* Seriously, what is the etiquette here?

I decide to just smile and nod.

"You said you'd listen to me," she says in a singsong voice as she leaves.

I am left staring unseeing at the pastoral landscape in front of me, stunned. What just happened? How did Laura Bolt know I was out here thinking about Aiden? Was it that obvious?

Ellie, you idiot, it's apparently so obvious she could tell by just looking at your picture.

And, oh damn. Because, like a seat belt clicking into place, it all just lights up in my brain, and I realize that the heaviness in my chest isn't because of the stress of the last two weeks. It isn't because

I got dumped, fired, ostracized, planned a huge event, and rescued another. It's because I'm in *love*.

I'm in love with Aiden and *really* homesick.

That's why every single mile that brought me up here felt heavier and longer than the last. That's why I'm wondering if Argos is still wearing his apple costume like Pumpkin and the PJs. That's why I can't breathe when I think about Aiden holding me in his arms while I cried.

I'm in love with him.

And Laura Bolt is right. I've made a mistake.

And I need to go make it right.

Expensive heels be damned, I turn and hurry as fast as I can along the cobblestones and down the little stone steps. I rush into the dining room again where Laura Bolt is talking on the phone. "I'm sorry," I yell, completely ignoring that she's probably on a multimillion-dollar business call. "I can't take the job, after all. Thank you so much for the opportunity, though."

Laura pulls the phone from her ear before saying, "Tell Aiden I said hi," and winking at me.

I spend the next fifteen minutes going over the plans with Cady, my assistant. She's younger than me but reminds me of me at her age. Really smart, with it, and going places. Everything is already set, so she's prepared to take over. She's got this. I'm sure of it. "Text me if you need me," I tell her. I will not leave her in the lurch.

After I go to my room and toss everything into my suitcase, I go to the front desk to ask about getting a train or a flight home. I want whatever is fastest this time.

Jim, the front desk manager, tells me that Laura has already asked him to have a car pick me up and take me to the nearby airport. My flight is booked. How she did it that fast when she was already in the middle of a phone call is a mystery I may never unravel.

"Ms. Bolt also asked me to give you this." Jim plucks an envelope from behind the desk and hands it to me. I open it and my eyes nearly pop from my skull, because inside is a check for an amount of money that is frankly indecent. There is a small note on top of it. *Thanks for fixing everything at the last minute. Best of luck.* It's signed by Laura.

I press it to my chest.

Then one of the bellhops materializes out of nowhere to see to my suitcase, and within minutes I'm inside another big black SUV and heading toward the airport.

I'm going home.

Chapter 26

I stand under the overhang in front of Aiden's front door. The mum planter sits by my left knee, and I stare at the brass Labrador door knocker. My giant suitcase lurks behind me. There is no goat to knock me over, but this is worse. My insides are a mess of nerves. The minute I ring the doorbell I will be caught on camera. Aiden's truck is here. He will see me. If he doesn't answer, what am I going to do? The car that drove me here from the private airport is already gone. I'll have to slink off down the street, and I'm not sure it's possible to slink given the size of my suitcase.

At least the rain has stopped. It's dark and cold, but my nerves and adrenaline are keeping me warm.

I had a lot of time to think on the way down here. And it turns out Sera was right. I did have the answers inside of me the whole time. I knew to turn down Steve's insulting offer, but I got confused when Laura made hers. It's not easy to say no to your ideal of success. But Mom was right too. Sometimes your definition of success changes. I mean, I still love the city, but the last two weeks showed me something. It's nice being completely in charge of things. It's terrific being my own boss. Having no commute. Wearing comfy clothes. Answering to no one and doing what I know I'm good at all day long. The Bolt job was amazing, but working for myself surrounded by my friends and family will be even more so.

And as for the Lovers card, Aiden *is* my soulmate. I think he always has been, since we were kids. The spider incident comes to mind. When you find the person who'll save you from what you're afraid of, don't let go.

And I won't. I'm totally clear now. I am here choosing the life I know I want, working for myself in my hometown. I only hope it's not too late to win back the man I love.

Okay. Time to stare fear in the eye. I ring the doorbell and hold my breath. Argos is barking. Uh-oh. I can't slink away from a barking dog. Can I? I may have to abandon the suitcase.

It feels like an eternity before the door opens. Aiden is standing there in jeans and no shirt. His hair is wet. He braces his hand on the door. His face is inscrutable. In case you're wondering if there anything worse than an inscrutable face at a time like this, no. No, there is not.

"Ellie," he says. His voice is also impossible to interpret.

"Hi," I manage around the giant lump in my throat.

"I thought you were in Vermont."

"I was." I peek inside. There is a fire going in the living room fireplace. And Argos is sitting there like the very good boy that he is. And I'm so nervous I'm tempted to tell Aiden that I just came back for my coat. It's freezing out here, and I would like it. But I already know Mom's got it and—

Oh, Ellie, just say it, you coward.

"I came back because I . . ." Am I having a panic attack? It's hard to breathe. I am dizzy.

"Because?" he prompts. He arches one brow.

"Because I forgot to tell you something." My gaze searches his face. I'm positive I look and sound like a deranged person. I wring my hands. And then it all just comes flying out. "I forgot to tell you that I love you. I love you, and I love the sense of belonging that I found here again in Harvest Hollow." I take a deep, gulping breath, fighting for air. "But most importantly, I'm sorry. I'm sorry I hurt you, and I'm sorry I was stupid. And I'm sorry I chose a meaningless job over what we found together. I realize now that being a corporate event planner isn't going to make me happy. It never would. Because that's not what real success is. Real success is living a life surrounded by the people you love and who love you back in a place that makes you happy while doing the things you love to do. And that's what the inn is for me. And that's who you are for me. And it always was, and you always were, but I just didn't realize it until I fell in love with you. And I know I don't deserve it, and I know I might be wrong to ask, but if there's some way—any way—you can forgive me, I'll spend the rest of my life making it up to you. Trying to, at least."

There. My heart is racing, and I feel like I just finished running a 5k. Did I miss anything important? I practiced this speech a hundred times in my head on the flight down here. But it all just came out like a big, jumbled mess. I can only hope I made all of my salient points.

Aiden's face is still inscrutable, but he opens his mouth. He's about to say something, when I remember one more thing I really need to say. "Oh, and Mom and Dad aren't going to take the Bolt Hotel Group offer. They're taking my offer instead."

He frowns. *"Your offer?"*

I nod too much. "Yes. Laura Bolt gave me a big bonus for fixing the event, and I'm using it to buy a share of the inn from Mom and Dad. Mom told me your parents turned down the Bolt offer too."

"They did."

"And your apple offer?" I hold my breath, even though I'm pretty sure I already know what he's going to say.

He brushes his hand up and down through the back of his wet hair. "Turned it down flat."

"Good. Good. Because you and I are going to be partners now. I mean it this time. And Charlotte too. I have a hundred ideas of how to make the inn and orchard more profitable, and we'll implement them together. I mean . . . if you want to." Oh God. I've just barreled ahead and assumed he agreed, when he actually has done no such thing. He needs to say yes first.

I stop. I stare at him. He may not want me back. He may tell me to get the hell off his porch. I have to wait. I need to know. I clasp my hands together and force myself to stop nodding.

Aiden's not moving. He's not talking. Somehow in my head this went better. In my mind's eye as I flew across the orange and yellow treetops today, Aiden would grab me and hug me and tell me he loves me, and that he's glad I came back, and that we will be partners forever.

"Aiden?" I search his face. I'm breathing so hard I'm shaky. "Say something. Anything." I've nearly forgotten we're still outside and it's freezing cold, and his abs are uncovered.

His voice is low. His countenance is wary. "What about not mixing business with pleasure?"

Oh yeah. That. That subject I kept harping on repeatedly for two weeks straight. No wonder he wants to know my current stance on that.

I shake my head. "I was focused on the wrong issue. My mistake wasn't mixing business with pleasure. My mistake was mixing business and pleasure with an asshole. You're not an asshole." Okay, maybe not the most eloquent reply, but it was heartfelt.

Aiden snort-laughs, and my belly flips. "I appreciate that," he says.

"I'm serious. Geoff was the problem. I mean, your mom and dad and my parents have mixed business with pleasure their whole careers. It seems to work for them."

His smile widens. "Good point."

"So?" I look up at him hopefully. I am searching his achingly familiar, handsome face. "What do you say?" I bite my lip. Waiting. Waiting.

Aiden blows out a deep breath. He slowly nods. "I'm trying to figure out if this is real or if it's a dream," he says. Because if it's a dream, I don't want to wake up."

Oh God. My face crumples. I close my eyes. Relief washes over me.

In two seconds, he steps forward, picks me up, and spins me around, and then he kisses me. He kisses me, and I kiss him back, grabbing his rough cheeks and slanting my mouth across his. He sets me down inside, picks up my suitcase with one hand, and swings it into the house. There are those arm muscles again. Swoon. And now I'm staring at his abs like it's my full-time job. It occurs to me that I'll never have to pretend not to be staring at them again. What fun!

I pat Argos's head and say hello to him. He is not wearing his apple costume, but he's smiling at me as if he's as happy to see me as I am to see him.

Aiden closes the door behind us and pushes me up against it and kisses me again.

"No shirt *again*, really?" I say.

He smiles against my cheek. "You have a bad habit of knocking on my door when I'm in the shower."

"I'd say that's good timing, actually."

He steps back and cups my cheeks. He rubs his thumbs across them gently. "You're not the only one who needed to apologize," he says. "I honestly questioned myself a hundred times whether I had the right to tell you I loved you before you had to make your decision about the job."

"No, Aiden, you had every right—"

"Shhh." He leans down and kisses my lips softly. "Let me finish."

I promptly close my mouth.

"It's no secret that I'm set in my ways," he says. "I don't like change, and I didn't like you coming back here and messing with the status quo. But it turns out we needed the status quo to be messed with. All of us did, actually. I see that now. But I had no right to be such a dick to you when you first got here. You were only trying to help, and it was wrong of me to hold things you said when you were a kid against you."

"Aiden, I—"

He grins at me. "I'm almost done."

I nod. "Go ahead."

"You showed me that opening myself up and trying new things

are the only way to make things better." He slides his hands down to mine and squeezes my fingers. "Thank you for teaching me that, Ellie."

"I love you," I breathe, just before his mouth captures mine again.

"I love you too," he says, the moment the kiss ends. "You're freezing," he says next, running his hands up and down my arms.

"Yeah, well, I forgot my coat." I shrug and smile at him.

He arches a dark brow. "I think I know a way to warm you up, if you're interested." He tugs me toward the bedroom.

"Ooh, yes, please." I'm already wondering if there's some way we can have sex on the book ladder, but I keep that to myself . . . for now.

"Hmm. I *did* forget my coat," I say. "Maybe I have dementia. I've got a test for that."

Epilogue

Two months later, Christmas week

I can't believe Mom and Dad and your parents aren't going to be here for Christmas this year," Charlotte says. She and I are sitting behind the front desk. The inn is decked out in full holiday regalia. There are stockings and garlands and fake snow on the mantelpiece. There are brightly decorated trees in every room. There are wreaths and Santa Clauses and little snowy villages along the door trim. There is mistletoe in every doorway and more evergreen garlands strung up the banister. The cinnamon is simmering on the stove, of course, and Sera has just brought in a fresh batch of gingerbread people. They smell so good. I want to stick my nose on the plate like a blood-hound. But I refrain. That would be unsanitary. And weird.

"I'm happy for them, but it won't be the same without them," Charlotte continues.

Mom and Dad and the Parkers are on a Caribbean cruise. Aruba, Bonaire, St. Lucia, St. Barts. The works. They'll be gone for two weeks. They just left two days ago. After working at the inn and orchard every holiday for over thirty years, we all managed to convince them to take a break. The money we made from the festival plus the money that's currently streaming in from the changes we've made to the businesses, including the lucrative new apple my boy-friend invented, easily paid for their trip.

Before they left, Mom and Lyn had a bit too much cider and admitted to me and Aiden that they'd invited me to help with the festival with the specific hope that Aiden and I would get together. Man, scheming mothers. But, of course, Aiden and I had to forgive them for meddling. They would not admit they had anything to do with the burst pipe or the apartment sharing, however. I asked a half dozen times, and all I got was the pish posh. I suppose I'll have to get Dad wasted one night before *that* truth comes out.

It's only been two months, but I'm happily settled in here. At first, I had all of my stuff in the attic apartment, because Aiden and I agreed that logically it made sense to wait and see how things went for a while before shacking up together. That lasted less than a week. Now I live in his house with him and Argos. It's a tight squeeze in the closet with all of my clothes, I'm not gonna lie, but we've made do. I've learned to wash dishes by hand without complaining. And I get to ride the bookcase ladder (and its owner) whenever I want.

The *Harvest Hollow Hot Sheet* had a field day after I returned. Aiden and I parked in the back row at the next *Gilmore Girls* night and made out like sixteen-year-olds. It was super fun and entirely premeditated. We were headliners the next morning. You have to have goals. And talk about a bold PR move. We decided it would be a rip-the-Band-Aid-off type of maneuver.

It's been an eventful two months for the inn and orchard. We've already implemented some of my ideas. First, we created a gift shop in what used to be a sitting area near the lobby. We sell stuffed apple dog toys, apple and pumpkin Halloween costumes for dogs and cats, and a whole host of other things with an apple-y autumn theme including T-shirts, postcards, key chains, and pillows. Oh, and tumblers. Big old Honeycrisp Orchard Inn tumblers. If you are in the market for an HOI tchotchke, we've got you. One of our bestsellers is a set of orange PJs (for people) that look like Pumpkin's set. Don't ask me why, but we can't keep them in stock. The minute guests see Pumpkin wearing them, they're in. The internet orders are ridiculous too. That's another thing I did, set up an online store to sell all the items we offer at the inn. The apple-scented face scrub is super popular!

We also offered Jesse and Sera ownership in the business. They both bought in, and now the brewery and bakery are theirs. We technically lease the space to them vs. pay them a salary. It's worked out great, because Jesse is making money hand over fist since he's been able to turn the brewery into what he always wanted, a full-service brewery/Biergarten. We have also heavily publicized Sera's "Karmic Bakery," and now people come from all over the region to try her magic love-potion cider and donuts. I mean who doesn't want some love potion? There's even a group on social media dedicated to the couples who've fallen in love after drinking it. It's advertising gold. I do not question it. She's got new products for the holiday season too: love-potion hot chocolate and magic peppermint brownies. They've been big sellers all month. She also offers tarot card readings (yes, my idea), and she's never made more money.

Charlotte is in charge of the inn. We gave her an equal share, and she's paying us all back in installments. She's been helping Mom run the place for the last two years, so she knows everything, and I'm happy to let her do it. I help out Charlotte when she needs it, but mostly I am the event coordinator, and I've never been happier. We have a barn wedding special and a baby shower extravaganza. We have bachelorette parties and bat mitzvahs and gender reveals. If people want to gather and have fun, we're the go-to place outside of the city thanks to Maria's continuing PR brilliance. Only, we're able to pay her now. She's still doing OnlyFans, though, because Manhattan ain't cheap.

We are all keeping a close eye on Charlotte and her new boyfriend, Miller. He's the guy who went to the drive-in with her in October. They've been together since then. Every once in a while, I see Sawyer looking at Charlotte longingly, but she seems pretty committed to ignoring him. I have no idea what happened between the two of them, but Sera and I are always hunting for clues. Any time we've tried to ask Charlotte about it directly, she's sidestepped the conversation. Aiden did a full background check on Miller, of course. Turns out he's a linens vendor. They met when he came to the inn to sell his wares. According to Aiden, he has no priors and a high credit score. He came to family game night in November and seemed nice. But I just can't shake the feeling that Charlotte isn't quite head over heels for him.

Speaking of head over heels, I never drank the love potion, but I couldn't be more gaga over Aiden. Turns out he's the best boyfriend ever, and even after two months, my stomach still flips every time I see him. Turns out a stomach flip is what you should be going for with a significant other. What seems like nausea at first is actually being smitten. Who knew? And I am a smitten kitten, I admit it.

There's only one downside to living out here. I don't get to see Maria as much. But we FaceTime and text, and I go into the city every few weeks for brunch. I invite her out here all the time, but wouldn't you know it, she's always busy. Hmm. Sounds familiar. I don't blame her, though. I love the city too, and with it so close, I go in whenever I want.

I invited Maria out here for Christmas, actually. She politely declined. She's going to LA like she does every year to see her ginormous family. She has to bring a second suitcase for all the presents for her nieces and nephews. I'll see her after New Year's. We're planning a girls' weekend.

I am putting the finishing touches on the New Year's Eve party we're throwing out here. We're doing another one of those drop-off-your-kids weekends, and it's sold out. Only this time, we're bringing in the big heaters for the barn. Otherwise, the staff and kids would freeze out there.

I'm going over the night's bookings, when the front door to the inn opens and Aiden strolls through with Argos at his heels. Aiden is whistling and looks as hot as ever. Seriously, will I ever get over how hot he is?

He's wearing jeans and a dark-green pullover and his brown work boots. His hair has grown out a bit, and a dark curl rests over one eye. That always gets me.

Argos immediately comes around the counter, pushing open the wooden half door with his nose. He needs to say hello to his good friend, Pumpkin. Pumpkin remains an internet sensation. Guests constantly ask about him. We let them take their picture with him for free these days. P-dog is always rockin' his orange PJs and ready for his close-up. Since they've been gone, Mom and Dad call every night to FaceTime him.

While Argos and Pumpkin press their noses together to say hello, Aiden strolls right up to the front desk and leans over it. He braces his forearms on top. "Hey, Charlotte. Can you handle everything for a little while if I take Ellie away?"

Charlotte's brows shoot up. "Depends on what you're doing with her."

"Nothing indecent, I promise," he says, laughing.

"In that case, I don't want to go," I reply, waggling my eyebrows.

Aiden laughs and holds out his hand and takes one of mine. "Come home with me."

"It's the middle of the afternoon," I point out, trying to squelch my smile.

"Yes, but I need to show you something." He is biting his lip in that way that drives me insane.

"What? Did your 'pipe burst' again?" I do air quotes and laugh at my own joke.

"Very funny," Aiden replies. "No. It's your Christmas present. I want to show it to you."

I cock my head to the side. "But Christmas isn't for three days. I don't want to open it yet."

"Yes, you do." He gives me a knowing nod.

He's being awfully cagey about this. "Why didn't you just bring it here, then?" I ask.

"It's too big. I can't fit it in the truck."

Okay, now he's got my full attention. I wasn't expecting an engagement ring this soon, of course, but what the heck did he get me that's so big he can't fit it in his *truck*? I've already learned that Aiden is the worst at keeping presents a secret. My birthday was the day after I came back from Vermont. He couldn't keep the secret even one day. He got me a new coffee maker and showed me how to use it. Of course, he makes the coffee every day now, but it was pretty cute at the time. And there is always pumpkin-spice creamer, though I have switched to peppermint mocha for the Christmas season and am loving it.

"Okay," I sigh. "Let's go."

"Send me a picture as soon as you can," Charlotte says, curious too.

Minutes later, Aiden and Argos and I are strapped into the truck and on our way home. Argos's seat belt connects to his harness. He has a red-and-green plaid harness for Christmas because the dog is stylish. I *may* have purchased it for him at a store in the city.

"Is it an elephant?" I ask, fiddling with the heat so the truck will warm up.

"No."

I flip on the seat warmers. They are my favorite thing about using a truck more often than riding the subway. Seriously. Seat warmers should be a thing everywhere. "A giraffe?"

"No."

I scrunch up my nose. "A moose?"

"No. And what's with all the animal guesses? Do you *want* a moose?"

I settle back into the seat and shrug. "They're the only things I can think of that are really big." I snap my fingers. "Ooh, it is a car?"

"No."

"A truck?"

"No."

"A giant donut."

"We already have one of those."

I snort-laugh. "A water buffalo?"

Aiden gives me a skeptical look. "What would you say if I said yes to that one?"

I shrug. "I would say I'm going to need a book about how to care for water buffalos."

"It's not alive, I promise," he assures me.

I tap my finger to my chin. Big and dead? What could it be? "A *stuffed* water buffalo?"

"No." Aiden laughs and shakes his head.

I am still thinking about the possibilities as we drive down Main Street, which, by the way, looks like the set of a Christmas movie. There are twinkling white lights in every tree and pretty red, green, and gold ornaments dangling from the branches. Mistletoe hangs above each business's door, and each streetlight is adorned with a big red bow. There's a Salvation Army bell ringer outside the general store, and Mrs. Wilkins has her famous life-size knitted snowman sitting out in front of the hardware store with a bucket of candy for children. Christmas carols are playing on the speakers along the town square, and as we pass town hall it begins to snow.

I snuggle into the heated seat and rub my mittens together, in love with the homey warmth currently settling in my middle. I missed this feeling for seven whole years. I don't intend to miss another second of it.

When we pull into Aiden's driveway, another little thrill of joy shoots through me. We decorated the house for Christmas the weekend after Thanksgiving. There are garlands with red bows all along the white picket fence and twinkling white lights along the rooftop. We even put candle lights in the front windows. It's cozy and warm and I love it here. It's so much more fun to decorate a whole house than a tiny apartment.

"Come on," Aiden says as he turns off the engine. He has a glint in his eye, and I'm squirming with excitement to see what my present is.

He holds open the little white gate for me like he always does, and Argos and I follow him up to the porch. The front door opens to our Christmas tree. We got a full-size one that nearly hits the ceiling. It's in front of the large window and filled with white lights and red and silver ornaments, including more than one apple-themed ornament, which, by the way, we also sell in the gift shop at the inn. The tree makes the whole house smell like pine.

Once the door closes behind us, and we shake and stamp off the little bit of snow we've accumulated, Aiden says, "Okay, close your eyes."

I immediately close them.

He takes my hand to lead me. We walk to the right which means toward the bedroom. If the present is in the bedroom, why didn't he just go get it? Did he not wrap it?

He helps me along and makes sure I don't bump into the walls as we go. Finally, we stop, and he puts his hands on my shoulders and pivots me around. I have no idea which way I'm facing.

"Okay, you can open them," he announces.

My eyes fly open, and then my mouth drops *straight* down because I am looking into a closet that is the size of a bedroom. Because it *is* a bedroom! Aiden has turned the guest room into an enormous closet. For me! All of my clothes are in here. There are shelves, and doors, and hampers, and rows and rows of shoes, and a little sitting area. It looks like something out of a reality TV show with really rich ladies. There is a whole section for my purses and another one for my sunglasses. And the shelves light up!

I am beyond shocked. "How did you do all this without me noticing?" I ask. He's had the door to this room closed for a while, but I didn't think much of it.

"It hasn't been easy. I had to do some of it while you were out. But the rest, we finished really fast this week."

"We?"

"Me and my buddies."

"You had your friends come over and help with this?"

"Yeah, I've been planning it for weeks. I had it sketched out and prepped. We just needed to do the installation."

My eyes are wet with tears as I turn to him and hug him fiercely. "This is the best present I've ever gotten." And I mean it. I think it's the best present anyone has ever gotten, and that includes those people on the TV commercials who get cars with big red bows on them. It's certainly better than a stuffed water buffalo. But there's always next year.

"So, you like it?" Aiden asks. I can tell that he's nervous.

I squeeze his arm, partly to reassure him and partly because, honestly, I can't get enough of touching his arms. "I love it. Like, *really* love. I couldn't love it more."

He looks relieved. He scratches the back of his neck. "I know you don't have enough clothes for it now, but I figure there's room to buy more."

"No woman has ever loved a sentence more." I kiss him. Then I wrinkle my nose. "Well, now what I got you is going to seem pretty lame."

"What is it?"

"That hand plane you mentioned last month."

"I already love it," he says loyally, pulling my fingers up to his lips and kissing them.

"Oh, and a hat," I say, giving him a very sly look.

"Like the one from the photo shoot?" he asks, returning my sly look.

"*Exactly* like the one from the photo shoot," I reply.

"Say the word, and we can go back to the greenhouse any time you want."

He pulls me into his arms and kisses me.

"Promise?" I ask.

"Promise."

Acknowledgments

It was an absolute pleasure writing this book and I want to thank the following people for their help along the way . . .

My amazing critique partner (and photographer), Mary Behre, who read the first chapters on very short notice and gave me invaluable feedback.
Your support and friendship over the years means the world to me.

My friend, Amber Wilson Mikalonis, who let me text her at all hours to run dialogue by her.
You're the best!

My wonderful literary agent, Kevan Lyon, and fantastic editor, Shannon Plackis, who trusted me to write this story.
Thank you for your faith in me.
Pumpkin, the Pug, wouldn't exist without you.

About the Author

VALERIE BOWMAN's debut novel was published in 2012. Since then, her books have received starred reviews from *Publishers Weekly*, *Booklist*, and *Kirkus Reviews*. Valerie grew up in Illinois with six sisters (she's number seven) and a huge supply of romance novels. Valerie now lives in Jacksonville with her family, including her mini-schnauzers, Huckleberry and Violet. When she's not writing, she keeps busy reading, traveling, or vacillating between watching crazy reality TV and PBS.